Sphenurus

A Bonded Changer Romance

Sue-Ellen Pashley

Paperback ISBN: 978-0-6488018-3-2

Printed in Australia by Ingram Sparks
Cover design by Vanilla Lily

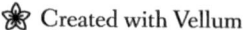 Created with Vellum

For my family, without whom life wouldn't be half as interesting or fun.

Lani

God, what the hell am I doing?

I grip the steering wheel and suck in a deep breath, letting it go in a long whisper of air. It does nothing to slow the thumping of my heart. Flicking down the mirror on the sun visor, I bare my teeth. No lip stick smear, no leftovers from lunch, I'm good to go. And yet, I can't seem to make myself get out of the car.

Which is ridiculous.

This is what I want. This is the freedom I've craved for the last two years. The chance to change my life. Not that it was terrible before, just...boring. The same room in the same house in the same town since the moment I was born. The same friends, the same places to go, the same opportunities, the same comments from my mother ...same, same, same!

I take another breath and wrench open the door. The heat curls its way into the car, battering the cooled air into submission, and I turn my face up to the sun as I get out, closing my eyes, enjoying the feel of it on my skin for a moment. More procrastination.

Opening my eyes, I smooth my skirt around my hips – black pencil skirt with red piping and red inset pleat at the back – and put my handbag over my shoulder. I'm ready to do this.

The house in front of me is nothing spectacular. Just a two story house – probably only a few notches up from a shack really, but I don't care. It's a house I've never lived in before and that makes it wonderful. My new home, for a while anyway.

I only make it half way up the driveway before the door opens and a guy walks out. My guy. At least, that's what we're trying for. That's one of the reasons I've moved up here.

He looks the same as he did when we talked on line, which is a relief to be honest. He's tall, which is definitely a must because there's no way I'm dating someone shorter than me; dark, straight hair that falls across his brow – almost black but as he steps out of the shade of the house into the morning sun, I can see shades of brown too; brown eyes that show his mum's Japanese heritage and a body that's lean and strong. Zac's a good match for me. The cousin of a guy I knew back in Tasmania.

He does that cute, lazy smile that's become a bit of a favourite of mine, and I smile back, standing still, so he gets the best view. I know I look good. I worked hard at it this morning before I left the hotel, obsessing over what to wear and taking extra time on my makeup but I've been worrying for the last three hours of the drive that he won't like what he sees.

And I want him to like me.

I want that instant feeling of connection with someone that every other person in my damn family seems to have experienced and is happy to tell me about, over and over. That bond that means two of our kind belong together.

I watch him as he comes closer. He *is* cute and I *do* get

butterflies. But I don't really know if this is a bond forming or if it's just nerves. What does a stupid bond feel like anyway?

He stops in front of me and puts his hands on my arms. His palms are slightly sweaty but I concentrate on his dark brown eyes and long eyelashes instead.

'Hey, beautiful. It's good to see you in the flesh at last.'

He leans forward and the butterflies increase. It's not like I haven't kissed anyone before – I've had my fair share of boyfriends, but I want this to work so badly. I want Zac to be the one.

His lips are nice on mine...firm, not too much moisture... nice. Our first kiss. I try to implant it in my memory. His hand goes around the back of my neck, inadvertently trapping my hair and I put my hand on his back and step in closer, trying to release the pressure on my scalp. And then, his tongue pushes between my lips. I resist the automatic reaction to pull back at the unexpectedness of it. Instead, I try to feel sexy, enjoy it. But all I can think is that this is the first time I've met him face to face and suddenly his tongue is in my mouth.

Sure, we've spent hours talking on-line and really, I probably know him better than any of my other boyfriends. He's made me laugh and I like how he thinks about the world and our place in it but...this is the first time we've even touched.

He pulls back and looks at me. 'You okay?'

I step back slightly and run my hands over my hair, sweeping it to the side.

'Sure. Just tired. It's been a long couple of days travelling.'

'Shit, of course, sorry. I'm just so excited you're finally here. Made me forget you came all the way from Tassie. Come on inside and I'll fix you something cold to drink. The heat can take some getting used to.'

He grabs two of my bags from the back of the car and I grab the third and my make-up case. It feels like a lot but it was amazing how many clothes I still needed to leave at home. It took me a week to pack, that's how hard the decisions were. My parents had to promise not to throw anything out. I trust Dad not to, at least.

Zac leads the way through the front door and up a set of stairs into an open plan area – kitchen to the side with a dining space and then the lounge area. But it's the view that makes me stop. I have to put the bags down so I can stare properly.

He looks at me and laughs. 'I know. You don't expect this when you look at the front of it, do you?'

I shake my head. Definitely not what I expected. Leaving the bags where they are for the moment, I walk out onto the deck built off the back of the house. The river stretches in front of me, blue under the afternoon sky, flowing past the jetty that reaches out from the yard. I could spend hours just sitting here, watching it go past.

Zac comes over and leans on the railing, smiling at me.

'Think you'll be okay staying here for a while?'

I smile back. 'I don't know, it's a bit of a step down.'

He laughs and a warmth spreads through me. I like him. He's a nice guy. Maybe this will be what I'm hoping for.

'Come on, I'll show you where you're staying.'

I follow him down a short hallway to a room overlooking the road. I feel a momentary stab of disappointment that it doesn't face the river but then, I'm not expecting to spend much time in here anyway. It's a nice enough room. Double bed, build in cupboard, which looks almost big enough, and a bedside table with a lamp. Simple. When I add some of my stuff, it'll be fine.

"It's great," I say.

Zac's standing in the doorway having put my two bags just inside the room. He jerks his thumb at the room across the hallway.

Sphenurus

"That's Matt's. He's the mate I told you about. Owns the house – I rent downstairs from him, where we first came in."

I give what I think is a sexy look.

"You'll have to show me."

He smiles that smile again and my brain almost does a sigh of relief that he seems to like me.

"You can count on it. How about a drink first though? And do you want to use the bathroom?"

Picking up my handbag, I nod. 'That'd be great.'

I follow him a few steps past my bedroom door to a stark white bathroom. It's modern and clean. I like it.

"This is mainly Matt's ensuite." He points to the door at the other end. 'But it's a shared bathroom as well. Just remember to lock both doors.'

I frown. 'Is he okay with having to share his bathroom?'

'Yeah, all good. He knows you're coming.'

It doesn't really answer my question but I don't want to push it because what if the answer is no? Zac leans forward and flicks my hair back over my shoulder. It makes me shiver.

"Do you want a wine? Beer? Something else?"

'I wine would be great.' And it would be. Just one. Enough to sand the edges off my anxiety but not enough to make me say something stupid. 'White, if you have it.'

'No worries.' He shuts the door behind him as he leaves.

I look in the mirror, making sure my makeup is still good, and grab a brush out of my handbag, running it through my hair in long sweeps. It's longer now than I used to wear it and I decide I like it – the colour, the way it curls at the end – some women pay good money to have it done like this.

I dab some more perfume on my wrists and I'm done. Ready to go out and spend more time with the guy that might be the one. God, it sounds weird saying that, even in my head. It's not like I'm old – twenty-two still gives me plenty of time to be in a long term relationship. But I'm sick of them lasting a couple of weeks and then fizzling out. I want to be in a relationship that feels like a grown up one. I'm ready.

I take a deep breath and open the door. I can hear voices – two males. Zac and I'm guessing Matt. I'm nervous again, twitchy, like I've got jumping beans where my organs used to be. What if Matt doesn't like me? It's his house, after all. What if he tells me to get out and I've got nowhere to live? I shake my head and pull my shoulders back. I'm not a coward. I just have to make the right impression.

Be what they want me to be.

They're standing on the deck, laughing at something. Zac's leaning on the rail again and the other guy is standing facing the river. He has dark hair, cut short, almost a crew cut, and is wearing a t-shirt that shows off the width of his shoulders. And he's tall – taller then Zac even.

My shoes tap on the wooden floor in the lounge room and Zac looks up, smiling. I'm almost at the sliding doors when the other guy turns around. And when his eyes meet mine – blue, blue eyes I could happily drown in– I stumble, my feet forgetting how to walk for a second. And I can't breathe – there's something lodged in my chest – something that's making it squeeze and twist like it's trying to push it out.

I want to walk over and touch this man's lips with mine, run my fingers through his hair, across his jaw, which has the start of a shadow colouring it, move the caress down his arm, marking his skin with my nails. I want to be near him. No, it's more than that. I need to be near him. As if every atom is my body is trying to pull me over there. And my heart's pounding so hard it feels like it's trying to fight its way out of my ribs to get closer to him. Holy crap! What is this? What's going on?

That's when it hits me.

Sphenurus

And I actually think I might throw up, right here, all over the beautiful, wooden deck.

The bond. Is this it?

The thing I wanted with Zac. The thing I was praying for. The thing my mother goes on and on about. The thing she doesn't think I'll ever be good enough to get, even though she never comes straight out and says it.

But that can't be right. It just can't be.

I can't have bonded with a human!

Matt

Shit! She's gorgeous – Zac's new girl. Stunning. Long hair that can only be called golden. Who has gold hair, for Christ's sake? And her eyes are this light brown – almost amber. They're wide as she looks at me. And her mouth – Jesus, those lips that were made to be kissed – is slightly open. I want to move over to her, touch her.

I don't, of course, but my fingers hurt where I'm holding on tightly to the rail.

Fuck, what's wrong with me?

This is Zac's girl. She's involved.

Not available.

Off limits.

Taken.

I don't know how else to say it to convince my brain to stop thinking about how long her legs are.

And then Zac's talking and I try to focus on what he's saying.

"Here she is. Matt, this is Lani. Lani, Matt."

That's my cue to talk, except I can't think of anything.

"Yeah, hi."

Smooth. Shit. I haven't been this tongue tied since...well, I don't think I've ever been this tongue tied! And now I just sound frigging rude!

"Hi."

Her eyes meet mine for a second and then slide away. Is she scared of me? Is that what it is? But that doesn't make any sense.

Zac raises his eyebrows, obviously wondering why I'm being such a rude arse to his girlfriend. I clear my throat.

'Did you have a good drive up?'

'Yes, thanks.'

It seems like a safe question...friendly...but she's still not looking at me. And her voice is cool, like I've done something to offend her. How can I explain it's only because I've been stunned by her beauty into a caveman-like level of coherence?

Zac puts his arm around her shoulders and she leans into him, wrapping her arm around his waist. My stomach clenches and it's all I can do to stop myself stepping forward and pushing them apart.

'Zac wasn't sure how long you were planning to stay.'

As soon as the words are out of my mouth, I want to shove them back in, mainly because they sound rude as hell.

But there's also a part of my brain saying, 'Good job.' It feels like I need to know for my own sanity – or, at the least, so I can get some control over my body's reactions to her. Stupid as it sounds, I've got the urge to ask her to stay forever but that other part of my brain is pretty insistently saying it wants her gone, gone, gone as soon as possible. Largely because I don't think I can stomach watching them be all cloyingly loving.

She looks at Zac and he's frowning at me. We've known each other since the start of high school and I know, just from that look, that he's wondering what my problem is. I wish I could tell him.

'I'll be gone as soon as possible.' Her voice has a definite chill factor to it. Not that I can blame her. It's not her fault my brain and body have suddenly decided to do their own thing. 'As soon as I find a job, I'll be able to get my own place.'

I take a deep breath, trying to bring my churning thoughts back to some sort of logical order. I'm an adult, not a frigging hormonal teenager. I need to get a grip.

'You're welcome to stay as long as you want. The bedroom you're in is just a guest room so it doesn't get used that often. You don't have to worry.'

'Okay. Thanks.'

There's an awkward pause. Christ, I hope this isn't going to happen the whole time she's here. Zac and I have a great friendship – easy – that's why, when I bought this place, I asked him if he wanted to rent out the bottom level.

'Did I tell you Matt owns a surf shop?' I'm glad Zac's here to fill the gaps because I still can't think of anything to say to her. 'He's a bit of an entrepreneur.'

I snort. 'I own a small business. Hardly an empire.'

'Yeah, but you're only twenty-five. There aren't too many people who can say they've done that.' He looks at Lani. 'He worked like a maniac while we were at school – weekends, all over the school holidays – saved every bit of money he made to be able to start his own shop. And he did it, just like he said he would.'

I don't know why Zac's trying to build me up to her but I wish he'd stop. Because I realise I'm actually holding my breath, waiting to see some sort of approval on her face. Which is pathetic. I don't even know this woman. And I don't need her to like me.

'It's no big deal.' My voice is short and Zac gives me that

look again. I sigh. 'Sorry, it's been a long day. I might just leave you guys to it. I'm sure you've got some catching up to do. I'll see you later.'

I smile at them but it feels fake. I'm hoping they don't realize that. Lani won't but Zac might.

I feel her eyes on me all the way in and I'm tempted to look back but I grit my teeth and keep my eyes straight ahead, heading for my room. It feels like my only safe haven.

I lay on my bed, arm over my eyes, trying to get her face out of my head and take a deep breath, imagine it filling my lungs like they taught in the yoga lessons my sister forced me to do after Mum died.

It's working – I can feel some of the stress leaving my body, relaxing into the softness of the mattress, until I realise I can hear them talking, probably murmuring sweet frigging nothings to each other – Lani's mouth near Zac's ear, her breath warm on his skin. I press my arm harder against my eyes. Fuck, I haven't been this hung up on a girl for a long time. And I don't think that I've ever been like this over a girl I've just met! It's weird. And uncomfortable... uncomfortably weird.

I hear Lani laugh – a soft chuckle that makes my insides melt away until I feel like I'm liquid mush. It almost makes me groan. I want her to laugh like that over something *I've* said. Actually I just want her. Full stop.

I swing my legs off the bed and head for the bathroom. I can't lay here anymore listening to them. It's like torture. Shedding my clothes, I turn the shower on full, the icy needles of water cooling me down.

Not that it stops me thinking about the woman standing on my deck. I grit my teeth, rubbing my hands through my hair. I need to get a grip. I'm not about to do anything to break up Zac's relationship...although they've really only had one over the internet so far. And even though there's a shitty part of my brain telling me that doesn't count, it does!

She came up here because she wanted to meet him face to face. She liked him enough to do that. And he's been bouncing around like a lunatic all week waiting for her to get here. He likes her. Really likes her.

And he's my best friend. One of the people I trust in this world. Just like he trusts me. So, she is off limits.

Totally.

I scrub my face with my hands, trying to bring my thoughts into order. Because as much as I say that, all I can picture is her being here in the shower with me. Shit. Turning off the water, I grab the towel, drying myself off like I'm trying to punish my skin.

I lean on the sink and look at myself in the mirror. I can do this. I can be in the same house with her for however long and control this pathetic...lust for her. I can do it for Zac. And for me too, because how badly I want her is actually kind of scary. Crazy scary, considering I don't even know her. Like a teenager fangirling over the latest boy band, for Christ's sake.

You need to get a fucking grip! I tell myself, scowling into the mirror.

I take a deep breath. Then another. It's good. Helps me to focus.

When the door opens, I turn without thinking. Only to be confronted by the very person I'm trying not to think about. Lani is looking at me, mouth open. I know it's only seconds that we stand there, both of us frozen, but it feels like longer. And then I'm grabbing the towel to wrap around me and she's backing out the door so fast I almost wonder if I imagined her.

Unfortunately, I know I haven't.

So Zac's girlfriend has just seen me naked. And part of me – a big part – hopes she likes what she saw. Shit.

Lani

I slam the door to my bedroom and wince as the sound echoes loudly through the house, imagining what Matt will think when he hears it. Leaning against the unintentionally firmly shut door, I put my hands to my cheeks, trying to cool them. I can't believe what just happened. Why didn't he lock the door, for God's sake? Did he do it just to torment me? God! God god god!

I can't get the image of his body out of my head. His skin, browned by the amount of time he must spend in the sun, the muscles in his shoulders as he stood at the sink, the curve of his back down to his buttocks, tight and firm, and then, when he turned... those abs, the line of hair as it crept further down... I put my hands over my eyes, pressing them hard, trying to squeeze the image of him out.

This can't be happening. Not to me.

I *cannot* be in love with a human.

It's just lust. He's hot, that's all. There's no denying that. It makes sense. But what I've got with Zac could be the real thing. I try to ignore the part of my brain that's sniggering at me. I do not want Matt, no matter what the image of him does to my insides.

I go over to the mirror that's hanging from the wall. My cheeks are still slightly pink but I look the same. That doesn't seem possible but I'm glad it is. I fluff my hair and then smooth it down again before straightening my skirt over my hips. Once. Twice. Three times. Just to make sure.

Zac is the reason I'm here. He makes me laugh and he really likes me – I can tell. That's what I need to focus on. I take a deep breath and open my door again. The bathroom door is open and there's no Matt in sight. Thank God.

Zac's waiting for me on the deck still, another glass of wine in his hand.

He smiles and holds it out to me. "For you."

I don't care that it's my second one. I deserve it. Taking a sip, I ignore the slight shaking of my hands. It's cool and fruity. The way I like it. I smile back at him.

'A girl could get used to this treatment.' I'm stupidly proud of the fact that voice seems normal.

'Just as well you've got me around then.'

We sit in the love seat that looks over the water. His arm goes around the back of the chair and he's fingers trace the curve of my neck, covering my skin in goose bumps. This is a good sign. It must be. Something that can be advanced anyway. A development my parents would be happy with. I angle my body more towards him.

'Do you have to work over the next few days?'

He smiles. 'No, I managed to get some time off so I can show you around. I thought it might be nice to get some time together before work gets in the way.'

'That sounds great.'

Better than great. The more time we spend together, the more chance we might have of a bond forming. A real bond –

the one between two of our kind not...well, not anything else. I hope it can happen like that anyway – gradually, lovingly tendered into existence, even if I haven't heard of it happening that way before. Realistically, Dad could only tell me how the bond was for him and Mum. Maybe theirs wasn't the normal way it works. I've never asked my brothers if it was the same for them.

I look around the veranda like I've suddenly realised we're still on our own. 'I hope we haven't made Matt feel uncomfortable?'

Even saying his name does things to my body.

'He'll be okay. I think he's in his room.'

My traitorous mind immediately pictures him lying on his bed, the towel wrapped around his hips still. Or maybe not even that. His tanned body, barely covered by a white sheet...

I figuratively slap myself. Focus, for God's sake. Zac. Remember? The man right in front of you.

'So, when do you actually need to go back to work?'

He grimaces. 'Sunday's my first shift back. I wanted to try and take a whole week off but they can't give me that much time. It's the busy period up here. At least we have three days together. Sorry it couldn't be more.'

I shake my head. 'It's okay. You have to take the shifts when you can.'

'Yeah, it's just a bummer that it's so soon. Especially since you don't know anyone else up here yet. I don't want you to be lonely. Maybe I'll see what Matt's up to on Sunday. He could keep you company.'

'No.' The word comes out more forcefully than I intended and I try to soften it with a small smile. 'I mean, he's already letting me have the room here for a while. I'd hate to ask him for anything else. He's done enough.'

Boy, has he!

'Nah, Matt's a cool guy. He won't mind.'

'No, truly, it's okay. I'll need to unpack anyway and maybe I can start looking for a job. Go around to the shops, put in resumes...you know.'

He turns slightly to look at me. 'You sure? I don't want you to think I don't want to be with you.'

I lean forward and touch my lips to his. Short and sweet. It's nice. Why do I keep using that word?

'I'm sure. It's all good. Don't worry.'

'You must be one of the easiest going girls I've ever met.'

I smile at him. He doesn't need to know that the thought of doing anything with Matt has my heart beating like it's about to explode into a million tiny pieces. And he definitely doesn't need to know that the sight of Matt's naked body still has my insides clenching with longing. Because none of that is true. That's what I've decided. If I don't acknowledge it, then it's just in my head. Not real. And I can deal with that.

'So we still have three days to do something.' I tilt my head at him. 'Anything you think I should see?'

He does what I think is supposed to be a sexy look. 'What? Apart from me?'

I laugh but I can feel my cheeks going red because, again, all I can think about is seeing a naked Matt. Damn it! Zac strokes my cheek with his fingers and suddenly looks serious.

'Hey, it's all good. We'll take this slow if you want. I mean, I know we know each other pretty well but it's different to actually being face to face. I'm not going to make any demands on you or anything.'

I nod and dip my head. He's a nice guy – respectful, funny. He deserves to have someone who wants to be with him totally. And I'm going to make sure that's me.

He leans forward, his mouth almost to mine when the doorbell sounds. He swears softly under his breath.

'Hold that thought, okay?'

I nod. Why does the adage of 'saved by the bell' pop into my mind? I want him to kiss me. I know I do. He is everything I should want.

Everything my parents – my mother – would be happy with.

I can hear Zac talking to someone and then there's a laugh so loud I hear it clearly from here. It's a woman's voice and I tense for a moment, suddenly wondering if it's Matt's girlfriend. It's weird that I hadn't even thought about that possibility until now. But why shouldn't he have one. From a totally objective point of view, he is gorgeous, obviously a hard worker and Zac likes him, so he must be a good person. Not that it matters to me. I have Zac. Who is also gorgeous and funny and nice...

So, I'm not going to dwell on the fact that, all of a sudden, I want to scratch this imaginary girlfriend's eyes out.

Zac comes out arm in arm with a woman who looks to be in her thirties. She's stunning. Tall with great curves that she really owns, long, dark hair that cascades down her back and blue eyes framed by dark lashes. Like Matt's. And she has on the most beautiful dress – rockabilly with a sweetheart neckline and lacing down the side. It's well made, that's pretty obvious from the detail I can see.

She smiles at me as she comes out to the deck and I can't help but smile back, even though I don't normally get on with other women. I don't know why. They all just seem to steer clear of me. All my good friends at home are guys.

Zac holds out his hand to me. 'See, Roxanne, didn't I tell you she was gorgeous? Roxanne, Lani. Lani, Roxanne, Matt's sister.'

I try to hide the relief that rushes through me, making my body hot and cold all at the same time. I'm trying so hard not to care but it feels like my body keeps betraying me.

"Hi. Nice to meet you.'

She moves forward to sit beside me and takes my hand. I don't automatically want to pull back, which is weird, because usually I don't like strangers touching me.

'For once, Zac wasn't exaggerating. You are gorgeous. Why on earth are you trading down to him?'

'Hey!' Zac says, but I can tell they're teasing each other.

'I don't know,' I say. 'I think he's pretty cute.'

He grins at me and looks at Roxanne.

'See? She thinks I'm cute.'

Roxanne laughs. 'Well, there's no accounting for taste.'

We laugh with her. She's that type of person.

'And where is my great lump of a brother?'

Zac shrugs. 'I think he's in his room.'

She cups her hands around her mouth. 'Matthew Trent James, get your ass out here now. Your sister is here to see you.'

I giggle – giggle for God's sake, I never giggle – but just the thought of Matt being ordered around like that makes it bubble out. Roxanne winks at me and I decide she's one woman I could possibly get on with. Someone to be like maybe.

It's not long before Matt's walking out through the lounge room. He's dressed, thank God, but I still can't look at him for long.

'I thought I heard the dulcet tones of my fair sister.'

'You bet your ass, baby.'

He comes over to kiss her, close enough to me that I can smell him – the aftershave he uses but his smell as well. Matt-cologne. He should market it. I only just manage to hold back a moan. It's not until he moves away that I'm game enough to take another breath.

'So, what do you think of the gorgeous maiden our Zac's managed to woo?'

She puts her hands out like I'm a prize on a quiz show and

she's the hostess. My cheeks go hot again. I don't think I've ever blushed as much as I have in the last few hours. It's ridiculous... as if I'm a teenager once more.

Matt's eyes meet mine for a split second and then his face seems to close off, like he's devoid of all emotion. Maybe he thinks I walked in on him on purpose – some sort of desperate female. Which is pathetic. As if I need to do that when I've got Zac waiting for me. Arsehole!

'She's gorgeous, no doubt about it.' But his voice is neutral. As if he doesn't really like me but is too polite to say it. That hurts me more than it should, given that I've decided I don't care what he thinks.

Roxanne just looks at him for a moment, eyes narrowed. Then she sighs. It sounds like a sigh filled with meaning, none of which I understand.

'So, Lani.' She's looking at me again. 'How long are you planning to stay in Noosa for?'

I can't stop my eyes from flicking to Matt before I answer her. When his eyes meet mine for that second, a jolt of awareness scorchers through my chest.

"I'm not sure. I'd like to move up here permanently but it all depends.'

'Of course you're going to stay,' Zac says with a grin. 'A few more kisses and you won't be able to leave me. Any guy will pale in comparison.'

I manage to keep myself from looking at Matt this time. Only just.

'Depends on what?' Roxanne is doing a good job of ignoring Zac.

"Well, I have to find a job for one thing.'

There's a muttering sound and we all look at Matt. He looks embarrassed, like he didn't mean to say anything out loud. Not that that's going to let him off the hook.

'What?'

My voice should clue him in to the fact that he's in trouble but it's like he takes it as a challenge. I can see his jaw tense.

"I just think most people would've had something lined up before they came all this way.'

For a second, I'm too stunned to say anything. Zac answers before my brain can kick into gear.

'Yeah, well, not everyone's a total control freak like you. I think it's cool that she came all this way without everything being planned out. It's spontaneous. Brave.'

I *want* to be pleased that that's what Zac thinks of me. But he doesn't know how hard it was for me to do this... how scared I was. How scared I still am. Scared of the fact that I know no one except for him, scared of not getting a job, scared of failing – of things not working out with us and disappointing my mother so she gets that tight, pinched look and I know I'm the cause of it. Again. Because what if she's right? What if I'm not good enough? I can't let that happen. I need this to be okay.

Roxanne snorts at her brother and then turns to look at me. She looks me up and down, surveying me.

'You like fashion.'

It feels like a statement more than a question but I nod anyway.

'Monday morning, come and see me in my shop. I sell clothes – mainly one-off pieces people can't get anywhere else. I need a new sales assistant. If that job's okay for you.'

I don't know what to say. It feels like there's an echoing silence in my brain for a few seconds while it tries to work out what's actually happened. And then it starts clamouring, jumping up and down, telling me yes, of course, take it, say something!

'Oh. That would be great. Just unbelievably fantastic.

Thank you so much. Are you sure though? You don't know anything about me.'

I know I should shut up but I can't seem to stop. Why would she do this? Offer me a job. Is it pity? I mash my lips together, trying to stop the flow of words.

'True. So an interview then. Right here, right now, since I'm asking you to start in a few days' time. Are you ready for Roxanne's quick questions?'

I don't know what that really means but I nod anyway.

'Where do you fit in your family?'

'I'm the youngest. Mum, Dad and two older brothers.'

Matt leans forward. 'So you're the youngest and the only girl?'

I nod. It's stiff. His tone of voice makes it clear he doesn't think this is a point in my favour. Whatever. I don't care what he thinks. He's not the one giving me a job.

'Okay. Highest level reached in your education.'

I look down and take a deep breath before answering.

'High school. Year ten.'

'And what did you do when you left school?'

I don't want to tell her. It makes me sound so pathetic. Like a spoilt brat. But I can't not tell her either.

'I did a year in a hairdressing apprenticeship but then, well, it wasn't really what I wanted to do. And I still haven't worked out what it is I *do* actually want yet, so...' I shrug. 'I've just worked in different places since then. Cafes, waitressing for private functions. That sort of thing.'

I want to tell her I love fashion. That I design and sew and make my own clothes but I can't. I'm not brave enough for that. Not with my mum's comments from over the years playing in my head. Roxanne is obviously a professional at this. And I'm just playing, like a kid.

She nods and the moment passes anyway.

21

'Ever been fired?'

'No. Never.'

'Great. Last one. Can you come in and do some training on Sunday for a few hours before you start?'

'You still want me?'

She smiles. 'I like to think I'm a pretty good judge of people. And I think you and I'll muddle along just fine. Besides, I really do need someone. I'm not making that up to make you feel better. I fired my sales assistant two days ago for stealing from me. So don't do anything to cross me.'

I take a big swallow and nod. She wraps her arm around me and laughs.

"Don't look so scared. I'm not going to eat you.'

Matt

I can't believe Rox has offered her a frigging job. As if it's not going to be hard enough to avoid her as it is, now she's got another connection to me. Shit. Could this day get any worse?

Rox leans forward, her elbows on her knees and looks at me. She has a way of doing that which makes me feel like she knows everything that's going on in my head. God, I hope not because she'd be really disappointed in me. *I'm* really disappointed in me.

'So, Matthew, what are you doing Sunday?'

I narrow my eyes at her. She's trapped me into doing too many things in the past for me to answer that question straight up.

'I'm not sure. Why?'

She sighs like I've insulted her.

'Such mistrust in your sister. I need you to look after Georgie for me if I'm going to show Lani the ropes and not chuck her in the deep end.'

I smile. 'Sure, Dan's rostered on to work in the shop. I'll look after pipsqueak for you.'

'Good. She was saying she needed some time with Uncle Matt.' She looks over at Lani who's watching us. 'Georgie is my daughter. She's five and loves everything Uncle Matt does – surfing and swimming – everything nastily physical like that.'

Lani nods but the smile she plasters on her face looks... contrived. The type of one I remember using on Rox when I was eighteen and she was trying to tell me how to still live my life.

I rock back in my chair, fingers tapping on the armrests.

'You don't like kids?'

Her eyes flick to Rox and she looks panicked for a moment. My chest tightens and I want to suck the question back in, so my shit-headedness isn't on such total display. What the hell's wrong with me?

'Um, I've never really had much to do with kids,' she says, biting her lip before she seems to realise what she's doing and presses them together instead. 'One of my brothers has a little boy, a baby, but I haven't really spent much time with him. They lived about two hours away from us in Tassie and no one else I know has had any kids.'

'Georgie's awesome.' Zac moves closer to her and puts his hand on her shoulder. She covers it with hers. I try not to notice how long her fingers are and how they curl around his. 'You'll love her. She'll have you wrapped around her little finger before you even know it.'

Lani looks up at Zac and then back to Rox.

'I'm sure she's cute.'

Rox laughs – that big booming one that always makes me feel like smiling... even when I'm in the shittiest of moods.

'Don't worry. Being enamoured with my munchkin is not

part of your job description. I'll pick you up Sunday when I drop her off if you like. Say around ten, ten-thirty?'

Lani nods. 'That'd be great.'

Rox stands up and my heart thumps in my chest, adrenalin invading my system like it's ready for an invasion, for Christ's sake. If she leaves it's just going to be the three of us again and I'm not ready for that. Not yet. I stand up too and she raises an eyebrow.

'I'll walk you to the front door.'

She cocks her head at me. 'Sure.' She turns back to Zac and Lani. 'Zac, see you Sunday?'

'Yeah, I'll be here in the morning before I go to work. Got to see the Georgie girl.'

She smiles at him and then looks at Lani.

'I'm glad you're going to be working at the shop.'

'I am too. Thanks so much for giving me a chance.'

Rox winks at her. 'See you in a couple of days.'

She links her arm through mine and is quiet as we leave the deck. It's almost a relief to walk away which is utterly pathetic since it's my house. Rox is still silent as we head down the stairs – unusual for her. I feel like I'm waiting for the guillotine to fall; big sister honesty with no holds barred. It's not until I open the door for her that she turns and actually says something.

'Lani's an interesting girl.'

I shrug but my heart is pounding out an uncomfortable beat, like a song that doesn't quite work. 'Is she?'

'And pretty stunning as well.'

I look out the door. 'Yep. I think she'll be good in your shop. Even though we don't really know her.'

She's quiet again and I look back at her.

'It seemed like you were a bit harsh on her up there before. Judgemental, even. That's not usually like you.'

I resist the urge to squirm. I'm an adult, for Christ's sake – I've got my life in order.

'Not judging. Just asking the questions. It's up to Zac what he thinks of her. He's the one who she's come up here for.'

I can hear a slight note of resentment in my voice, which is ridiculous in a grown man. I'm praying Rox doesn't pick up on it. She moves closer instead and wraps her arms around my waist. I hug her back, remembering all the times she did this for me when Mum died, even though it must've been killing her too.

'Just be careful, okay?'

I pull back slightly, looking at her.

'Careful of what?'

'Zac's one of your best friends. It would be terrible if a girl came between you. Just be careful how you treat her.'

It sounds like she's talking about the whole judgement thing but I wonder if there's something else. Something she senses in me – my guilty conscious, maybe. Which royally sucks, because if Rox is picking something up then Zac could be too. Maybe I need to move out of my own god-damn house just to be sure.

'I'll be careful.'

She smiles at me. 'I know you will. Anyway, I have to go and pick up Georgie from care. I just wanted to come around and see Zac's new girl quickly. I'll see you Sunday?'

'Okay.'

I shut the door and turn around, looking at the stairs. I'm tempted to just take off – go for a surf or a paddle. Leave the two of them alone. But I need to at least tell them I'm going. Rox is right. I *have* been rude. And judgemental. It's not Lani's fault she's had this effect on me. I need to stop being an arse-hole. This isn't me.

So I take a deep breath and walk up the stairs.

Lani

Three days. Three days of just relaxing and having fun and seeing Noosa. Three days with Zac.

And it's been...nice.

I've enjoyed it. I really have. It's not like I have to convince myself of that. Zac's been funny and thoughtful and a great tour guide. And I love Noosa. Love the beaches and the cafes and the easygoingness of it. This is what I wanted.

But each time we've been out, all I can think about is whether Matt will be home when we get back. It's driving me crazy.

He's barely said two words to me in that time. As soon as we get back from wherever we've been, he takes off again – out on the water or into work or to his room. He hasn't been rude... he just hasn't been here. Which is also driving me crazy. Because I want to talk to him, hear what he thinks, see him smile, watch the way he moves. And that's okay. He's Zac's best friend – it's normal to want to know him better...

He's sitting on the deck when we get back Saturday afternoon, a magazine laid over his lap, feet up on the balcony. He looks relaxed. Happy. Until he sees us. I watch his jaw tighten and he immediately sits up, legs down, like he's wary of something. Me? Perhaps he can sense how much I want to trace his face with my fingers, follow the line of his chest, down, down...God, what if that's it? What if he thinks I'm a total bitch – here to be with his friend but wanting him? And he'd be right. I need to get it together before I wreck everything.

'Hi. How was the drive?' It's a normal greeting – the words are right – and yet, it sounds off. Like he's too tight.

Zac takes my hand and smiles at him. 'Good. We checked out a few of the beaches, went for lunch. Nice, hey?'

He looks at me for confirmation and I smile back, even if my brain is only half in it. The other half is wondering how long it'll take Matt to leave.

'Yeah, it was nice.'

'Well, good. I'm glad the coast is putting on such great weather for you.'

Banal conversation about the weather. Safe. Even if it doesn't fill the almost urgent need that's sitting my chest, my throat, making everything tight.

'It has been lovely.' See – easy.

He flicks the magazine shut. 'Well, I was about to go out for a paddle. I'll leave you guys to it.'

'You don't have to go.' The words come out too fast. Wrong. I take a breath – in and out, smiling at him. 'I mean, this is your house. I feel like we're constantly chasing you off.'

He smiles, his eyes flicking to mine only briefly before looking away again.

'You're not chasing me away. It's a nice afternoon to be on the water, that's all.'

'Okay, have fun.' Zac's already leading me out to the double chair, passing close to Matt. He watches us for a moment, just like I'm watching him, and then shakes his head before walking inside.

I turn quickly, ignoring the sense of loss swelling in me. I need to make the most of my time with Zac.

Zac.

Someone like me. Maybe it *is* better that Matt isn't here. Then I can give all my focus to the person I'm supposed to. I sit next to him and his arm goes around my shoulders. I make myself snuggle in and his embrace tightens.

'It's been an awesome day. I've enjoyed being with you.'

'Me too.' I'm slightly buoyed by the fact that I'm not lying. 'So you have to work tomorrow?'

'Yeah. My shift starts at twelve.'

'Okay. I think Roxanne's coming at ten to pick me up.'

'How awesome is that? Roxanne having a job that's just perfect for you. You know, with your interest in clothes and fashion.'

'It feels like it's all coming together.'

He rubs my shoulder. 'Like it was meant to be.'

I laugh. A low one that I hope sounds sexy. And then, nothing. Neither of us talk. I don't know what to say which is weird because on the internet, it was easy to keep the conversation going. That was one of the things I loved about talking to Zac. It was stress-free. But over the last three days, there are times when it's been...awkward.

I turn my head instead and he quickly takes up the invitation, bringing his lips to meet mine. His kiss is soft, gentle, like he's trying his hardest to be respectful. It's...nice. I'm so sick of that word! I want it to be so much more than that! I need it to be. I turn my body further around and put my hand on his thigh. The muscles are hard under my touch. He's in good shape.

His hand goes up on the side of my head, sliding up until it covers my ear. I struggle not to pull away, knowing he doesn't realise what he's doing – that I hate my ears being covered. Hate it. I only last a few seconds before I sit back.

Zac touches my hand.

'That was nice. I'm looking forward to more of them.'

God, now he's saying it too! I smile back at him. It feels forced, too tight, so I look out over the water instead. The sun is starting to set and the changing colours on the river look beautiful.

'This is such an amazing spot to live.'

Zac's thumb rubs over my palm. 'Sure is. I was pretty excited when Matt asked me to come and rent part of it. There's no way I'd be able to afford something like this on my own.'

'One day, maybe.'

He laughs. 'I doubt it. Not on a waiter's wage.'

'You don't want to do anything else?'

He shrugs. 'Not really. I like not having too much stress. Then I can fly as much as a want. All I need is enough money to meet the bills and I'm good.'

I tell myself it's a great attitude to have. Except there's a part of me that wants him to have some ambition. Wants him to think about being financially secure, having a nice life, a house of our own, like my mum and dad. Which is so hypocritical because I haven't found that ambition in myself yet either. But it just seems more important for a guy. That's what Dad's always said. I shouldn't need a guy to look after me though. Another thing to work on – get better at.

A movement down on the grass at the river's edge catches my eye. It's Matt and he's carrying something. A board. The shape of his body, without a shirt to hide anything, is silhouetted in the afternoon light. It makes everything in my body clench. Clench and twist and twang. And when he steps onto the board and uses a paddle to push himself along, I can't stop watching him. His rhythm is hypnotic.

Zac clears his throat next to me and I feel the heat rush to my cheeks as I turn to look at him. He's watching me and there's a guarded expression on his face that wasn't there before. Or maybe that's just my own guilt.

'I've never seen anyone do that.'

I blurt the words out as if I need to explain myself before he gets the wrong idea. I don't want Matt. Well, it's obvious that my body finds him attractive and, if there were different circumstances, I might be interested in seeing where it goes – purely as a bit of a fling. But there aren't different circumstances and I want what Zac can offer. One of my own kind. A future, like my parents have. Safety. No secrets.

Zac looks out, watching Matt for a moment.

'It's a stand-up paddle board. They're fun. You should ask Matt to teach you – I'm sure he'd jump at the chance.'

His tone is slightly off and my heart is telling me that this isn't going well. He needs to want me. Because if he doesn't, I've come all this way for nothing. No bond. No future. And another way for Mum to remind me that I never quite measure up.

'I'd prefer if you taught me how to do it.'

There's a pause – so small I almost miss it – but there anyway.

'Sure. I can teach you.'

I turn my body so I'm facing him again and put my legs on his thighs. My skirt rides up but that's okay. My legs are one of my best features. And I want him to notice them. I don't want him thinking about what sort of person I am. I want him to want me and forget about everything else – forget that I was just checking out his best friend.

He runs his hand up my calf muscle, stopping just above

the knee, his thumb on the inside of my leg, drawing little circles. My heart's pounding for a whole different reason now. I sit up, straddling him on the chair, legs either side of his and look down at him. His pupils have dilated and I know he wants me. I can feel it. And he's forgotten about how I was looking at Matt. For the moment anyway.

'God, you're so sexy.' His voice is husky, rough, and my body is thrumming with the power I have to do that to him.

I bring his hands up on either side of my hips and lean down, my lips only just touching his. Teasing. I hear his breath catch in his throat and move to the side of his mouth, his jaw, to just under his earlobe. His hands tighten around me, digging into my hips.

'Jesus, Lani, stop. Okay. We need to stop.' But it doesn't really sound like he wants me too.

'Why?'

'Because...' He clears his throat again. 'And I can't believe I'm saying this, but because we should take this slow. I don't want you to feel like this is payment for me organising for you to stay here or anything stupid like that. I want you to feel comfortable and...I don't know...ready, I guess.'

'I'm not thinking it's payment.' I whisper it in his ear and I can feel him shiver under me.

And then his hands come up and are grabbing the top of my arms, pushing me back. He's breathing hard and shuts his eyes for a moment, as if trying to get control, before opening them again.

'I'm trying to be all respectful and shit. You're not playing fair.'

I smile at him. 'Aren't I?'

He groans and pushes himself up, so we're standing together, hip to hip.

'No, you're not. Come on, I'm taking you out to dinner.'

I thread my hands around his back.

'Are you sure that's what you really want?'

He laughs. 'Not at all. But we're doing it anyway.'

I laugh with him and let him go, smoothing my skirt down.

'Do you want to have a shower and change before we go out?'

I nod. 'That'd be great.'

'Ladies first then.'

I touch his arm as I walk past, my fingernails gliding over his skin, and he groans again. And I'm proud of the fact that as I walk across the deck, I don't look out to the water. Even though I want to.

Because Zac and I are good again. And that's all that matters.

Matt

I push the paddle through the water, moving the board along, keeping my balance against the slight ripple caused by the breeze. I love this time of day – it's just the sound of the water under me and the birds starting to roost in the trees, settling down for the night. It's peaceful. Except today, and for the last three days, it's been hard to find the calmness I usually enjoy.

It's hard to find any thought that doesn't include something about Lani.

Lani's face when she walked in on me in the bathroom on the first day she was here – pink cheeked, mouth slightly open, amber eyes wide.

Lani's hair and her face and her body and those legs that I just want to run my hand up.

Lani working for my sister and what that means.

Lani kissing Zac and how pathetically at a loss that makes me feel.

Jesus, I feel like I'm back at high school with a crush on the popular girl and hormones running wild. I see the way she

34

looks at Zac, the way she touches him and smiles at him. Probably the only thought she has for me is wishing I was out of the way.

Which I'm going to have to continue to do more of, I think, for my own sanity. Until I can work out how to be around her without feeling like my hormones are running the show.

I'm a frigging adult, for Christ's sake. I take a deep breath, focusing on the flow of the water, on the rhythm of my stroke, centring myself.

As I come even to the parklands that line the water's edge, I steer the board towards the bank and pull it up onto the grass, just as the last of the sunlight is starting to sink into darkness. Saturday evening, the area is full of families and kids running around, having summer barbecues, filling the air with the smell of cooked sausages and onions. Tonight the distraction is welcome rather than annoying.

I sit down, leaning back onto one of the trees, and watch life go on around me.

'Well, look who's away from the shop for once.'

I don't need to turn to know who it is. Karli. My ex of six months. The last person I want to see. She sits down next to me without asking if I want company. But then, thinking about what other people might want was never one of her strong points.

'Aren't you going to say hello?'

I try to keep the sigh in. 'Hi, Karli.'

I don't turn to look at her. I stare out at the water instead, wishing she'd go. The few times I've seen her since the breakup have left neither of us happy. She doesn't get the hint though, even though it feels like I'm basically slapping her in the face with it.

'So what have you been up to?'

Normal chit-chat. I can't do it with her. Actually it's more like I don't want to do it. I don't want to be friends, despite how long we were together and how much history we've had. I don't know if I'll ever be in that place.

I shrug and finally glance over at her. She's looking at me in a way that makes me want to put a shirt on. Yet, she didn't want me enough six months ago to stay faithful. And that thought still has enough power to make me feel angry and sick and rejected. Not as much as it did back then but the taste of it is still in my mouth, bitter and metallic. It's all I can do not to just get up and leave but I'm not giving her that power.

'Not much. Working.'

She laughs. 'Yeah, I can believe that. Since that was basically all you did for the seven years we were together.'

I choose not to respond to that. It's an old argument that, from experience, I know I can't win. The main reason, apparently, that she felt she needed to be with someone else. She pulls her hair back and weaves it into a plait at the side of her head. I wait. This usually means she's got something to tell me. I'm guessing it's probably not something I want to hear.

'Anyway, I wanted to let you know that I'm in another relationship. Before you heard it from someone else or saw us together.'

I wait for my reaction – a punch to the guts, a pain in the chest...it's there, but less, like it's more of a habit rather than real pain. The 'moving on' that I've been waiting for. It's a relief actually.

'Okay.'

There's a pause – it feels like I'm supposed to say something else but I don't know what she wants from me. Maybe I never really did.

'That's it? You don't want to know who it is? Or, I don't know, want to talk about how you feel?'

I get it now. She wants a reaction. Some emotion. Something that tells her that I'm not over her. It's all about Karli and what she needs. I'm glad I'm past wanting her.

'Tell me who it is if you want, Karli. I don't really care.'

She takes a deep breath – a portent for a deep, dark secret obviously. Something she's nervous about. I feel myself tense.

"It's Brent.'

Brent. The guy she used to work with. The guy she had the affair with. The one she promised meant nothing to her when we were still in the middle of the break-up fall out. I almost smile – an I-was-right-all-along one – but I manage to keep it in. And anyway, if I really look at this objectively, they belong together. Both of them worry about a lot about what other people think. Both of them are big into the image thing. The best clothes, the best cars, the best holidays. Everything material.

'Okay.'

There's a moment when she's silent and I wonder if we're finished. But I should know better.

'Are you alright?'

'Yes, Karli, I'm fine.'

She looks almost disappointed by that. But maybe I'm just being a bastard.

'We're going on a holiday to Melbourne.'

'Great.' It was one of the things we used to argue about the most. Karli always wanted to go on holidays. A weekend here, a few weeks there. And it was just never possible with the shop. Not as much as she wanted anyway.

'Like I said, I just wanted to let you know before you found out from anyone else.'

'Okay.'

'Stop saying that! I didn't mean to hurt you. You know that.' She rushes the words out like they're uncomfortable in her mouth. I've heard them before though. Over and over.

I sigh. 'I don't know what you want me to say, Karli. We've been through this. And I don't really want to go through it again. I'm done.'

She's quiet. Almost long enough that I start to wonder if she's actually heard me this time.

'What about you? Have you found someone else?'

'No.'

An image of Lani pops into my brain, standing on the deck, looking unsure when she was first introduced to me. But I can't have her so I ignore that. Not that I'd be telling Karli anyway.

She touches my arm, her hand on my skin for longer than it probably should be. I shift slightly and it falls away.

'You know, sometimes I really miss you. Miss us.'

I know she wants me to say I miss her too. But I don't. Not now. Five months ago, that probably would've been a different story. Now, though, I've had enough distance to know better.

'You're with Brent.'

She lets go of her hair and laughs. I know it's not a real one but I'm sick of trying to work out what she actually means. It's not my job anymore.

'Yes.'

The silence is turning awkward when she smooths down her hair and stands. I stand too. She moves forward, her hand on my arm again. I don't have time to react before she leans in to kiss me. It's only because I turn my head that it lands on my cheek. I want to rub the feel of her lips from my skin. It's like it's burnt me somehow, branding me. She straightens up and looks at me, sadness in her eyes. I wonder if it makes me a terrible person that that gives me a momentary stab of satisfaction.

'Are you sure? About us not being together? About not giving it another chance? I've changed, Matt. Grown up, I think, in the last six months. I know I did the wrong thing. I accept that.'

I step back, away from her.

'Don't, Karli. I don't want to do this. It's over. Done with.'

She nods and, once again, her face is sad. And, for reasons I can't explain, this time it makes me feel like a bastard.

Lani

I look out over the water and feel really good...happy. Zac's brought me to a restaurant on a boat, moored to a jetty overlooking the darkening river, highlighted by the moon. It's a great way to finish the third day of my new life, before all the trappings of actual life get in the way.

I push the last of my wild mushroom risotto away, too full to finish it even though it's amazing. Zac smiles at me, running his hand through the hair falling over his forehead, even though it falls back in place straight away.

'I can't believe you're here. I know I keep saying that but, honestly, I didn't think it'd actually happen.'

I cock my head at him. 'Why?'

'I don't know. You've been in Tassie your whole life, your family's there, your friends. It's what you know. I guess I just thought I wouldn't be enough to get you up here.'

I laugh. 'But they're all the reasons I wanted to move. Everything was the same. All the time. I needed a change – something new.'

'So it wasn't my good looks and charm then?'

'Well, they certainly helped,' I say, rubbing my foot up his calf under the table.

He arches one eyebrow at me. 'I'll take that as a compliment, will I?'

'Okay. If you want to.'

He laughs and sits back, drink in his hand. I toy with the stem of my wine glass, feeling the condensation under my fingertips.

'Can I ask you something?'

'Sure. Anything.'

I take a deep breath. 'Do you believe in the whole bonding thing? Do you believe it's real?'

It's hard to look at him. I want to just keep staring at my wine. And I want him to say yes. Yes, and that he's felt it with me. I want to be good enough, interesting enough...I don't know...whatever it is that sparks the bond. I finally bring my eyes up.

'I guess. Sort of. I mean, I've heard that it happens but I've just never seen it. It didn't happen for my mum and dad. Or any of my mates yet.'

I don't know what to say. I've never heard of that before – of one of our kind getting in a serious relationship...a long term one...without bonding.

'But how did they know they were right for each other without the bond?'

He laughs. 'How does anybody know?'

There's a sinking feeling in my stomach...an aching that has nothing to do with the food. I take a sip of wine, letting the sweetness sit on my tongue for a moment. It doesn't help.

'My mum and dad have it. The bond. And my two brothers. And some friends.'

'Really. Shit. I thought it was a pretty rare thing.'

I shake my head, waiting to see what else he says. Waiting

to know what to say, what to do. I don't want to push it...push him...but I want him to want it as much as I do. Because maybe that's what makes the difference – how badly you want it.

'Hell, must be the air or something down there, hey?'

I lick my lips and choose my words carefully.

'There was even a guy I knew in Tasmania, Nick, who bonded with a human. That's what he believed anyway. I don't know. It doesn't seem right.'

I hold my breath, waiting for his reaction. It's important. Or it feels like it should be anyway.

'Really?'

I nod, waiting for a further response from him – how he feels about it – but nothing comes. He just takes another sip of his drink.

I sit up straighter in my chair. 'I think it's disgusting.'

He frowns at me, obviously confused. And now I don't know what to think.

'Disgusting? That seems a bit harsh.'

The butterflies swarm in my stomach, taking off in a massive wave. I want to impress him, be like him, agree with him. But I don't know that I can. My mum and dad thought it was wrong. Most of my friends thought it was weird. So how can he say he thinks it's okay? But then, he thought that the whole bond thing was almost mythical. Maybe he just doesn't understand.

'She's human though. If they get together – like a serious, long term relationship; have kids – they won't be able to carry on the gene.'

He shrugs. 'So? I don't think it's that big of a deal. Some people can't have kids anyway, no matter how much they want them. The only thing that'd be crap about it is trying to keep it a secret. It's hard enough keeping it from Matt now we live in the same house and he's only a mate. It'd suck to have to do that to your partner.'

My mouth is open slightly and I snap it shut. I can't believe he's saying this. He has to be wrong. Has to be! It's so selfish to think like that. To just care about yourself and not worry about passing the gene on... That's what the whole bond is about. Or at least, that's what Mum and Dad have been telling me my whole life. How important it is to make sure the gene gets carried on and our kind continue.

And I don't believe that Nick and Grace have a true bond anyway. That's what he was probably just telling himself so he didn't have to take responsibility for his decisions. And that feeling I got when I saw Matt, when I think about it now, it can't be a bond, no matter how intense it felt. No matter how much it made me want to forget everything but him. It's lust. Pure and simple.

'Are your mum and dad happy?'

'I guess. Happy enough. They argue a lot but I think that's just them. Different cultures, different backgrounds, so that gets in their way sometimes. They broke up once, when I was about four or five, but got back together. They say they love each other. They must, to get back together and stick with it.'

I tell him the story of my parent's love but it feels like they're the words I should be saying. My head is in a whirl. All my life I've thought the only way for us to find someone – to be with someone in a serious relationship – was to wait for the bond. Then you'd know...for sure. I feel sick. Like everything I've known has somehow shifted, disorientating me.

Can I still be with Zac without the bond? Not just messing around but really be with him? Do I want to be? I don't know. I'd be the only one in my family not to have a bond – another disappointment for my mum to subtly point out, like she's only trying to help me when she says the things she does. It's too hard. Too big.

'What's the bond supposed to feel like anyway?'

He doesn't sound like he's making fun of me – he looks truly curious.

I take a deep breath and force a smile, acting like everything's okay. Putting on my face...my mask.

'My dad's always said that when you see the person, it's like it sucks the breath out of you and when you breathe back in, you're breathing in your future with them.'

I can feel my cheeks going red. I can't help it. To me, it's always sounded so wonderful...so romantic, but saying it out loud to someone who doesn't really believe in it or understand it...it sounds lame.

Zac reaches over and grabs my hand. He smiles.

'Breathing in your future with them, huh? That sounds great.'

I smile back. It doesn't feel as forced this time. Maybe it'll be okay. Maybe I just need to breathe and relax.

'Did you feel that when you saw me?'

No. That's what I should say. But I can't. I'm not ready to give up on it yet.

'I'm not sure,' I say instead and that feels at least like a partial truth.

He presses his lips together and nods. 'Is that a deal breaker for you? If there's no bond?'

My throat is suddenly dry and I take another sip of my wine. He's watching me. I put the glass down carefully on the wet circle that it's already made on the tablecloth. It fits perfectly. A match, of course. No doubt that it would be.

'I don't think so.' And for a moment, it feels like I really mean it.

Matt

Georgie's still playing under the sprinkler when I pull up at Roxanne's, the summer heat lasting into the night. She's squealing in a way that makes me smile, even though I don't really feel like it. Infectious. Oh, to be back to the time in my life when running under the sprinkler was all I needed to make me happy.

Rox is sitting on the bench by the door, watching her, a glass of wine in her hand. She raises it in salute to me as I get closer.

'Cheers, little brother, what brings you over tonight? Something that couldn't wait until tomorrow?'

'Do I need a reason to visit?'

'Of course not. But there usually is.'

She's probably right, which I guess makes me a bit of a crappy uncle and brother. I sit down next to her and take the glass from her hand, stealing a sip before handing it back. We sit in silence for a moment, watching Georgie. I love that Rox always gives me space to talk. I lean forward, elbows on my knees.

'I ran into Karli this afternoon at the park. She was up for a chat.'

'Oh.' That one word holds every element of understanding I was counting on.

'Yeah.'

'That must've been interesting. And what did she have to say?'

'She and Brent are officially together. She wanted to tell me before I found out from someone else or saw them together. She thought it'd be the right thing to do.'

'Mmm. Well, she's all heart, isn't she?'

'She also wanted to know if there was any chance of us getting back together. Because, apparently, she's changed and she misses me. Misses us.'

'Shit. She really asked you that?'

'Yep.'

'Unbelievable.' She takes a sip of her wine, and eyes me over the glass. 'What did you say?'

'That there was absolutely no chance! Jeez, Rox, do you think I'm that stupid? After what she did...' I shake my head.

'Well, I thought that'd be the answer but I just needed to check. You guys were together for a long time. And you loved her.'

'Loved being the operative word.'

'How did she take it?'

'Honestly, I don't really care.'

We sit in the night air for a while longer, watching Georgie run around. I laugh when she runs over to me, trying to give me a hug and make me wet. And then she's off again, worried only about having as much fun as possible before she needs to come inside.

'How long has it been since you've broken up? Six months?'

I nod, still watching Georgie.

'And is there anyone else you're interested in now?'

I turn back to Rox, feeling the creases between my eyebrows set into place.

'What?'

'Just thought I'd ask. You know, big sister nosiness and everything. Is there anyone else?'

Her voice is deceptively innocent. I don't trust it.

'No.'

'Okay.'

She takes a towel off the chair arm and holds it up.

'Come on, Georgie. Time to go inside.'

'Aw, really. Just a bit longer?'

'No, miss. Come on. Dinner and then bed.'

Georgie drags her feet as she walks over, disappointment obvious in every movement. It makes me want to laugh although I manage to keep it to a smile. She wouldn't be happy if she thinks I'm laughing at her. Rox wraps her in the towel and then pulls her in close, tickling her until she is giggling. Happy. A family. And even though they're mine too, I feel lonelier than I have in a long time.

Lani

We've started our after-dinner coffee when it hits. The intense pain comes on so abruptly I'm unable to draw breath for a few seconds and I grip the edge of the table in an effort not to cry out. Zac doesn't look like he's doing much better.

'We need to get out of here,' he says after the first wave of agony passes. He rises from his seat and holds out his hand to me.

'I can't believe I forgot the aurora was due tonight.' Stupid. All I can put it down to is the long trip and the fact that my mind's been pre-occupied.

'I thought it was happening tomorrow,' Zac says, stopping for a moment as another wave hits us, thankfully not as intense as the first one.

Not that the reason for our confusion – for being caught unawares – matters. It's happening...that's all there is to it. This is the part I hate about what I am. The pain that comes from the forced change that the southern aurora brings on. Afterwards is fantastic – a buzz that lasts for ages – but this pain... this I hate.

We hurry to the front desk to pay and the waitress looks worried when a soft groan makes its way past my clenched teeth. The pain feels like it's ripping through my organs, slicing and dicing. She looks at Zac.

'Is she okay? I hope it's nothing you've had here tonight?'

He shakes his head but I can see how much it's costing him to hold it together and not show his pain. Hopefully it's not obvious to her. I shake my head. It's all I can do and even though I feel rude, I can't talk. If I do, all my control will be lost.

Zac's breathlessness could be taken as concern for me. 'I'm going to take her to the hospital. Appendicitis, maybe.'

She takes his credit card to press against the machine and the beep seems to take forever. Hurry, hurry, hurry. God, please hurry.

'Can I call you an ambulance?' Concern is clear on her face and in her voice.

But Zac is taking my hand again and dragging me out as he answers.

'It'll be quicker if I drive.'

And then we're out. Out in the fresh air, out into the darkness. Out into the park filled with people. God, how could we have been so stupid! And there's no way either of us can drive. Not with pain that feels as if it's trying to crush our bodies like an empty tin can before it forms it into something else.

'Where?'

It's the only word I can manage. He grunts in return but then, he's said so many more words than I was able to manage, I'll definitely forgive him.

And then we're running. Well, sort of running. Enough that it's taking us away from people...away from their immediate sight, anyway.

Zac pulls me in behind a clump of trees right on the river. It doesn't offer a lot of cover but there's no light so hopefully we won't be seen. I strip my clothes off, laying them as best as I can over the tree branches, hands shaking with the effort that this takes. But it's my favourite dress – there's no way I want it getting wrecked.

We're naked just in time. The changes are coming fast now, tearing through us, creating ripples in our skin, our bodies shaking. It feels strange to be so affected by the southern aurora without being able to see it like I can in Tasmania. There's no doubt it's happening though – the painful change it's forcing onto our bodies is testament to that. But to not be able to see Mother Nature's light show...especially when I know my family will be...a feeling of homesickness swamps me for a moment.

It's only a few minutes before the change finishes and I'm no longer human. I'm the other part of my soul. The other me. I spread my wings, delighting in the freedom now the pain has stopped. My feathers are a golden brown in the moonlight, unlike Zac. It's weird to see his black feathers when he still looks so much like me. All of my family are whistling kites – Haliastur sphenurus – but he's a black kite. Another part of his mother's Japanese heritage which has been passed on to him. He is beautiful.

He cocks his head at me and I know what he wants.

To fly.

I spread my wings again and we take flight, flapping hard to get the altitude we need and then soaring through the warm Noosa air. I call to him and he calls back. It's joyous. Amazing. There's nothing like the Aurora change, after the pain has passed. My body is awash with energy.

We head down the river and it's not long before we meet other changers. I know what they are as soon as I see them –

they are the perfect image of their soul bird but all of them are slightly bigger, slightly...more. And I can feel them. Feel their difference. We swoop with them, diving and rising and gliding. Playing. Like a party. An aurora party.

It's early morning before the need to fly begins to wane. We land on the headlands of the national park, where all of the other, more organised changers obviously came before the aurora began, and change back to our human forms.

The only problem, of course, is that our clothes aren't here. Not that it's a huge deal. After a lifetime of changing in front of those who are like me, nakedness doesn't hold the same embarrassment that it does for other non-changers. It's only as I think that thought though, that images of Matt pop into my head and I feel the heat on my cheeks, remembering my body's reaction to seeing him naked. So maybe nakedness is only a big deal if you want someone and you can't have them.

Stop it! The thought is harsh, grating, but my brain almost sniggers at me. I decide my brain's an ass.

One of the guys who lands with us offers to drive Zac back to the spot where we changed last night. A much better plan than having to try to get dressed where we shed our clothes without the cover of night to hide us – those trees won't offer a lot of protection in the soft morning light – and getting arrested for public display of nudity is not on my must-do list. Especially since I'm supposed to be starting my new job.

Zac kisses me before he goes, cupping my chin with his hands.

'We won't be long. And Saxon said he'll stay here and keep you company until we get back.'

I smile at the red-headed guy standing to my right who's already started to get dressed. He smiles back – one that seems to take over his whole face, and offers me his t-shirt.

'It's still pretty clean. I only put it on last night before we came down here. Just thought you might like it in case we get any early morning bush walkers.'

'Thanks.'

I pull the shirt on. It's not huge but it covers me enough for decency. We're silent as we watch Zac and the other guy walk away. Saxon clears his throat and I turn back to him. He's rubbing his hand back and forth in his hair, making it stick up.

'You haven't been in Noosa long?'

I shake my head. 'Only a couple of days. I met Zac through friends and we've been talking on-line. We thought it might be nice to meet and see how things go.'

He nods. 'That's great. It's important to find someone you have lots in common with. Another changer. Makes it easier to be in a relationship, don't you think?'

It's as if he's talking in my general direction but not really *to* me. He seems nice, just...distracted. And sad somehow, underneath the smile. Maybe it takes one mask wearer to recognise another.

'My parents were certainly happy when I made the decision to come up here.'

His lips quirk up at the sides but the smile doesn't touch the rest of his face this time. His mask is slipping.

'Yeah.' He sits down on a log behind us. 'Hey, I know this is weird since we've only just met, but can I ask you a question? It's sort of personal.'

I'm not sure I want to say yes. But he seems like a nice guy and I don't know how to say no without sounding like a bitch.

'Okay.'

'You and Zac, have you got a bond?'

I try to smile. Try really hard. But all I can think of is my conversation with Zac in the restaurant.

'No. We haven't. Not yet, anyway.'

'And do you think that matters? I mean, do you think you guys can still be happy without it?'

I play with the hem of the shirt for a moment, pleating it between my fingers before letting it go again.

'No, I don't think it matters. I think you can be happy together without a bond.'

I really want to believe that. I want to be happy with Zac, even if it's just a normal relationship, one based on the fact that we like each other and get on and...it will be fine without the bond. Not the same but fine. It worked for his mum and dad. Maybe it could work for us.

And yet, this morning, sitting here with the euphoria of the change colouring my blood, it seems harder to ignore what I felt for Matt – my reaction to him on that first day. It seems to be getting harder to ignore the overwhelming weight of wanting him. If anything, it's intensified, like my emotions are super charged.

Saxon nods, like everything I've said makes perfect sense and I've convinced him of the truth of my words. I wish I felt as convinced, despite how much self-talk I'm doing.

'I think you're right. I hope so.'

I don't tell him that I hope so too.

Matt

The early morning sun is still dancing on the river when I get back to the house after my surf. I stow the board under the veranda to dry and rinse myself under the outside shower. The cold water is refreshing after the warm ocean, and I stand there for a moment, letting it drip down my skin, before drying off. The good waves this morning have got me feeling pumped and I take the stairs two at a time, still drying my hair.

Lani's sitting on the deck, cup of something in her hand, legs curled up underneath her. The sight of her pulls me up short and I almost take off into my room before I manage to stop. This is my house, for Christ's sake. I need to harden the fuck up and get over this stupid...I don't even know what it is... obsession I have for her.

'Morning.'

She looks up, startled, and puts her feet down, as if she's about to run. I try not to notice how she looks in her pjs or how pink her cheeks are...

'Sorry. I didn't mean to disturb you. I didn't think anyone would be up.'

I shake my head and manage a small smile. 'You're not disturbing me. I've been for a surf already. Usually I'm the only one up at this hour. Zac's not really a morning person.'

She smiles but it's tentative, like she's still not sure whether to trust me or not, which sucks. It'd be good if we managed to get on. Even a friendship, if that's possible. For Zac's sake, mainly. But for mine too.

'No.'

I point at her cup. 'What are you having?'

'Oh, tea. I found it in the cupboard. I hope that's okay?'

She rushes the words out. Nervous. I want to take her in my arms until she relaxes, but squeeze the towel I'm still holding to give my hands something else to do instead.

'Yeah, that's fine. Make yourself at home. Use whatever you want. I'm going to make myself one now. Do you want another?'

She looks down at her cup like she's not sure what she should say. Then she holds it out, her face serious.

'Okay. Thanks.'

I nod and take it from her. It feels big, which is so fucking ridiculous. I'm just getting her a cup of tea, for Christ's sake. Maybe it's because it feels like we've taken the first step in our friendship. An interaction without Zac being around.

I try not to keep looking at her while I'm making the tea but when I do glance up, she's looking in at me. She turns away quickly, her hair hiding her face and my heart pumps harder, as if it's urging me on.

I cut up fruit too – enough for both of us – and carry it all out, handing the cup to her. Her fingers graze mine as she takes it and I've never been more aware of such a small touch. It's like every cell in my body knows her, wants her, and this slight contact isn't enough to sate their need – they want more. Her eyes, when she looks at me, are wide, startled, and then she's turning her head away again, like it's too hard to look me in the eye. And I know all I can do is ignore it. That's my only choice.

We're silent for a moment, the birds calling out in the trees and the flow of the river the only sounds filling the morning air. There are so many questions I want to ask her but I don't know how to start. Tongue tied in a way I haven't been around a woman for a long time.

'Do you surf every morning?'

She's still sitting stiff in the chair but I'm definitely giving her points for actually being able to strike up a conversation. One of us has it together enough at least.

'Yeah, most mornings, as long as the surf's okay. Part of the perks of owning a surf shop, I guess. And I like the way it makes me feel.'

She nods and there's silence again.

'Do you like the beach?' I blurt the words out. It's the only thing I can think to say.

'Yeah, I do. I love being near the water. It's not usually as warm as this in Tassie though. Well, not for as long.'

I shake my head. 'I can't imagine living anywhere else. I'm not a cold weather sort of guy. Give me the heat any day.'

She laughs. 'You'd definitely have to wear more clothes.'

And then, as soon as she's realised what she's said, she goes so red she could be a port side beacon. I raise my hand to my chest, self-conscious suddenly, of being here with her with only my board shorts on. Her eyes follow my hand, looking at me, and then they flick up to my face before she's staring out over the water again. Yep, definitely makes me a shitty friend that I want her eyes back on me. I take a deep breath.

'Listen, I'm sorry about the other day. About not locking the door to the bathroom. I'll be more careful in future.'

She's shaking her head and her hands go up to her face, covering her cheeks.

'No, I should've knocked before I went in. It was my fault.' She shakes her head and takes a deep breath. 'Let's just forget about it. Never mention it again, okay?'

I smile. 'Great idea.' I watch her – watch the way she moves the cup in her hand, like she's not even aware she's doing it. 'I feel like we didn't really get off on the right track on that first day. What do you say we start over?'

Her teeth bite into her bottom lip for a moment and I stop breathing, waiting for her to say something. Finally, she nods.

'I'd like that.'

'Okay. Hi, I'm Matt. I live here with Zac.'

'Hi Matt. I'm Lani, Zac's girlfriend.' She says it like she's trying to make sure everyone believes her. The words stab into my chest like a hot iron.

'And how long have you known Zac for?'

'Well, I've known him for about five months but I only met him face to face four days ago.'

I nod slowly. 'Internet relationship. They're happening more and more from what I hear.'

She frowns. 'It's not weird.'

'I never said it was. I'm guessing it can be a really good way to meet people.'

'It is.' There's silence for a moment. 'So, what about you. Are you in a relationship?'

She's still, like she's waiting for something.

'I was. It ended about six months ago.'

'You're not with anyone now, then?'

I shake my head. And there's silence again. I want her to fill it. I want to know what she thinks about the fact that I'm single. And desperate, obviously. Shit. I'm being nice – delightful, in fact. And yet, all it's doing is fucking with my mind.

This is pathetic. I *can* be friends with her. It has to be possible. And yet, when Zac walks out, I can't stop the feeling of missed opportunities.

Lani

A noise startles me and I turn to see Zac standing there, hair dishevelled, in a pair of boxer shorts. He looks like he's just got out of bed, even though I know he's as full of energy as I am after the change last night. And that the hair and the pyjamas are just for show – maintaining the secret. Both of us.

It's terrible that my first thought is I'd wish he'd stayed in bed for another thirty minutes. I want to hear more about Matt. And logically, I could. I could keep asking questions in a getting-to-know-my-boyfriends-best-friend kind of way...except I'd prefer Zac wasn't here for that.

Matt looks disappointed that Zac's here too. Or maybe that's just me projecting.

I feel horrible – guilty in a way that makes my face hot. Zac has been nothing but wonderful – supportive, loving, funny, nice. I get up and wrap my arms around his neck. Doing the right thing.

God, what is wrong with me! Not doing the right thing – I want to do it. I have everything I want here in Zac.

Except the bond.

There's no getting around it. Not unless my parents have played it up more than they should've. Maybe this feeling of being a good friend is what it's all about. Maybe that's all it is.

Zac pulls back a little and gives me a still half asleep smile. He's good at this.

'That's a nice way to start the morning. But it's so early. What's with you people getting up at stupid o'clock?'

I laugh. It doesn't feel as forced as it could've.

'It's eight o'clock. Not really that early.'

He groans and rubs his face.

'Zac's never been a morning person.' Matt's leaning back in his chair, looking at us. 'I can remember being late for school all the time because I used to pick him up on the way and he was never ready. Used to drive my mum nuts. She was forever telling me to just go without him.'

Zac frowns at him. 'Hey, you're supposed to be my mate! That means you should only tell stories that make me look good.'

Matt laughs. 'Full and open disclosure, bud. She needs to know what she's getting into.'

The conversation feels awkward somehow. Like they're joking but there's a small part of them that isn't.

'He also can't make a decent cup of tea to save his life,' Matt says, holding up his cup. 'Don't ever feel tempted to get him to make you one. I don't know what he does to it but they're just terrible.'

Zac winks at me. 'Yeah, that one's true. But I pour a mean glass of wine.'

'He's pretty crap at surfing, no matter how many lessons I've given him.'

'Also true.'

'And he's always been a bit of a flirt.'

'Hey!'

Matt shakes his head. 'No denying it, Zac. It's true. Although now you've got the girl that should change, right?'

'So terrible surfer. Big flirt.' I smile at Zac to let him know I'm okay. Be the easy-going girlfriend I want to be. 'What else?'

Zac looks at him. 'Come on, be nice.'

Matt pops a grape into his mouth and nods. 'And he's loyal and a good mate and, most of the time, one of the best flatmates I've ever had.'

'See, you're getting the whole package with me.' Zac puts his arm around my back, caressing my side. I lace my fingers through his, stopping the movement.

'And what about you, Matt.' My heart is pounding as I look at him. I feel daring and bold, which is stupid. It's only a question. I swallow past the lump in my throat. 'Since I'm staying in your house. Where's the full disclosure for you?'

His hands grip the chair. I don't think anyone else would notice but I seem to notice everything about him – like I'm keyed in to every micro movement he makes.

'He can't sing to save his life,' Zac says, 'and for a smart guy, he's really crap at cooking. Like, really crap. But he's a pretty good mate, especially when he gives me somewhere as awesome as this to live.'

Matt nods. 'That's true. All of it.' He stands up, tapping his hand on the rail of the veranda like he's adding an exclamation point to his words, his face serious. 'And I'm loyal. My mates, my family, come first.'

'That's true, too,' Zac says and he looks just as serious.

I step away from him – it all feels too much. Overwhelming. 'Well, I guess I'd better go and have a shower before your sister gets here.'

They nod and I make my escape. That's what it feels like

anyway. I grab my toiletries bag and lean against the closed bathroom door, hand to my chest.

I should never have come. This isn't how I imagined this happening. I was supposed to meet Zac and just *know* – want to be with him without any doubts. Instead, I feel like I don't know what I'm doing – don't know how to act, who to be. As if the Lani I was at home doesn't fit here. I want Zac to like me and for us to have a bond. And I don't want to like Matt. Not like that anyway. Not in a way that feels like I want to be with him...all the time. Not in a way that feels suspiciously like a bond.

Nothing is going to plan.

I make sure I lock the other door as well – the one leading to Matt's room. I'm tempted for a second, to open it and see what his room looks like – whether it's organised, what's on his bedside table, where he sleeps – but click the lock before I give into the urge.

The water is cool on my skin and I shampoo my hair with more vigour than I normally do. I scrub my body too, until it's red and tingly, and then turn off the water, standing in the shower for a moment longer to let the coolness of the water on my body get sucked away by the day's warmth. Wrapping the towel around myself, I sneak a look out the door before hurrying to my bedroom, shutting myself in.

I grab the clothes I'd already chosen to wear back when Roxanne offered me the job, but anxiety rubs against the inside of my stomach, creating friction, making me jittery and nauseous. I want to get this right. I want this job.

I'm applying the last touches of make up when I hear the knock at the front door and freeze, the anxiety spiking, stabbing into me. What if I'm not good enough? What if Roxanne sees straight through me, knows it's all an act? Realises that I'm just Lani. Nothing special.

I shake my head and put the smile on my face that's always worked before, checking the mirror one last time. I can't stay in here all day.

There's giggling coming from the lounge area and I take one more deep breath before heading out. Matt has a little girl on his shoulders – the source of the giggles. Her red hair is tumbling about her head as he swoops her around like she's flying. I stand at the edge, watching them, not wanting to intrude, but Roxanne sees me anyway and walks closer.

'Wow, you look spectacular.'

She's dressed casual – shorts and a shirt, nipped in at the waist. Different to my tailored pants and red pleated shirt, showing one shoulder. Too different.

'I'll go and change.'

She grabs my arm. 'You'll do no such thing. You look awesome.'

'But I'm overdressed.'

She laughs. 'Honey, it's nice to see that someone who's going to work for me actually has style.'

I don't say anything else but I feel like I've made a wrong step. Even the euphoria from the change last night isn't enough to get rid of that feeling. And I wish I could just turn around and go change without anyone noticing.

There's a squeal from Matt's passenger and we both turn to them.

'Stop, Uncle Matt. Stop.'

He looks over our way and his eyes narrow, as if he's assessing me. My chest is aching, twisting, making it hard to breathe.

The child on his shoulders, Georgie, I'm assuming, flicks the hair out of her eyes.

'Who are you?'

I smile, trying to act natural, wanting her to like me.

'I'm Lani. I'm going to be working for your mum.'

She squirms on Matt's shoulders and he puts her down. Hands on her hips, she marches over to us, looking up at me.

'Are you Uncle Matt's girlfriend?'

I laugh. It sounds nervous and I cut it short.

'No. I'm actually Zac's girlfriend.'

She tilts her head. 'Why?'

Why? That's a really good question. It takes a moment for me to think of an answer.

'Um, because I like him.'

She nods. 'Zac's fun. But Uncle Matt does lots of cool stuff. And he owns a surf shop. If I was older, I'd want him to be my boyfriend.'

'Georgie, enough.' Roxanne shakes her head and looks at me. 'Sorry. She has a tendency to say whatever comes into her head. I'm trying to break her out of it.'

I shake my head and smile, even though I want to turn and walk away. I don't want to hear that she thinks Matt's a better boyfriend. I don't want to think about it.

And yet, I can't help it.

Matt

She looks amazing. The red shirt makes her lips seem even redder. And her hair is just touching the skin on her bare shoulder – I want to go over and whisper my lips along her collar bone until she throws back her head with desire.

Shit!

And then Georgie asks her if she's my girlfriend and my stupid, pathetic heart trips over itself, even though I know she's going to say she's with Zac. Which she does. Of course.

Shit again.

Rox is watching me and I smile and step forward, scooping Georgie up in my arms once more.

'Hey, ferret, be nice to Lani. She's our guest.'

Her little fingers dig into my arm as she turns to look at Lani again.

'Do you like surfing?'

Lani's eyes flick to mine and she gives a small smile.

'I don't know. I've never tried it.'

Georgie's eyebrows furrow down. 'You should try it. It's lots of fun. Uncle Matt's teaching me.'

Lani smiles at her. It looks like it's forced. Nothing like a barrage of questions from a five year old to put you on edge if you're not used to it.

'He sounds like he's a great uncle.'

Georgie nods at her, serious.

'He could teach you to surf.'

Both of us take a step back like the idea is going to rear up and slap us. Lani laughs like she's about to have an anxiety attack. I wonder if it's the thought of spending time with me or if it's something else – like maybe she can't swim. Which would make me feel better.

'I'm sure your uncle's too busy to teach me.'

I take a deep breath, knowing I'm being stupid, but I can't help it.

'I'd be happy to teach you to surf if you want to learn.'

She looks at me like I've told her I could photograph her naked – eyes wide, lips open. Actually, no, better to not even joke about that thought. That's dangerous territory.

'Oh. Okay. Maybe one day.'

She's blowing me off and my stomach sinks with disappointment. But it's for the best. Sensible.

'Alright. Enough talk about surfing and what you're teaching my precious daughter.' Rox is shaking her head and Georgie looks at me and giggles. It's an ongoing thing – I think that's what makes it more fun for her. The fact that her mum pretends she hates it.

'Is there a precious daughter here?' Zac comes up the stairs, dressed in his work uniform.

'Zac!' Georgie wiggles in my arms and I put her down. She runs over to him and he picks her up and turns her upside down. She laughs – it's a routine they do every time they get together – but I'm not looking at her. I'm watching Lani as if it's a habit I can't break. She's watching the two of them like she's not sure what to do. As if she's out of her depth.

Rox must see it too because she steps forward and touches Lani's arm again.

'Shall we go and leave them to it. They'll be messing about and acting stupid the whole time she's here.'

Lani smiles at her – it looks like one of relief. 'Sure.'

Zac puts Georgie down and goes over to Lani. I can feel myself tensing. I know what's going to happen – it's perfectly normal; what they *should* do as a couple. But I still don't have to like it. He wraps his arms around her and pulls her in close – hard up against his body – one hand against her lower back, where it curves in, the other at the nape of her neck. He leans in to kiss her and she kisses him back. Eyes closed, enjoying it.

She smiles at him when it stops and he pushes the hair off her shoulder, running his fingers along her skin, just like I'd imagined doing.

'That's because I probably won't be here when you get back. I've got a shift this afternoon, remember? So I just wanted to give you something to think about until I get back tonight.'

'That was definitely something to think about.'

But her eyes flick to me again as she finishes saying it. Just a quick look. Hardly noticeable. But it's enough to set my heart pounding.

This is going to be harder than I thought.

Lani

There's not that much for me to learn with the shop. The computer and eftpos systems are the same as the ones I've used before, and the shop itself isn't that big. But the clothes...oh my God. I feel like I've found my place – a place where it all makes sense.

Everything's handmade and while most of them have a few in each size, there are one-off pieces as well. I think I've touched every item of clothing in the store, running my fingers lightly over them, bringing them out, looking at the design and material and the way it falls. And then there's the shoes and the accessories. I can hardly contain myself.

Roxanne's been watching me the whole time. To be fair, she's been going through everything I need to know but I can feel her eyes on me in the quiet times too. I'm not sure what she's hoping to see in me and it makes me nervous.

'So, what do you think?' she asks finally and I smile at her. A real one.

'I think it's amazing. I love how you've got everything set up and the clothes are fantastic. Thank you so much for letting me work here.'

She smiles back at me. 'I'm pretty proud of it. You really like it that much, huh?'

I nod. 'The clothes are beautiful. Do you make them all yourself?'

'Most of them. There are some other dress makers I pay to do things for me too but all of the one-off stuff – that's all mine.'

'You're really talented. I've never seen anything like these.'

She laughs. 'Oh, you can stay for as long as you want.'

I laugh too. I feel good. Like I could fit in here.

'Who taught you how to sew?'

Her smile winds down a little.

'My mum. She was a dressmaker herself. Used to make and sell wedding dresses. They were amazing.'

'Was? Doesn't she sew anymore?'

The smile is gone now – replaced by a wistful look.

'No. She died nine years ago. My dad died when Matt was a baby – God, I don't even think he was a year old – so it was just Mum and us for a long time. And then she got cancer. By the time she was diagnosed, there was nothing they could do except make her comfortable. She died four months after.'

'That must have been really hard.' I'm sure it was difficult for both of them but the focus of my thoughts is Matt. He must've still been a teenager. Still young. Still needing a parent.

She nods. 'Yeah. It was. Took us ages to recover from it. I looked after Matt, made sure he finished school, had food, everything he needed, but I partied hard too. Trying to forget how sad I was. How much I missed her. That's how I fell pregnant. Had a bit too much to drink and decided to have some fun with a guy I'd met at a party.'

I don't know what to say to something so personal – or what

she expects me to say anyway – so I just stand there, the hem of a gorgeous blue skirt in my hand.

She shrugs. 'Anyway, it was the best thing that happened to me. Made me wake up to myself. I had another little person to look after – someone who was relying on me to get my act together. I had the chance to be the type of mum that my mum was.'

I look down at the material, noticing the almost invisible swirls in the fabric, even though it's as if my mind is only half looking at it.

'She was a good mum?'

'The best. Loving and fun but tough when she needed to be too.'

That sounds like the type of mum you'd miss. The type of mum it'd be nice to have.

'And what about Matt? How did he handle it?'

There's a pause. Only a small one but it makes me look up.

'He got really focused. Worked every available hour he could, even though it meant that basically all he did was go to school and work. I tried to make sure he had some sort of social life but it was hard when I wasn't doing great either. He was determined to own his own shop. Maybe it was something to do with the fact that if it was his, no one could take it away from him. But what do I know?'

I try to imagine a younger Matt – grieving his mum, wanting to have something that was his – and feel my heart constrict at the thought of how sad that must've been.

'What was he like when he finally got what he wanted? Did it make it better for him?'

Roxanne cocks her head to the side. 'I guess. He was able to get some sort of balance happening in his life anyway. But probably still not as good as it should be. He still works too much. That's what his girlfriends have complained about anyway.'

I chew the inside of my cheek. I want more information but I don't know what Roxanne will think of me if I keep asking questions. So I don't ask them. I drop the fabric and look around.

'What time do you want me to start tomorrow?'

'Nine? And then you can work through until five.'

'Great.'

And it is. More than I expected. She points to a door at the rear of the shop.

'Come on, I'll show you the back.'

The door leads to a narrow but sunny hallway, lit by the horizontal window that runs the length of the wall. She takes me past two closed doors.

'Bathroom. Kitchen. Use them whenever you need.'

At the end of the hall is a huge, open plan room, the same size as the shop front. Long windows at the end flood it in light and give a view out to the small courtyard filled with plants.

The room is amazing. One I could've only imagined in my dreams. Well, in my designing dreams, anyway. A huge work bench sits in the middle of the room, dominating the space, and I run my hand over the wood, feeling the grooves under my fingers.

A sewing machine and overlocker are set up over to the side under the light, with cotton reels in a rainbow of colours lining the wall next to them, propped up on wooden pegs. And a mannequin takes pride of place in front of the windows, side by side with a rack of half-finished clothes that I just want to look at, right now.

I turn to Roxanne. 'This is amazing.'

'Yeah, I think so. Pretty much my dream room for creating gorgeous clothes. You know how people cut out pictures of the things they want in their house. I used to cut out pictures of things for this room. Bit sad really but it's everything I wanted. I love working in here.'

'I can see why.' I can hear the wistfulness in my own voice.

'Do you sew?'

I shrug. Yes, yes, yes. That's what I want to say. 'A bit.'

She doesn't let me get away with that though. 'What do you make?'

I lean my hip against the bench, trying to look calm, cool, rather than like my heart is thumping, pounding, as if it's egging me on just to say it – to tell her. I take a deep breath.

'All of my clothes.'

I feel like I'm going to throw up as I wait for her to say something. I resist the urge to lick my suddenly dry lips and concentrate instead on the solidness of the wood as I lean into it.

She narrows her eyes at me.

'You mean that shirt.' She nods her head at my clothes. 'And the skirt you wore on the day I met you?'

I nod and watch her, waiting to see if she thinks that's a good or bad thing.

'From a pre-made design?'

'No.' It's really hard to say that one word. I can't believe how vulnerable it makes me feel – like I'm standing in front of her naked. Actually, that would probably be easier. Much easier.

'So you did the design yourself?'

'Yes.'

She raises her eyebrows and nods. 'I'm impressed then. You're obviously really talented.'

I can't believe the words have come out of her mouth and, for just a second, I think she must be teasing me. But the expression on her face tells me she's serious. I swallow against the lump that's made its way up to my throat. Dad's always told me I'm good but he doesn't know much about fashion. It feels like he's just being nice – supportive. And mum has always been able to find fault in anything I've made her. The cut or the fit or the choice of colour. The 'but' at the end of every comment. The add on that tells me it's never quite good enough, no matter how much I try or how much I drive myself crazy trying to make just one thing she won't be able to pick at. It's like a true talent for her though – a super power.

But Roxanne can sew. She knows about fashion. She knows about doing a good job. And she's not my mother.

'Do you think so?'

She steps closer, her hand hovering over my shoulder.

'May I?'

I nod and she turns the strap over, looking at the seams – the finish. She follows the pleat down from the top, pressing the fabric together between her fingers. She shakes her head and my heart drops, like a car on a roller coaster. Mum was right then.

'You should be sewing, creating – doing more of this beautiful stuff. Not working in my shop.'

I try to smile, even though my lips are so tight they feel like they're about to crack; try not to let the thoughts scrambling around in my brain come to the surface and show on my face.

'Oh, okay then. Thanks for the tour anyway. I hope you find someone.'

The smile is forced now, hovering just on the edge of manic, but I don't think I sound that way. I think I've pulled it off. I should have known that it wouldn't come that easy. It never does. Just for a second though, I was hopeful.

She frowns at me. 'I'm not saying you can't have the job.'

My lungs forget how to work.

'You're not.'

'God, no. I really need someone and honestly, you're perfect. So if you still want it, it's yours. But you obviously love clothes and you've got a good eye. You've got talent. You should do something with that as well. Do you draw your designs or are they just all in your head?'

'I draw them.' Mountains of them, piled high in folders that stopped being able to accommodate the number of designs ages ago.

'Can I see some?'

My eyes are stinging with the salt of the tears that are threatening to show themselves, giving me away. They've got no chance though. I've had years of mum's comments to practice holding it in, pretending, pretending, pretending. I can do it now without trying. Because I want her to think I'm strong. Professional.

'Sure. If you'd like to.'

'Good. Then maybe we could look at selling some of your stuff as well. Especially if it looks like this. I'm happy to supply the fabrics you want and just take a small commission to cover some costs for the shop. But we can work that out once you've settled in.'

A shot of equal parts panic and euphoria blast through my veins, making me hot and cold, all at once. I try my smile again. It feels less false this time. And yet, what if I'm not good enough? What if she sees the designs and hates them? I can't get excited. Not yet. I hold the smile back, stiff again.

Roxanne takes a step back and leans against the bench as well.

'So, I guess I have to formally ask – are you happy to start tomorrow?'

'Yes, I'd love to.'

'Welcome aboard then. How about we have a coffee to celebrate?'

She starts to move back towards the kitchen area and I follow her.

'I'd love a tea, if you have it. I don't actually drink coffee.'

She shakes her head. 'You're as bad as Matt. He doesn't drink coffee either.'

I file that information away, even though there's no reason I'd need it.

'Really?'

'Yep.' She fills the kettle up and clicks it on before turning to look at me. 'How long have you and Zac known each other?'

I stiffen slightly. I hate answering this question but I want to trust her.

'I got to know him through a friend of mine back home. Zac is his cousin. We've been talking on-line for about five months. But it was only the other day that I actually met him face to face.'

She raises her eyebrows and I wait for the judgement – for her to tell me that it's not a real relationship and I don't really know him, just like everyone else has done. Even Zac's cousin thought I was nuts to move up here rather than just having a holiday to see how it went. I couldn't explain that I needed more than that.

'You're braver than I could ever be. To come all this way without knowing if you actually click in person.'

I resist the urge to squirm. It was the opportunity to click that I was hoping for. That's what brought me here. The clicking that hasn't happened. At least, not with Zac. And I refuse to acknowledge anything else.

'I don't know that I was brave. I don't really feel it. I just needed a change. Something different.' I run my fingers over the smooth top of the kitchen bench, not able to say out loud what I really was hoping from coming here – just to be some-where people didn't know me and didn't expect the same thing from me all the time. Expect me to be the Lani they'd all decided I was.

The kettle finishes boiling and I look up as she turns to fill the cups she's set out.

'A change can be good,' she says. 'Stir things up a bit. Make us work out what's important, who we are.'

'Yes,' I say and even though I can't think what else to add, it feels like she understands what I'm hoping for – a validation that maybe my decision wasn't as stupid as Mum thought it was.

'Come on, let's go back to the sewing room.'

She puts the cups on the wooden bench and drags two stools from the other end. I wait until she sits before I do. She wraps her hands around her cup and sighs as she takes a sip of her coffee.

'That's good. How are you finding your first couple of days of living with two boys?'

I smile. 'I used to live with my two brothers. I don't think it can be any worse than that. I haven't noticed any smelly sports socks laying around, so that's got to be a step up.'

She laughs. 'At least I only had one brother to contend with.'

I trace the handle of my cup, not looking at her. 'What was Matt like as a brother?'

'Pretty good, all in all. Even before our mum died, he wasn't too annoying. But then, I'm nine years older than him, so we weren't ever really in each other's pockets. We were at different stages of life, I guess.'

'But you looked after him when your mum died?'

'As much as possible. There were some things he refused my help on. Even though he was still at school, he was sixteen, nearly seventeen. I guess he felt like an adult – probably more than his friends did given he'd had to watch Mum get really sick and then lose her so quickly. It was hard – wanting to protect him for Mum's sake but knowing that he was pretty grown up and probably doing better than I was. There were a lot of things he didn't think he needed my help with and he was probably right.'

'Like what?'

'Maintaining the house, mowing the lawn, doing his own washing. And yet, he managed to keep up with his school work, too. I kept on waiting for his grades to drop or for him to lose it but he never did. He even got a job all by himself and made his own way there for every shift. I've never seen anyone as determined as he was.'

I want to ask more questions – a lot more – but I take a sip of the tea, trying to keep the words from coming out. I can't do this. The more I know of him, the more I like what I hear. The more I like who he is. The more I think about what it would be like to be with him.

Roxanne puts her cup down and folds her hands in front of her on the table.

'He's only had two serious relationships.'

There's something in her voice that I don't quite understand but it has my heart squeezing in, like it's trying to fold up into a smaller version of itself. I don't know why she's telling me about her brother's relationships and I feel like I should stop her – change the subject somehow. And yet, I don't want to.

'Really.' Casual. Like I don't care.

'Yeah. The first one started just before Mum was diagnosed. It lasted for about a year. She wasn't too bad – stuck by him when Mum died, tried to help him. I think she wanted to be there for him more than he wanted her to be.'

'Oh.' I can picture him, putting up a wall, determined, hurting but not wanting to show it.

'His next girlfriend – Karli – she was okay too, especially at the beginning. He was with her for a long time and I think they were planning to move in together. They broke up about six months ago after she cheated on him with someone she knew. I could've killed her.'

Why do I feel like there's some sort of warning in there? I look up at her but she's not looking at me – she's toying with the handle of her mug instead. And I'm not sure what I'm supposed to say. I wait for her to talk again.

'Zac and Matt have been friends for a long time.'

I nod, trying to swallow past the kink that's developed in my throat. 'Yeah, they both told me that. Their friendship's obviously really important to them.'

She picks up her cup again.

'Zac's a nice guy.'

I keep my face even, even though I don't know where she's going with this. I feel suddenly uncomfortable... and stupid. Like I'm missing something important.

'He is. That's why I thought it was worth a try. The relationship, I mean. Coming up here.'

'Do you still think that?'

I sit back a little – it's my turn to play with my cup. It's ridiculous that I almost feel cranially naked, as if she can see straight into my brain.

'I think it's too early to tell. We need to give it some time and see how it goes. But I like him.' That, at least, is the truth.

She must see the look on my face because she holds up her hand, palm facing me.

'Sorry. I should shut up. It's none of my business. It's just hard not to be the protective older sister. And Zac's been around so long, he feels like another little brother. Just tell me to butt out in future.'

I give her a half smile but my comfort at being here has well and truly gone. Fled with all the half messages that seem to be swimming in the air around me. Half messages that don't make any sense given she really has no idea of the war going on in my head, my body. This is only the second time we've been in each other's company, for God's sake – she can't know...can she?

I stand, needing to get away. Clear my head.

'Well, thanks for the tea. If that's all you needed to show me, I guess I'll see you tomorrow.'

She stands too. 'I can drop you back to the house if you like. I've got to go back and get Georgie.'

I shake my head. 'It's okay. I packed my bathers in my bag. I thought it'd probably be a good opportunity to go to the beach for a while, since Zac's working.'

She nods but looks confused. That makes two of us then.

'Okay, sure. I'll see you tomorrow then.'

Another half-smile and then I'm gone, down the hallway, grabbing my bag on the way through and out the door. The sun and the fresh air make me feel lighter already, like Roxanne's half warnings are being diluted.

I know it probably isn't the best end to the morning with her but I'll make it up to her tomorrow. Hopefully we'll be so busy we won't have time for any more talking.

The beach is only a block away and I hurry down to the bush that pushes its way to the line of sand. I dump my bag, hiding it behind a set of lower plants. I wasn't lying to Roxanne – I do want to check out the beach. But not in the way she was probably expecting. After the forced change of last night, I just want to fly again. I want to see my new home from the air, want to know how it looks in the daylight, rather than under the shadows of the moon. I look around, checking no one else is around me, and then strip my clothes off, the warm sea breeze caressing my bare skin.

I sigh as I feel the change take me over. It's time to fly.

Matt

The water is bath temperature. It swirls around my waist, the waves washing into me, pushing me towards the beach. I hold the end of the board, keeping it close to me while Georgie clambers back on. We've been doing this for an hour and she's showing no sign of wanting to give up.

She lays on the board and I untangle the leg rope from around her little foot. She looks back at me, hair plastered flat to her head but glowing a dark red in the sun.

'Okay, Uncle Matt. I'm ready.'

I nod at her and look back at the waves rolling in. There's a set coming through that'll probably give her a good run and I look back at her and smile.

'Looks like a good one. Ready to go?'

She looks forward again and nods, her arms tensing as she grips the board. Her determination only makes me smile more. I look back again, watching the first wave get closer...closer... and then push the board, giving her the momentum she needs. She paddles hard, little arms pumping in the water. And then she's on it, jumping up, balancing and turning the board in a way that tells me she's a natural. She pumps her fists and lets out a whoop as I body surf on the next wave, following her in.

She falls off and, just for a second, my heart stutters, like it does every time she disappears. But then her head's bobbing up again and she turns to grab the board. A huge smile splits her face.

'Did you see me?'

'I sure did. That was an awesome ride.'

She clambers back onto the board, sitting astride it, and I grab the edge to stop it floating away.

'I even turned it. Did you see?'

'Yep, I saw you. You're a natural.'

'Do you think Mum would buy me a board? We could come to your shop and I could pick one.'

'If your mum says it's okay, maybe I could get you one for your birthday.'

She squeals and leans over to hug me. 'You're the best uncle ever.'

I laugh. 'Yeah, yeah.'

'Can we go again?'

I'm about to say yes when I see Roxanne on the beach, waving at us. Without Lani. I try and ignore the sense of disappointment that washes over me in its own distinct wave.

'We might have to put it on hold for another time, ferret. I think your mum wants to talk to you.'

She whips her head around and waves at Roxanne.

'Did you see me?' She's yelling at the top of her lungs and Roxanne puts two thumbs up. I grab Georgie around the waist and pull her off the board, holding her body against my hip, face down. She giggles.

'Put me down, Uncle Matt.'

'Wow. I've never had a talking board before.'

She giggles again and I smile. 'I'm not a board. I'm Georgie.'

I shake my head. 'I must be hearing things.'

I help her grip the board as it gets shallow and deposit both of them on the sand, smiling at Rox.

'Did you see me, Mum?'

Roxanne smiles at her and pushes the wet hair out of her eyes before pulling her in close, getting water and sand all over her.

'I did. That was amazing. You were up for ages.'

She bends down to take the leg rope off her daughter, laughing at the drips Georgie's directing her way. It makes my heart ache for a moment. Mum should've been here for this – meeting her granddaughter, watching her grow up into an awesome kid. It's moments like these that I realise how much I still really miss her, even though it's been years since she's been gone.

Georgie taps her mum on the head and then points down the beach.

'It's Maddi. Can I go and say hi?'

There's a family further down the beach – one of Georgie's friends, I'm guessing – and Roxanne nods.

'Stay where I can see you though.'

'Okay.' There's not even a backward glance as she goes racing down the beach and I smile at my sister.

'And just like that, I'm forgotten.'

She smiles back at me. 'Don't feel rejected. It happens to me all the time. Did you have a good morning?'

'Yeah, it's been great. She has so much energy though. I think I'm going to need a nanna nap this afternoon.'

Roxanne just laughs.

'And how did your morning go?'

She looks at me and then down at the sand. 'Yeah, it was great. I think Lani will fit in really well.'

'Oh. Good.' But all I can think is that that means she's probably going to be here for a while. And that she might move out. I can't work out if that'd be good or bad. Probably a bit of both, if I'm honest.

'I think she's very unsure of herself though.'

I frown at Roxanne. 'What do you mean?'

She shrugs and then sighs. 'Oh, I don't know what I mean. Forget I said anything.'

I look out over the waves, trying to not ask but I can't do it. The words force their way out of my mouth.

'No, you obviously have a reason to say it. I thought she seemed pretty confident.'

But then I think back to the look on her face this morning and I'm not so sure about that anymore.

'I don't know. God, I've only seen her twice. But sometimes...' she wrinkles up her nose as she's trying to magic the words she wants, 'it's sort of like she's being who she thinks you want her to be. Like it's an act.'

I feel my jaw clench. 'Like she's trying to trick us? Or Zac anyway?'

'No, I don't mean in a bad way. More like she's not sure of herself. Like's she trying really hard to be what she thinks she needs to be in that situation to make you like her. Like she's trying to fit in but isn't really sure how to do it.'

I try and work that through in my head – thinking about what she's said, how she's acted. I don't feel like I've known her long enough to get a good impression though. How the hell does Roxanne do that? But I trust what she says...she's always been a good judge of character. It's like a sixth sense or something.

She's looking up to where Georgie is still playing with her friend. The silence is easy, like it usually is between us. She sighs and turns back to me.

'I think you'll have to go easy on her. Treat her gently.'

I want to take a step back, away from what I see in her eyes, but that'd be a dead giveaway. 'You'll have to tell Zac that.'

She hesitates for a moment before nodding and looks away again, out to the ever-moving water. 'I just thought you should know too.'

There's silence again but this one feels heavy, filled with unsaid stuff. Which is crap. Rox is usually the one person I can tell most things to but I don't want to tell her how I'm feeling about Lani. That'll just get me in deeper shit because saying it out loud makes it real. And being with Lani isn't an option open to me.

Roxanne rubs her hands together, brushing off the sand that she'd collected from hugging Georgie.

"Well, I guess I should get my gorgeous girl and take her home. Thanks for having her this morning.'

'I'm happy to have her anytime. You know that.'

She touches my arm. 'I do. You're a great uncle. Mum would be proud.'

I feel my eyes prickle and narrow them, as if the sun's too bright. Jesus, what is it about today that means Mum's on our minds?

'Oh, by the way, Lani said she was going to come down to the beach. You might see her.'

I resist the urge to turn my head and look for her. Roxanne smiles, like she knows what's going on in my brain.

'Just remember what I said.' And then she kisses my cheek and is gone.

I watch her walk across the sand, scooping Georgie up in her arms, and my heart constricts in my chest. Even though I know I'm a part of that – part of that closeness – I'm still sepa-rate. Not part of that tight little shell that holds them together. Sometimes I want that more than anything else – that sense of belonging – more than I want the shop, more than I want to be successful. That's why I really tried to fix it with Karli, I guess. It just wasn't fixable.

I shake my head and turn to pick up the board. Crap. Ever since Lani's been here, I've become an emotional ship wreck – all the torn apart planks of my ship floating to the surface so I can't ignore them. It's pathetic.

And that's when I see her, coming out of the bushes at the end of the beach. She's stunning, the blue bikini showing off the shape of her body, accentuating her legs, the shape of her breasts, the curve of her back. Jesus! My suddenly tight chest makes it feel like I can't even breathe properly. All I can do is watch her and hope she comes over. To me.

She stops to pick up something from the sand and her hair falls across her face as she looks down to inspect it. I have an irresistible urge to go over and push it back, tuck it behind her ears. Just to feel how soft her hair is, to let my fingers trace over the nape of her neck, across her shoulders...

She looks up and sees me, stopping where she is. And I just know she's going to turn and go, like a startled bird about to flap away to safety. So I raise my hand. Stupid but I can't help it.

'Hey. How did your morning go?'

I don't know why I'm doing it to myself. I should just let her go. Keep myself safe. Keep myself sane! But it's too late now. Every step she takes closer to me makes my chest hurt that bit more, like there's a belt around it, slowly being notched tighter. Sweet torture.

She stops when she's a few metres away and folds her arms across her chest, digging her feet into the sand like she's trying to bury herself. She gives me a small smile, one that just touches the corner of her mouth, before looking away.

'It was great. I can't wait to start tomorrow. Roxanne is really talented.'

I nod but can't think of anything to say. All I can think of is the way the sun touches her skin.

'How did your morning with Georgie go?'

I smile. It's more about the relief of having something to say, I think.

'Yeah, good. She got up and had a good ride this morning. She was pretty excited.'

Her eyes flick to me and then away again, like she has trouble looking at me. I run my fingers through my hair.

'So, do you want me to teach you to surf?'

Jesus, what is wrong with me? I'm just blurting out stuff that I know isn't going to lead me to a good place. But then, like a frigging miracle's happened, she's nodding her head and my heart feels like it's going to explode.

Lani

I don't know why I nod. I really don't. All I can say is that it feels like every part of my body is fizzing, like baking soda mixed with vinegar, just by being this close to him. And I react without giving my brain a chance to think.

He smiles at me and I feel great and terrible in equal measure. Great that he's smiling at me, that he wants to teach me, great that I get to spend time with him, get to be close, maybe touch him even. And terrible because I really want that to happen. And that's so not fair to Zac – he should be the one I'm asking to teach me, even if he says he's terrible at it.

'You said you tried to teach Zac to surf?'

His smile seems to falter for a moment. Or maybe it's just my imagination.

'Yeah, a couple of times now. He's not too bad. No actually, he is. It's not his thing. But he gave it go.'

There's a pause. One that's long enough to be noticeable.

'He'd probably know enough to teach you though. If you wanted him to do it rather than me?'

'No.' I've said it too quickly. 'I mean, if he's not really into surfing, maybe he won't be interested. And we're here now...'

It sounds lame, like I'm making excuses. Which I am. But he nods, like it all makes perfect sense to him.

'Sure. And it's a great day for it. Nice swell. Good for beginners. Be a shame to waste it.'

I unfold my arms and push my hair back, over my shoulders. His eyes follow my hands and the fizzing in my body gets worse. It almost feels too much. Too much without being able to touch him anyway, especially when he's standing there bare chested, the line of hair starting just above the waist band of his shorts before it disappears. I realise I'm staring and look down at the sand, giving a few seconds for the redness to go from my face.

'So, what's the first step?'

He clears his throat and runs his hands over the top of his hair again.

'Well, first I usually teach people to be able to jump up on the board. It's harder than it looks.'

I take a step towards the water but he stops me.

'No, we do it on the beach first. It's easier without trying to keep your balance on the water as well.'

He lays the board on the sand in front of me, digging out some sand to accommodate the fins. He's close. Close enough that I can see the grains of sand on his chest – like he's seasoned with the things he loves. I swallow hard and look down at the board. It's white with red and blue stripes up the middle. I focus on it, trying to make my brain stop thinking about wiping the grains away from his skin. About leaning down for the barest of tastes with the tip of my tongue...

'Okay. Lie on the board, face down, like you're going to paddle with your hands.'

I give myself a mental shake and lie down. The board,

against my stomach, is cool in comparison to the heat of the sun on my back. He lies on the sand next to me and I turn my head to look at him. It feels intimate somehow. I don't move. And for a moment, neither does he. His eyes seem darker this afternoon. I wonder if it's the light or if they change with his mood. That's all I get a chance to think before he looks away.

'What I'm going to do now is to get you to hold the sides of the board and then, in one movement, you're going to come up to a crouching position.'

He puts his hands flat against the sand, the muscles in his upper arms firming, taking his weight. I have to remember to keep breathing. And then, in a way that's purely athletic, he's on his feet, one more forward than the other, arms slightly out.

'Think you can give it a go?'

I nod, wanting to be able to do it, wanting to impress him. I grip the sides, pushing myself up slightly and take a deep breath, before jumping up. Not really elegant and nowhere near as smooth as his but I'm up! I turn to him and smile.

'How was that?'

He smiles back. 'Not bad for a first timer. Try it again.'

I do and this one's a bit smoother, like my body understands what I want it to do now.

'Good. Again.'

He sits cross legged on the sand and I lay down on the board once again. But one of my feet isn't quick enough this time and I can feel myself starting to overbalance. I grab at the board to stop the fall but miss and then I'm going over, toppling into his lap, my face in his groin. I don't know which one of us moves quicker but this time, there's no hiding the red of my face.

'I'm so sorry!'

He's shaking his head, turning his body away from me slightly.

'No, it's all good. I think you just missed your footing a bit that time. It happens.'

There's a silence between us again. And I so don't want a silence. It just makes this more awkward.

'Maybe I should try it in the water.'

'Yeah, good idea, we'll get in the water.'

The relief is easy to hear in his voice and now I'm worried that I've hurt him. He swings around, away from me, and swoops down to pick up the board, holding it between us.

'Come on. We'll see how you go in the water.'

He almost speed walks down the beach and I have to jog a little to keep up.

'Shit.' He says it so softly I'm not sure I've actually heard him correctly. My stomach twists itself in knots at the thought that I've done something wrong. Something that means I'm not good enough. Lani – the girl who's never quite tough enough or kind enough or smart enough.

He does slow down though, so I can walk beside him.

The water is beautiful. Clear and warm. It's not until we're up to our waists that he stops and turns, moving the board around so it points to the beach. And that's when he actually looks at me. I don't know what he sees in my face but he's suddenly serious.

'Shit. Are you okay? You didn't hurt yourself?'

I shake my head, trying to smile. 'No. I'm fine. They breed us tough in Tassie.'

'You sure?'

I nod, turning to the board. 'Do you want me to get up?' My voice sounds light, easy. Not fake at all.

'Um, yeah. Let's try some paddling.'

I pull myself up and lay across the board. His hand touches my calf slightly as he comes around to the side. It feels like a bolt of electricity running through my muscles straight up to my pelvis, like it's an electrical highway, and I suck in a breath, holding myself stiff. God. And that's from an accidental touch, not even for a few seconds! What's going to happen when he really touches me? I shake my head, trying to clear the persistent images running through my head – of him moving his hand up my leg, higher and higher, leaning down to kiss the dimple at the bottom of my spine. God, it's hard to stop the groan that's trying hard to escape and I clench my stomach in an attempt to get my body under control. Zac. I need to remember Zac and how nice he makes me feel.

'Okay, we're going to wait for good wave and then I'm going to push the board and I want you to paddle until you feel the wave catch you. Don't worry about standing up yet.' His voice sounds strained. Forced. Maybe he doesn't want to teach me anymore. I'm about to ask if he wants to stop when I feel him start to push, one huge heave, and I'm shooting through the water.

'Paddle!'

My arms dig into the water, paddling hard like there's something chasing me. And then I feel the wave catch me and suddenly, I'm on it. It's pushing me, taking me into the beach, and I use my hands to steer me along, until I feel the sand brush along the bottom of the board, bringing me to a stop.

The laugh that bursts out of me makes me feel light, happy – for the first time in I don't know how long, I forget how I might look to anyone else watching or what they might be thinking. I'm buzzing and I haven't even stood up on it yet.

Matt is wading over to me and I stand up, grabbing at the board as I do.

'Oh my God, that was awesome!'

'One of the best feelings in the world when the water pushes you with it. That was great paddling. You've obviously got good muscle strength.'

His eyes move down to my arms and I bring them up, tensing them either side of my head.

'A lifetime wrestling with two older brothers. They'd want to be strong.'

He laughs and a warm glow washes over me – I'm the one making him laugh. Just me – Lani, without having to try so hard.

'Do you want to go again?'

I float the board back into deep water, looking at it rather than him.

'Do you still want to teach me?'

'Sure. If you still want to do it?'

I look at him. He seems genuine.

'Okay then.'

The afternoon seems to fly by but I love it. We talk and laugh and by the end, I've stood up twice. And the second time was longer than a couple of seconds.

I collapse on the beach when we finally wade out, feeling the sand stick to my back.

'God, I don't know if I'll be able to make it back to the house. My legs and arms feel like jelly.'

'Do you want me to carry you home?'

I laugh. 'You might need to.'

And then I think of Zac. My boyfriend. The one I haven't given any thought to for the last few hours and my laughter fades.

'Are you okay?'

I sit up. Matt is standing next to me, end of the board dug into the sand, hand on his hip. He is delicious. Everything I want. And that's the problem. He's still human. Still not what I need. And I have Zac.

'Sure. I'm just thinking I should get back and have a shower. Maybe wander up and see where Zac works.'

It's like his face goes blank for a second. And then he nods.

'Yeah, he'd probably enjoy it if you went down and had a drink there or something. He can show you off to everyone he works with.'

There's an edge to his voice. One that makes me feel horrible. Like I'm the one doing the wrong thing. I stand up.

'Thanks for the lesson. It was great.'

He smiles at me but it doesn't reach his eyes this time. 'You're a natural. You probably would've picked it up without me.'

I don't know what to make of that and I concentrate on brushing the sand off my arms.

'Are you going back to the house?'

He shakes his head.

'No, I might go down to the shop for a while. I've had staff running it today. I should go and see if everything's okay.'

'Oh. Well. I guess I'll see you back at the house later then?'

He shrugs. 'Maybe.'

I stand there for a moment, unsure. Unsure of what to do to make it okay between us again. It's clear I've done something to upset him and my brain gnaws at the thought that he's been suddenly reminded of what a bitch I am – that he thinks I'm playing both him and Zac. And the joy that's buoyed me up for the last few hours drains away.

'Thanks again.' My voice is soft and I don't know if he actually hears me but I turn away and start to move back up the beach to where I hid my bag.

'Lani.'

I turn back, heart pounding, hope flaring in me like a lit match. I don't know what I'm hoping for though. I don't know much really – not when I'm around him. But he's just holding out a key.

93

'You'll need this. To get in the house. Don't worry, I've got a spare at work.'

I walk back and take it, smiling, smiling, smiling. Faking it.

'Okay, thanks. See you later.'

And I turn before he can see the tears in my eyes that seemed to have come from nowhere.

Matt

I push the board up on top off the roof racks and pull the tie-down straps harder than they need. They creak in protest.

Shit. I'm a fucking idiot. Why the hell am I doing this to myself? Doing it to Lani and Zac, who both deserve more than the shit I'm creating in their new relationship. The longer I spend with her the more I want her. And not just because she's gorgeous – even thinking about that makes things stir again and I have to adjust my shorts – that's all I've been doing all afternoon, like a fucking teenager! But because I like who she is. The way she laughs, the easy way she chats when she's not thinking too hard – just letting herself be, the way she kept trying out there until she finally stood up...even her loyalty to Zac, which sucks for me. She's a good person.

Roxanne was right though. There's this uncertainty to her. A fragility that's emotional rather than physical, like she has to keep checking if she's saying the right thing, doing the right thing – trying to make what she thinks is the right impression. Which just makes me want to protect her. Show her that she's good enough, even if what she thinks isn't the same as whoever she's with.

I lean my back to the car and rub my face with my hands. Christ, I wasn't looking for anything like this. When things ended with Karli, I thought it was probably a sign that I needed to just be on my own for a while and concentrate on the business. Probably what I still need – I have to to keep reminding myself that she's not available. And that it's not that complicated really. I can't have her. That's it.

I slide into the seat and start the car. The drive to the shop only takes a few minutes and it does nothing to stop the torment in my head, imagining her heading back to the house, getting in the shower, washing the sand and salt water from her body before going to see Zac, his arm around her as he introduces her to everyone. I shake my head as if that's going to stop my thoughts. Fat chance of that.

The car park at the shop is nearly full and I park in my reserved spot out the back, taking just the keys with me as I go inside. There are people milling around everywhere and Dan, my second in charge, is finishing with a customer.

He turns to face me and smiles. 'Hey, boss. How was the water?'

'Good. Georgie managed to get up.'

His grin gets wider. 'Awesome. You'll have to bring her in and let her choose her own board one day.'

'Yeah, don't worry, she's already hit me up for that. How's it been in here today?'

'Busy. I ended up calling Sam in this morning to help. Hope that's okay?'

'Sure.' I look around, feeling that warm glow of satisfaction that gets me every time I think about the fact that it's mine. Not the banks and mine. Mine. No one can ever take it from me. 'Listen, you can take off if you want. I'll close up.'

'You sure?'

I nod. I don't want to go home and risk running into Lani. See her getting ready to go to Zac.

'Okay, great, I'll take you up on that then. Lisa will be happy to see me home early.'

I smile but it's more of an automated response than a real one. Which is crap. Happy relationships should be a good thing but it makes me feel even worse.

A furrow mars his forehead. 'You okay?'

I look at him and then look away.

'All good. I was just thinking about an idea for the shop. Something I've been mulling over for a while.'

'Oh yeah. What are you thinking?'

I gesture to the front of the shop.

'I noticed when I was driving in here that the place next door has finally gone up for sale. I was thinking I could knock through the wall, maybe expand the shop a bit and add a coffee shop. Give people another reason to come in.'

He nods his head slowly. 'Doesn't sound like a bad idea. And you could still keep this half open while you were renovating.'

'Yeah. Depends how much they want for it though – be stupid to overcapitalise.'

He laughs. 'You say that like there's a chance it won't happen.'

It's my turn to frown. 'Well, it might not.'

He rolls his eyes. 'Don't take this the wrong way but you always get what you want. In the four years I've been working for you, you've never given up on something when you really want it.'

I laugh but it doesn't feel real. Because I'm not going to get what I really want. Not this time. Not that I'm going to tell Dan that. No one needs to know. I'll get over Lani. Especially if her and Zac move out. And then, I just won't see Zac as much. Or visit Roxanne's store. And hope that Lani and Roxanne don't become friends... Shit. I'm screwed.

I start to organise the counter so I don't have to look at him.

'Are you getting out of here or not?'

'Sure, sure. Don't need to tell me twice.'

He collects his things from under the desk and is about to head out the door before he stops and turns back to me.

'Shit. Nearly forgot to tell you. Karli came in.'

My hands go still but I don't look at him. All he knows is that we broke up. Not why. That's my business and I'm not a big sharer.

'Yeah?'

'Yeah. She said she wanted you to call her.'

'Did she say why?'

There's a pause and I finally look over at him. He scratches the side of his face, like he's trying to work out what to say.

I sigh. 'Just tell me, Dan.'

'Well, it was a bit personal.' I raise my eyebrows and he takes a deep breath. 'She said she still loves you. And she wants you to give her a call before she goes away for the weekend.'

With Brent. Fat chance. But that's not Dan's problem.

'Okay. Thanks.'

He gives me a tight nod and then turns to go. I shut my eyes for a second, as if that's going to make all this shit go away. How the hell did everything get so complicated?

Lani

My boots tap on the pavement, a staccato rhythm to my disjointed thoughts. I could've driven to the restaurant but I needed a walk. I chance to sort out my thoughts even though I haven't been able to do that so far. My brain keeps rebelliously turning back to Matt – his eyes, the way his face changes when he smiles, his patience while he was teaching me to surf, the feel of his touch on my leg, his grace and athleticism in the surf. The way my heart squeezes and twists at the thought of more of that.

I press my lips together. I need to stop it. Bond or no bond, it doesn't matter. It doesn't! I *cannot* be with a human – not if I ever want to be able to face my mother again. And even if I did choose Matt and was still somehow, unbelievably, able to be a part of my family, I don't know if I could live with the constant passive-aggressive comments and sighs and disappointment. There's no doubt in my mind that I'd mean even less to her than I do at the moment if I chose to be with anyone other than a changer.

And a human would never be accepted into our family.

Not as a lifetime partner anyway. I couldn't do that to Matt even if I was free to choose him.

Mum was bad enough when Nick got engaged to Grace – the couple I knew in Tasmania. And they weren't even part of our family. God, I'd never be able to go home. All I can imagine is Mum turning her back on me, refusing to talk to me, look at me. My chest aches with the thought of the sort of rejection I have no doubt she's capable of. Even though I know Dad would be okay. Probably. Maybe. But I don't know that I could even be sure of that.

Because there's still the need to carry on our genes. Make sure changers don't die out...the responsibility for making sure our kind continue...blah, blah, blah. It's been drummed in to me all of my life. And both my brothers have married other changers. Both of them are doing the 'right' thing. Both of them make my mother happy. I don't know how they do it.

In the end, I can't be with Matt. No matter how much my body wants it. No matter how much *I* want it. The bonding process or whatever it is – it got it wrong. It has to have.

The restaurant where Zac works is half full already. People chatting, laughing, having a good time, sitting around dark wood tables, and surrounded by pots of trees with fairy lights threading through the branches before being hooked to the ceiling over the seating. It looks like a magical land.

I stop at the entrance until one of the waiters comes over. She smiles at me.

'Can I help you?'

'Yeah, hi. I don't have a reservation but I'm Zac's girlfriend so I was just hoping that I might be able to sneak in with a table for one...'

'Oh, you're Lani. Pleased to meet you. Zac's told us all about you. Come with me. I'll find a table in his section for you.'

I follow her through the restaurant to a table further at the back. It's set for two but she takes one of the settings away as I sit down.

'I'm Greta, by the way. I used to go to school with Zac. Well, he was in the grade above me anyway so I went to school with him but not with him, if you know what I mean.'

'Oh, so you'd know Matt too.'

I don't know why I say that. The plan is not to think about him let alone talk about him!

Greta puts her hand up to her chest and rolls her eyes. 'Oh my God, isn't he the sexiest guy? What I wouldn't give to have him keep me company for a couple of nights. And those eyes... man, oh man.'

I want to rip her throat out, right then and there. The thought rushes through my head unbidden and something of it must show on my face because she actually takes a step back.

'Oh, sorry. That was pretty tactless. I mean, Zac's cute too. And he's a nice guy. I didn't want to...I mean, you know he's cute...but, you know...'

She looks really uncomfortable and I don't know how to make it better. Even a smile doesn't seem to fit on my face.

'Who thinks I'm cute?'

It's Zac. Greta actually looks relieved and I feel terrible. I try to smile at both of them, wanting her to like me.

'Greta was just talking about the fact that you guys all went to school together. And she was agreeing with me that you were cute.'

He puts his arm around her shoulder and my heart doesn't even react. How is that possible? I like Zac. I do!

'I know, Gretski, that you want me but I'm taken. I'm so sorry. Do you think you'll be able to cope?'

She rolls her eyes and pushes him away, laughing.

'Whatever. And don't call me Gretski.' She smiles at me as she goes to walk away. 'Nice to meet you.'

I smile back at her, it feels less awkward this time, and then turn back to Zac. He leans down, hands on the table and kisses me. It is soft and sweet. That's it. Nice. Again. I don't want nice. I want a heart pounding, can't-help-but-want-more, stomach clenching kiss. And I want it from Matt's lips.

And that's it – the truth in all its stark reality. It creates a hollowness in my throat, my chest – a dark emptiness like nothing I've ever felt before. And so, I do what I always do when I don't know how to react, I put on my mask and smile.

'I didn't know you were going to come in tonight. This is a nice surprise.'

I shrug, still smiling, smiling, smiling. 'I just thought it'd be fun to see where you work. That's okay, isn't it?'

'More than okay. Order anything you want. It's all on me.'

I shake my head, feeling the darkness spread. What am I doing? Zac deserves more than this but if I tell him that, then maybe he'll leave and there'll be no chance to be happy with a changer and Mum will tell me I stuffed it up again – like normal, and I'll know I'll never be good enough to get it right.

I suck in the breath, my smile getting slightly bigger like a macabre parody of a real one. 'That's sweet but you don't need to do that. I'm going to start working with Roxanne. I have my own money.'

He silences me with another kiss. 'I want to. You're my girl. White wine to start with?'

I nod, lips stretched wide, trying to ignore the guilt that's tracing through the hollowness. He is the sweetest guy – nice, kind, funny, one of my own kind – why don't I want him? I should want him. I *can* want him. I just need to give it time and never, ever see Matt again. He can just be a lovely dream – an interlude before my real life starts.

Zac tucks my hair behind my ear as he goes. It's a romantic gesture, so I wait until he's out of sight before I pull it back out.

Sphenurus

He brings me wine and another kiss and I watch him as he moves around, serving people, making them laugh, handling everything with ease. I can see why he likes his job. He's good at it. And yet, to want to do this for his whole life...

I shake my head. God, I sound like my mother. It's enough to make me feel nauseous.

He comes to take my order but I'm not hungry anymore, even though I didn't have lunch.

"Come on, babe, you've got to let me get you something apart from wine. Let me impress you with my serving style.'

I laugh and am honestly a bit surprised that it doesn't sound manic. 'Okay, the prawns then. Just an entrée size.'

It's only ten minutes before the food's ready and, as he puts it down in front of me, he sits in the other chair.

'Are you allowed to sit and talk to me while you're working? I don't want to get you in trouble.'

He looks around. 'Don't stress. Everyone's good. So, how did your day go?'

I put a prawn in my mouth, enjoying the spices it's coated in, and finish it before I talk. Deciding what I want to say. And how to say it...

'Good. Roxanne asked me to start tomorrow. And she said she wants to look at some of my designs.'

'That's awesome. I told you they were good.'

'She hasn't seen them yet. They could be crap.'

He reaches out and covers my hand with his. 'Don't keep on doing that.'

I frown at him. 'Doing what?'

'Putting yourself down. You've got talent. That's obvious.'

I nod. It's easy for him to say. I take a gulp of wine so I don't have to answer.

'And how did you fill in your time this afternoon? Did you miss me?'

I look around me. There are people close enough to hear so I lower my voice.

'I went flying. I thought I might explore everything in the daylight. It's a beautiful area.'

He strokes my hand. I have to consciously think about not pulling away.

'Did you go over the national park? That's my favourite spot.'

I nod. 'It's amazing.'

'And then you came here?'

The guilt flares in me again and I take another drink of my wine.

'No. I ran into Matt at the beach when I came back. He offered to teach me to surf – he'd been down there with Georgie, I think – so I thought I'd take him up on it.'

He smiles. It seems genuine and it makes me feel even worse.

'Yeah? That's great. Did you manage to get up?'

'Twice. But only for a few seconds.'

He laughs. 'That's great on your first go. I was pretty shit at it and unfortunately, I can't even blame it on Matt's teaching. Wish I could've been there to see you.'

Does it make me a terrible person that I'm glad he wasn't? Yes, of course it does. I'm a bitch. I take another gulp, finishing the glass.

The people a few tables over have finished their meals and he squeezes my hand as he stands up.

'Duty calls. Do you want another glass?'

I nod. It seems to be helping keep the guilt at bay. And by the end of the prawns and the fifth glass of wine, I'm feeling okay again. Relaxed, easy, unwound...like I could say or do anything and not worry about what anyone else thinks. Not think about what my mother would say or how she would look at me or how she would sigh. Not think about anything except what *I* want.

So maybe it's time to go home before I do something stupid.

I stand up and the floor under me feels slightly uneven. Like it's moved since I've sat down. I grab the edge of the table, holding on until it comes right again. Maybe the fifth glass wasn't a great idea. Perhaps even the fourth one...

And then Zac is next to me, grabbing my hand. I pull away from him. Mainly because I need to hold onto the table again. He grins. It's nice but not as devastating as Matt's. I go to tell him that and realise I probably shouldn't. Only a few words escape from my mouth before my brain brings it up to speed with our decision.

'Hey, my gorgeous lady, how about I call a taxi and get you home? I don't think it'd be a good idea for you to walk home all on your own.'

I shake my head, holding the table just a little bit tighter.

'No. I'm fine. A walk home would be good. Help me to clear my head with the fresh air and...stuff.'

I frown. There was something else I was going to say but my brain isn't playing nice. The fifth glass was definitely a shit decision.

Zac shakes his head. 'I can't let you do that. Not on your own and I can't leave yet. Let me get you a taxi, okay?'

I let go of the table, standing tall. Balancing, although my boots are making it hard.

'No, see? I'm fine.' My tongue doesn't seem to want to work properly now either and I have to concentrate on each word.

He laughs and wraps his arm around my waist.

'I can see that. But I think you still need a lift home. Will you let me do that? Will you let me be a good boyfriend?'

I turn my head to look at him as he leads me through the restaurant, past everyone else having a good time. Everyone else there with people they love. And yet I'm not. Am I? It's hard to concentrate. Even that hollowness seems to have disappeared, which is nice. I like Zac, I really do, but I don't love him and I don't know that I can. Is that what I was thinking before? He's gone blurry for some reason and I squint my eyes to look at him better.

'You are a good boyfriend, you know. You're the best. You're funny and you're lovely and you're a nice guy.'

He squeezes my side as we walk out the entrance. 'Well, that's good to know.'

I shake my head. It's not good. Not at all. Because I should want him. But I know I don't.

'It's not fair though. You're a good person. A nice person. Very *nice*.' I touch the side of his face – hard to do when I'm also concentrating on walking. 'But I don't want you to be *my* boyfriend though.' The words are out of my mouth before I can catch them. Is that a good thing? I don't know. I can't think. My brain feels thick, like the thoughts need to fight their way out.

He stops. 'What?'

I step back a little so I can see his face and his arm drops from around my waist. And I know I am the worst person ever. Definitely *not* nice.

'It's not right. You are cute and funny and nice and...' I lose my train of thought and have to stop for a moment, frowning. 'Nice. Gretski says you're nice. And she's right. You are a really nice person. But there's no bond, Zac. No *bond*.'

There's a long pause and I have to squint again see what his face looks like – what he's thinking. It's blank. I don't know if that's good or not.

'I think maybe we need to get you home to bed, hey? We'll talk about this in the morning.'

I shake my head. That thought scares me. I don't want to talk about it in the morning. It'll be too late then, even if I'm not sure why. That's how it feels though. I have to tell him – now, while I'm feeling brave.

'It's not working Zac. I need a bond. I want that. I wanted that with you but it's not...Mum...she won't...' It's like my brain keeps running out of steam.

'So what does that mean? You don't want to go out with me anymore?'

I shake my head again and stumble a little this time. I can feel the tears start to prickle in my eyes and my chest is tight and aching, the hollowness back again and making everything feel like it's going to cave in.

'I'm sorry. So sorry. I like you. I really do. I don't want to hurt you.' I wipe my eyes. There's black stuff on my hand. I can't work out what it is until I realise it's probably my makeup. It doesn't matter though. I need to make him understand. 'But the bond, Zac.'

He's still, just watching me. He looks hurt and I didn't want that. He's so nice – so *good* – and he doesn't deserve to be in pain. And yet, I'm doing that. I can't help it.

'You might never get it, you know. You might never have a bond.'

I need him to understand that it's not him I'm rejecting. Maybe that will make him hurt less. I lean forward and grab his arm, bringing my finger up to my lips.

'Shh, don't tell anyone, okay? But I've already got it. That's why I can't be with you. The bond happened. And you're a good guy, Zac. The best. I don't want to hurt you. It's not you. It's the bond. Okay? It's the stupid bond.'

He's quiet again and I can't work out what he's thinking from his expression. Did it make it better for him to know? Or have I made it worse. Probably that one. That's what I always do. Stuff things up. Stuff it like a well packed chicken. I put my hand to my mouth to stop the giggle that's sitting on my tongue.

It wouldn't be good to laugh. Zac might think I'm laughing at him and that'd make him feel bad.

'Who with?'

I frown at him. 'What?'

I notice his jaw clench but his words are still patient – calm. 'Who have you bonded with?'

I take a deep breath – it feels like a big thing to say out loud. 'With Matt. Isn't that crazy? A human!' And then I remember who I'm talking to. 'I'm so sorry. I didn't mean for it to happen. Didn't want to hurt you. You're so nice and friendly and funny –'

'With Matt? You've got a bond with Matt?'

I nod. He sounds...angry. Maybe. It's too hard to work out. I go to touch his face again but he pulls back.

'Sorry. Sorry. I didn't mean for it to happen. My mum...' I can't remember what I was going to say about her. 'Matt doesn't know though. You can't tell him, okay? Mum would hate it – hate him. I don't know what the bond thought it was doing...'

Zac shakes his head and waves at a passing taxi.

'Just go home, Lani. We'll talk about this in the morning, okay? Just go home and sleep it off.'

I nod. Sleep. That sounds good. I don't want to hurt him. I don't.

'Okay. Okay.'

He puts me in the taxi and tells the driver the address, which is good since I can't find it anywhere in my brain. He hands him some money too and then leans in, helping me with my seatbelt which doesn't seem to want to go together.

'We'll talk about this in the morning, okay?'

I nod. 'Sorry,' I say again and he just nods before shutting the door. And then the taxi is driving away. I turn, looking back at him. He watches the car until I can't see him anymore.

Matt

I'm getting dressed after a shower when I hear banging in the kitchen. Loud banging. Like the place is being trashed. I race out, still tugging my shirt down, but pull up short when I see Lani. The sight of her actually takes my breath away.

She has her hair up at the sides and it hangs down her back in waves. I want to wrap it up in my hand, just to feel the softness; thread my fingers through it as I kiss her mouth, her neck... And she has a white dress on – short, clinging in all the right places – God, she is gorgeous.

And obviously drunk.

I can tell by the way she sticks her tongue out at the side, concentrating while she pours herself a glass of wine. And the way her make up is slightly smeared. It's weird that that makes her seem more attractive.

'Are you okay? Need a hand?'

She swings around so quickly that she knocks the glass and white wine flows over the bench, dripping down the cupboard.

'Oh no, oh no. I'm so sorry. I've made a mess. I've made a mess of everything!'

She has her hands out in front of her like she's trying to keep the wine back through the force of her mind. And she sounds like she's about to cry. I grab the sponge off the sink, squatting down to clean up the liquid that's already made it to the floor, following the line up the cupboard.

'It's okay. I startled you. It's my fault.'

She watches me as I clean up. I can feel her eyes on me still when I turn, rinsing the cloth out. My heart is squeezing in my chest like the sponge in my hands. The few hours apart hasn't made it any better. I want her still – drawn to her. It's all I can do not to turn around and kiss her. When I finally turn back around, she's still watching me, her eyes wide, body still.

'Would you like me to pour you another one?'

She nods and, for a second, she looks scared, which doesn't make a hell of a lot of sense. I can't think of anything I've done which would have her looking like that.

Our fingers touch when I hand her the glass and I swear I feel an electric spark. Jesus, I've turned into a romantic sap. Stupid. And yet I run my fingers against my shirt to help get rid of the feeling. She's still watching me.

'Are you okay?'

She nods and then shakes her head. And then she takes a big gulp of wine. At least half of the glass and I'm nervous and excited in equal measure at the way she seems to need the alcohol to be brave enough for something...

'You might want to slow down.'

I can see the sheen of moisture on her bottom lip and want to kiss it away, stroking her lip with my tongue, wrapping her in my arms, pressing her up against me...I take a half step back.

'I broke up with Zac.'

My eyes snap up to hers. The air feels thick between us,

like a storm's about to hit and the humidity has become a physical thing, making it hard to draw a good breath in.

'Did you?' My voice is husky and I clear my throat. 'Why?'

She shrugs and in doing so, almost loses her balance. I grab her arm and she clings to me. Every place where her skin touches mine feels like it's about to self-combust.

'Come and sit down.'

I lead her out to the veranda. It's quiet, except for the soft lapping of the water on the bank.

'Why did you break up with Zac?'

I'm holding my breath, waiting for her answer. She looks down at her wine and then back up at me.

'It wasn't right...I mean, he's a nice guy and he's funny and sweet and friendly...' She shakes her head like she's trying to make her brain behave. Probably hard when it's battling the alcohol.

When she looks at me again, there are tears in her eyes. I want to wrap her in my arms but I think if I do that, she'll stop talking and I need her to talk. I need to know where her and Zac stand before I do anything that could be considered crazy. Stupid.

'I should want him. He suits me. He's one of us. But I don't want him.' She takes a deep breath and her eyes lock on mine again. 'I want you.'

My heart stops for a second, like it's gone into shock, before it jump-starts again, running across my rib cage like a prisoner with a cup against the bars.

'You do?'

She nods, slowly, and licks her lips. I'm mesmerized by her tongue. It's only when she stands up that I realize I still haven't said anything. I don't know what to say. I've been struck dumb – caught unawares – sure that she liked Zac. Loved him even. I can only watch as she walks over to me, putting her legs either side of my chair and sitting on my lap. I grab her around the waist before I can even think what we're doing...what she's doing...it's pure reaction and yet, I don't want to let her go.

Holy Christ!

It's all I can do not to pull her lips down to mine. But I can't. She's drunk. There's no getting away from that. And I don't take advantage of drunk women. Especially when there's a good chance they might regret what they've done in the morning. But it is so hard. This is what I've wanted from the moment I saw her – for her to say she wants me as much as I want her.

She's watching me, her eyes serious.

'You're no good for me.' Her voice is low, husky and it makes everything in me tighten, harden. Jesus, she must feel that. 'Being with you won't carry on the gene. And my mother will be furious. So disappointed in me. I'm a bad daughter. Really bad. Always have been even though I try hard.' She takes a deep breath. 'But I can't help it. I can't help the bond. I want you.'

I don't know what the hell she's talking about but it doesn't matter – drunk ramblings, maybe. I've had my fair share of them. All I can concentrate on is her lips coming closer to mine with every word she says.

Until they're touching mine and I can't hold back anymore.

I thread my hand through her hair, my fingers resting at the back of her neck, pulling her closer. She groans and my body responds to her, like a call from a siren. I feel like I'm drunk on her. Who needs alcohol?

I brush her lips with my tongue and taste the sweetness of the wine she's been drinking, overlayed by the taste of her. The sweetness of Lani that I could live on.

My free hand travels up her back, tracing her vertebrae in the backless dress that allows me free access. She leans in closer to me, her hands going under my shirt, pushing it up, her skin on mine like she's branding me, marking me as hers. She sits back a little, giving herself room to take my shirt off. That's when a little bit of sanity comes back to my brain. Enough to make me put my hands over hers, holding them against my chest, stopping her.

'Stop, Lani. Wait.'

Tears are in her eyes again as she tries to pull her hands out. I don't let her, sure that she'll leave and I won't be able to explain.

'You don't want me.' She says it like there's no doubt – that it could be the only reason I've stopped it going further.

I give a choked laugh.

'Jesus, are you kidding me.' I pull her towards me, my hands going around her upper arms, and kiss her again, hard, trying to show her my need, before letting go of her. She's breathing heavy, matching my own.

'I want you so bad it hurts. It's taking all my will power to hold myself back. But we need to stop.'

'Why?'

I take a deep breath. It's shaky. I can't believe I'm actually saying this.

'Because you just broke up with Zac. Tonight. And you've had a bit to drink. If we're going to be together, I don't want it to be because you're on the rebound or because you're not thinking clearly.'

She shakes her head and tries to lean down to kiss me again. I hold her away. I don't know how much longer I can resist her if I keep kissing her.

'Lani, stop. Please.'

I stand, scooping her up in my arms. She has me so worked up that it's hard to walk, so I stand there for a moment, looking down at her. She runs her hand down the side of my face.

'It's okay. I'm thinking clearly. I know I want you.' The

longing I can hear in her voice matches mine. Fuck! But I can't do it. It's not right. I start walking towards her room, my eyes on her the whole way. Just as well I know the layout of the house so well. She watches me, her amber eyes wide, like she's drinking me in.

I lay her on her bed, pulling the throw from the end and putting it over her.

'Tomorrow. Get some sleep now and we'll talk tomorrow.'

It's hard to get the words out of my mouth. She looks beautiful laying there. All I want to do is lay down next to her, hold her in my arms, continue to kiss her. Jesus, even if we don't do anything, the thought of holding her the whole night has my brain doing a happy dance. But not yet. Not until we've talked and I know Zac knows how she's feeling and is okay with what I want to do. Although how could he be okay? How could he not be hurt and pissed off?

'Fuck.' The word comes out as a whisper and I'm hoping she hasn't heard it and read a different meaning into it.

I lean down, softly kissing her forehead. She catches my hand, holding it as I stand back up.

'Tomorrow,' I say again.

And then I turn and walk out before I change my mind.

Lani

The sun glinting through the gap between the window and blind is shining in my eyes. I groan and roll over. My head hurts, like my brain is too big for my skull, and my mouth is so dry that even when I move my tongue, there's no saliva to make it feel better. I put my hand across my eyes and another groan leaks out of me, making my skull vibrate. I hurt all over.

And then it comes flooding back to me.

Everything.

Breaking up with Zac.

Telling him about the bond with Matt.

Then getting home somehow – a taxi, I think – and telling Matt how much I like him. God, I think I even said something about the bond and passing on genes!

And sitting on Matt's lap.

And kissing him.

Kissing him!

All of this and I'm not really sure, lying here now, that I've actually broken up with Zac. Not really.

Because both of them said they were going to talk to me in the morning. Which is now!

God, oh God, oh God! What have I done?

I roll over, burying my head under the pillow. Maybe if I just lay here all day, everything will go away and I won't have to talk to anyone or face anyone or explain myself...

And then I remember it's Monday. Shit! My first day of work. I bring my head back out and gingerly grab my phone from the bedside cabinet. It's only seven. Thank God. I flop back down and lay there, looking at the ceiling.

What am I going to do?

The only thing I'm sure of is that I can't stay here anymore. That is just way too complicated. And, for the moment, I need it uncomplicated. Because I need to work out what I want. And I truly have no idea what that will look like.

Sure, I want Matt. Want him so much that it actually hurts my body to think that I might not be able to be with him – an ache that feels like it goes all the way down to my bones.

But all my life I've been told how important it is to carry on our genes. I've been told how disgusting it is to be with a human. I know that if I go down this path with Matt, my mum will never speak to me again. Actually, it might be my whole family, but it will definitely be my mum. And as much as she's a pain in the ass – as much as she makes me feel like I can never do enough to make her truly happy with me – she's my mum. And I want her to love me. I want to be good enough for her.

So Zac is still the best person for me. Even if I don't want him. And God knows if he'll want me now.

I sigh. It's too hard. All of it. Especially when my brain doesn't really feel like it remembers how to function properly this morning.

Sitting up, I look around the room. I can't stay here. That's the most I can think about. I'm just glad I only brought three suitcases with me and that I haven't really had time to unpack yet – it's only going to take me a few moments to put the stuff I have taken out back in my bags.

And if I just take my essentials with me this morning, I could perhaps ask Roxanne to get the rest later. Even though I hate asking her to do that as my new boss and it means I'm going to have to explain things to her. Well, some things maybe. I don't think I'll tell her about the kiss. It feels like it's the only way I'm going to be able to get out of here as quickly as I need.

Running away. Just until I can work things out anyway.

I sigh. Even though it's the first day of work, I don't want to take the chance of having a shower. Just in case Matt's in his room, sprawled out on his bed, the sheets only just covering him... I shake my head, trying to dispel the image.

Grabbing my suitcase, I fold the clothes I've taken out, trying to make sure that things don't get too crushed, leaving out the lime green swing dress I'd planned to wear today.

I look in the mirror and grimace. The damage from last night is definitely showing. The makeup I didn't get around to taking off last night is smeared over my face and my skin looks blotchy. So not just damage control on the emotional part of my life then – there's a physical need for it too.

I grab the makeup wipes from my toiletries bag and pull them gently over my skin. No point in making the blotchiness worse. The dark circles under my eyes look worse now that my face is naked and I lay my palms against my cheek. It'd be nice to not have to put makeup back on but there's no way I can turn up for work looking like I've been dragged from the gutter.

Years of practice means everything's reapplied in ten minutes and I look vaguely normal again. I drag the brush through my hair, wincing at the pull on my scalp and what it's doing to my headache. Winding it up in a loose bun at the nape of my neck relieves some of the pressure and I turn to take the dress out of the cupboard, pulling it over my head. I feel like I'm on automatic pilot, limbs doing what they need to do even though my brain isn't really engaging. And then I'm finished and there's nothing else to distract me.

I look around the room. Apart from the dishevelled sheets, it's like I've never been here. As if I never existed in this room... in this house.

I push two of the suitcases against the wall and grab the smaller one and my toiletries bag. Opening the door seems huge. What if Matt's out there? Or Zac? Or both? God, what am I going to say if they're both out there? I don't know if I'm brave enough to do it.

All I can think about is how sweet Zac was last night at the restaurant and then his face when I told him I didn't want to be with him. And then Matt...the smell of him when he picked me up, the feel of his lips on mine, the need that seemed to overtake me, how much I wanted him. Like I've never wanted anyone before. Ever.

I take a deep breath, reaching for the door handle with a trembling hand. And then I turn it.

The house is quiet. I stick my head out, looking both ways. There doesn't seem to be anyone awake. Or at least, there doesn't seem to be anyone in the living area. I pick up the bags so the wheels don't clatter against the wooden floor, my shoes in my other hand for the same reason. I walk carefully down the hallway, each step as slow and light as it can be. Silent. The living room and kitchen are empty and I let out the breath I'm holding. Because even though there's a small part of me hoping I'd see Matt, there's a much, much bigger part of me that's relieved I can just sneak away.

I start down the stairs and the third one creaks loudly in the silence. I freeze for a moment, waiting. But there's no response – no one is running out to see what the noise is, no condemnation of me as a coward. I hold my breath and hurry down the last of the stairs on tiptoed feet, and then I'm out the front door. Shutting it quietly behind me, I almost run to the car, shoving my bags on the back seat. I can't help looking back at the house before I climb into the driver's seat. It's still quiet.

I can't believe I'm doing this. And yet, it feels like it's the only option. I need to get my head together before I see either of them. Otherwise, I'm going to do more damage than I managed last night. I need to work out what I want – not what Mum or Dad want or what I think I *should* want. But I'm so used to thinking about my responsibilities to our community and how to make my mother happy that it's hard not to continue to do it.

I wince as I start the car, the sound loud in the quiet morning air, even though I know it's not really that loud, and back out of the driveway. It's harder to do that I thought. Tears sting my eyes, threatening to come out and wreck my newly applied makeup, and I wave my hand in front of my eyes, fanning them away.

The drive to Roxanne's shop seems to take forever and yet, when I pull into the car park in a street next to it, only forty minutes have passed since I woke up. Why does it feel like a lifetime?

My stomach is in knots, twisting like a yoga master. There's no way I could handle anything for breakfast, even though I probably should after only having the prawns last night. But I might be able to stand a tea. With lots of sugar. Hot and sweet and comforting. And a bottle of water. With a couple of paracetamol.

There's a cafe a few doors up and I hurry along the side-walk, praying that neither Matt nor Zac will go by. Which is ridiculous. Why would they? Except maybe if they realise I've left and are looking for me. God! I don't know what I'd do...

what I'd say...if that happened. So I just keep my head low, looking at the cracks in the cement.

Being inside the cafe offers me some protection, and I breathe deeply, taking in the smell of brewed coffee. Just that makes me feel a little better, even though I hate drinking it. The woman behind the counter tries to make conversation but my brain still doesn't want to function and I respond to most of her chatter with one word answers and vague smiles. It doesn't seem to worry her.

I clutch the takeaway cup of tea to my chest as I walk back, the warmth sinking into me, defrosting me, even though the weather is still definitely summer-hot. It's just my brain...and maybe my heart...that feel like they're frozen.

Getting back in the car, I sift through my bag until I find the paracetamol, taking two with the bottle of water I bought with the tea, before leaning my head back on the headrest, eyes closed, taking sips of tea, ignoring the world as much as I can. The warm drink is delicious and slowly, at a snail's pace, it feels like my brain is starting to work again.

But when Roxanne's car pulls up next to mine, all of my slowly emerging thoughts flee in panic. Like they're abandoning the sinking ship maybe. Cowards. She smiles at me when she gets out of her car.

'Wow, you're early. Are you trying to make a good first impression? Because I have to tell you, I'm impressed!'

I don't know if it's the expression on my face or the bags that are evident on the back seat that clue her in, but the smile drops away from her face and she looks at me – really looks at me – as I get out of the car.

'Are you okay?'

I take a deep breath and try for a smile. It's not the type of smile that's going to fool anyone but it's some attempt at acting professionally at least. I don't want to fall apart in front of my new boss on the first day, regardless of how supportive she's been. Especially since she's related to the guy I can't seem to get out of my system – one of the reasons I can't get it together. I need to show her I can handle things. That I'm mature and in control...despite the fact I feel anything but.

'Yeah, I'm okay. It's been a big night, that's all. Zac and I broke up so I thought it'd be less awkward all round if I left this morning before...well, just before anyone was up. I'll try to find somewhere else to stay this afternoon, after work.'

Not to mention I kissed your brother and I want him so badly it feels like my ovaries might explode. I'm still with it enough that I don't say that out loud though, so snaps for me.

She reaches out to touch my arm and I struggle to keep it together. It's almost a relief when she drops her hand again.

'You've had a tough time of it then? Did you talk to Zac this morning?'

I shake my head. 'He wasn't up when I left.' I don't tell her I didn't check – that I didn't want to see him.

She nods. 'It must've been hard, considering you came up here to be with him.'

I shrug. Nonchalance...taking it all in my stride...even though I'm not. Even though I'm running away. Even though I'm not sure what I think.

'It's okay. Sort of. I'll work it out.' I take a deep breath. 'I just need to find somewhere to stay and I'll go from there. You don't know anywhere that might be suitable?'

She nods. 'I've got the perfect spot. You don't even have to go looking – well, as long as you like it, I guess. My place has a granny flat. It's where Matt stayed when he initially bought the shop. After Mum died and we'd sold the house. It's just sitting there empty. I use it for storage more than anything else.'

'Oh, I don't want to put you out.'

Because although it sounds fantastic – easy – I don't know

that I can do it. I feel like I need space. From him. Space to think. Roxanne shakes her head.

'You're not putting me out. And the rent will help me.'

It doesn't feel like I can say no. But maybe I don't need to. Maybe I can use it for the next couple of days so I don't have to accept something else in a panic of need. It'd be easy. Get my head together. Breathe. Think. And work out what I want from there. Hopefully.

Matt

Even an early morning surf hasn't cleared my head. Usually being out on the water, sitting on my board as the waves roll in under me, paddling hard when I see the right swell, heart thumping and the feel of all that power under my feet when I get up – usually that's enough to fix most things going on in my head. But not this morning. This morning, all I can think about is Lani and what happened between us last night.

And how much I want her break up with Zac to still be true and not the result of a drunken argument which can be resolved in the clear light of day.

I trudge back up to the house. It's quiet but then, it's only six. Zac never surfaces this early and I'm not expecting Lani to either with the night she had last night. I hesitate at her door, wondering if I should knock so she's not late for work but the thought of seeing her – and the possibility of seeing regret on her face from the kiss last night, from what she said about wanting me...

I don't want to even think about it.

I head to my room and shut the door, leaning against it for a second. Shit. It feels like everything is royally screwed up. I strip my damp shorts off and use the towel I've thrown over my shoulder to finish drying off from the shower I had downstairs. I don't know what to do with myself. I need to get dressed and get into work but I don't want to leave things like this. I won't be able to concentrate at work if I do.

But there's no one up to sort it out with! And even though I said I'd talk about it with Lani in the morning...what if she doesn't want me anymore? What if she's not over Zac? Or what if she doesn't want me but remembers I wanted her?

Christ.

Not that I know what I want to say anyway.

Especially to Zac...hey man, how did you sleep? By the way, sorry, I kissed your girl last night. Hope you *were* actually broken up. Because the thing is, I want to kiss her again. In fact, I want to do more than kiss her.

I shake my head. This is not who I am.

I grab some clothes and pull them on like they've done something to insult me. I can't be here. I can't deal with it now. It's still quiet when I go down the hallway but now that I've made the decision to go, I just want to be out of here. It's only when the front door closes behind me that I actually breathe.

The day at the shop drags, even though there are more than enough customers to keep me busy. I reach for the phone so many times to either ring Roxanne's shop just on the slight chance I'll hear Lani's voice or ring Zac to find out what the hell's going on that I lose count. But each time I put it down before I dial. Because I don't want to speak to Lani before I speak to Zac. I need to know that it's definitely over for him. Finished. No thought in his head of them getting back together. Otherwise it's going to make me the type of person I hate. Maybe I'm already that person.

And I don't want to speak to Zac over the phone. That just seems like a really shitty thing to do.

It's close to six before I manage to get away. My chest is aching on the drive home, like a vice is squeezing it, pressing my ribs closer together, tighter and tighter. All I can picture is the two of them, curled up on the seat on the veranda, having sorted everything out. In love again.

But Lani's car isn't there when I drive in, which I guess means she isn't here either. It's almost a relief. A relief and a loss, all at the same time. Man, I'm so totally screwed.

I can hear Zac banging things in the kitchen on the way up the stairs, like he's pissed with the world. It doesn't make me feel any better. He looks up as I get to the top of the stairs.

'Hey.'

There's something in his voice that makes me feel like crap. But maybe it's just my guilty conscience. I hope that's all it is. I swallow against the lump in my throat.

'Hey.'

He puts the bowl his holding on the bench. 'Have you heard?'

I try and keep my face blank.

'Heard what?'

'Lani dumped me. Last night at the restaurant, as she was leaving.'

'Shit.' I try to look concerned. Try to feel concerned. That's what a good mate *should* be feeling. But instead, my heart's doing somersaults in my chest, back flips and front flips and cartwheels. Celebrating. They aren't together. She's free.

I'm a shit, shit person.

'She said something when she came in last night but she was pretty drunk. I thought it might've just been the alcohol talking.'

He picks up the bowl again and then puts it back down like

he doesn't know what to do. Every muscle in my body tenses, waiting for whatever he's going to throw at me – words, the bowl...

'So, you saw her last night?'

I lean on the bench, trying to look like I'm not tight, not on alert, and nod.

'What did she say?'

'Just that you weren't together anymore. That you'd broken up.' And then she sat on my lap and kissed me. And I kissed her back. Really kissed her. Wanted to kiss her. I'm trying not to feel guilty – they *had* broken up. But it's not working.

'Did she tell you why?'

I shake my head – lying by omission. But I don't want to make him feel worse. He just nods.

I clear my throat. 'So, how are you going?'

He looks down at the eggs he's cracked into the bowl.

'Honestly, I don't know. I mean, it's pretty shitty. No one likes rejection. And I thought we were getting along okay. More than okay actually. I thought it was going really good. So it was a bit of a kick in the guts.'

'But?'

I hold my breath, waiting for his answer. Praying that there *is* a but.

'But I haven't known her that long. Not really. It's not like she's been my girlfriend for years and then has an affair on me, like Karli did to you. I keep on thinking about what you went through and how crappy that was. And I have to keep reminding myself that it isn't as bad as that. Even though it still feels crap.'

Shit. My stomach feels like it's in a rinse cycle. And he's giving me a hard look. Like he knows what I've done. I don't know what to say, so I say nothing. He looks away.

'So, you know, I guess I'm okay, considering.'

Sphenurus

I stand up straight again and let out a quiet breath. Centring myself.

'Is she still here?'

He shakes his head, and everything in me clenches.

'She's gone?'

He must hear the shock in my voice because his face gets serious and he puts the bowl back on the bench with exaggerated care.

'You sound worried about that. About her.'

'Well, yeah.' I struggle to think of a plausible reason, mind scrambling like it's trying to find something sparkly in a bucket of sand. 'I mean, Roxanne just hired her. She needed her in the shop. It'd be a pretty crap way to show her thanks if Lani just up and left.'

He gives me that look again.

'She's still in Noosa. She's just not here. In the house.'

That knowledge doesn't do much to slow the thumping of my heart.

'So where's she gone?' I try for casual.

He sighs. "She text me before. Must have been after she finished work. Told me she was sorry, she wished it had worked out, blah, blah, blah. Said she'd been at work and that Roxanne offered her the granny flat at her place. She's going to be staying there for a while.'

'Are you going to go over and talk to her? Try to work things out?'

I'm praying he's going to say no, which only makes me feel worse.

He turns his back to me, getting something out of the drawer.

'No. There's not much point. She was pretty clear about how she felt last night. There's some things it's pointless to fight against.'

When he turns back, he looks really tired, like the night has suddenly caught up with him. 'Listen, I have to ask you something.'

I freeze, alerted by the tone of his voice. I don't think this is going to be a question I'll like. 'Okay.'

'Do you like her?'

My mind's racing, trying to work out what I should say here to do the least amount of damage. In the end, I decide on the truth...sort of. 'Sure. I mean, she's a nice girl.'

'No, not that. I mean, do you like her? Want to be with her?'

'Jesus, Zac, why would you ask that?' Shit. Shit! He knows. He knows about the kiss. Maybe he even saw us. Or she's told him. Christ!

He shrugs, like his question means nothing. No more than asking me if I liked the waves this morning. But his body language is saying a whole different thing – he's stiff, tight... waiting. And I feel like I'm matching him.

'I'm not accusing you of anything. I know you wouldn't do anything behind my back. It's just...' He shrugs again and I want to walk away. Run. Because I did do it behind his back. I kissed her, held her, touched her. Wanted her. And it doesn't matter that they'd broken up. I mean, it did. But not really. 'Well, she said last night, when she broke it off, that she liked you.'

I have to force the words out of my suddenly dry mouth.

'Did she?'

'Yep.'

The silence hangs in the air. It feels like it's wrapped in ice, making everything cold and stiff. His eyes don't move from my face. And I know I can't run from it. It's not fair to him or to me or to Lani. He deserves the truth. Or at least, the truth of how I feel. Even if it makes me look like a total dick...the worst friend he could have. Even if it makes him hate me. He deserves to know.

I take a deep breath and look him in the eye. 'Yeah. I like her.'

He shuts his eyes for a second. That makes me feel worse than a thousand angry words would. But I can't take back what I've said. And I don't want to. I should tell him that if he wants her, I'll back off, give him a chance. But I don't want to say that either. My lips tighten, like that's the only way I can keep the words in.

'You should go see her then. Take over the rest of her bags for her or something. Talk to her.'

I don't know what to say to that. There must be a catch. I stay quiet, waiting for it. He looks at me and then his eyes slide away, back to the bowl on the bench.

'You should. If she wants you and you want her, then you should go see her.'

This is more generous than I think I could ever be. More generous than I deserve. The chance of seeing her, of being with her...I want that. And yet, Zac and I have been friends for a long time. And this is going to hurt him. It can't not. And he's been there for me in the really tough times...when mum died and when Karli left. He was there for me and yet, all I'm thinking about is being with Lani.

'I don't want this to wreck our friendship. We've known each other too long. Been mates too long.'

I feel greedy, asking for both Lani and his friendship.

'It won't. I'm telling you to do it. You should go see her. See if you can be together.'

No. It can't be that easy. I don't deserve to have all of this. I can't do this to Zac. I shouldn't. And yet, I really, really want to take him at his word. Believe that he'd be okay with it.

'Are you sure?'

He laughs. It sounds off, like he's not good. Like he's just saying it but doesn't want me to actually do anything. Fuck.

'No. Not one hundred per cent. But you should go see her. She's meant to be with you.'

I don't know what to make of that. Zac's never struck me as a 'soul mate' sort of guy. But I don't want to argue with him. I want to believe him – believe he wants me to see her.

And I want to be the person she's meant to be with.

I just don't know if that makes me the type of person I want to be.

Lani

It's been four days since I moved out of the house. Four days and in that time, I've sent a text to Zac and had one awkward phone conversation with him which neither of us really knew how to end. Four days and I've made myself comfortable in Roxanne's flat. Four days and I've heard nothing from Matt. Not even through Roxanne. He's been totally silent. Which I guess is a way of communicating. It tells me loud and clear that he doesn't want anything to do with me. I've embarrassed myself, made myself vulnerable, split up with Zac – and all for no reason.

Well, no, that's not true. Zac deserved to be with someone who really wanted to be with him. Someone who doesn't think about another person the whole time they're with him. So, that's something at least.

Still, even though I love the job and Roxanne has been enthusiastic about the designs I've shown her, and the granny flat is perfect for me, I feel like I'm breaking into little pieces. Like a block of ice with shards splintering off, cracking, warping, getting smaller and smaller.

Because he kissed me in way that made me believe he wanted me, too – told me that he did – and yet, we haven't talked about it like he said we would. Which must mean he doesn't really want me – it means I'm not enough. My mother is right.

And the stupid, pathetic bond doesn't mean anything if he doesn't want me back. It's useless. Actually more than that, it's agony. Agony to have it and know it's not returned. How can it work like that? It's supposed to be a bond...a bond between two people. A joint connection. A shared thing.

Except obviously it's not.

And the only reason I can come up with is because he's human. Maybe he doesn't feel it. Maybe Nick was just lucky that Grace wanted him back.

I flop on the bed that Roxanne told me was Matt's old bed. In fact, I'm surrounded by things that used to be his. It's like sweet torture. I want to shut my eyes and pretend I'm somewhere else – or *someone* else. But it's Thursday and I promised my parents I'd talk to them, even though it's the very last thing I feel like doing.

I pull myself up and sit on the edge of the mattress, contemplating what seems like the mammoth task of actually having a conversation with them. Well, no, if I'm honest, the hardest part is having the conversation with my mum. Especially now she knows I've broken up with Zac. I text her that news yesterday so, hopefully, she'll have had time to process it. She hasn't answered me so I don't know what sort of response I'm going to get today. I can make a pretty good guess though. I hope I'm wrong. But then, I've always hoped that when it comes to her, for as long as I can remember.

I drag my fingers through my hair, pulling at it, before standing and looking in the mirror hanging over the chest of drawers. I'm a mess. Like my mask has slipped, showing the real me. That, at least, is something I can fix.

I brush my hair, slowly, carefully, tucking it behind my ears, smoothing it down so it looks perfect. It's a start. Powder next, reapplied over the dark circles that are starting to show through after a long day. And lipstick, a light shade of pink that takes the attention from my eyes and from the sadness that even my mother should be able to see, although it's doubtful she'll acknowledge it. I take my time, making sure everything is fault-less. I look good. My reflection shows nothing of what's going on inside me and I nod at myself. Ready.

Taking a deep breath, I open the computer screen. The video app is already flashing. They're waiting for me. I click on the icon and put a smile on my face as their images appear before me. My dad's smile is what I'd expect. And so is my mother's scowl.

'Hey, possum. How's it going up there in the warmth?'

'Hey, Dad. It's good. The job's great. I'm really enjoying it. Roxanne, my boss, is awesome. And the clothes she makes... they're just fantastic. Really beautiful.'

Prattling on and on until I run out of things to say. There's a pause. That small space for Mum to say something. She doesn't. She's looking off to the side like she doesn't really want to be here and I feel small. Insignificant.

Dad clears his throat.

'Where are you staying now?'

I sit up straighter and try for the smile again. It's harder to keep on my face.

'I'm at Roxanne's place, my new boss.' I put my hand out like a hostess on a game show. 'This is the granny flat I'm renting off her. It's perfect for me.'

I don't tell him I don't know how long I can stay here. That's not something that we've got around to discussing yet.

I'm avoiding it for as long as I can. Avoiding making any decisions, for that matter.

Dad nods. 'It looks nice.'

Mum sniffs. 'It's nice of her to offer you something when you...well, when you made the decision you did. It's good that you have someone who has their life together enough that you can take advantage of it.'

And once again, I've failed. She never says in outright – well, not often. But she doesn't need to.

'Yes.' It's almost a whisper.

'Is she one of us?' There's no warmth in my mother's voice. No concern for me. I knew there wouldn't be but there's still this small piece of me that keeps hoping, hoping, hoping. Stupid.

'No.'

She purses her lips like I've done the worst thing possible.

'Don't be like that, Nora. It's not like she's in a relationship with her or anything. She's just staying at her place.'

My mouth goes desert dry as images of Matt ricochet through my head. I feel sick but there's no way I can end the call yet.

Mum's mouth goes tighter for a second, if that's even possible. 'Well, she's chosen not to be with Zac anymore so heaven knows what she'll choose to do next.'

I grip the edge of the desk. 'It just wasn't right, Mum. There wasn't a bond.'

'There may have been, young lady, if you'd just given it time. You give up too soon. You always have. School, hairdressing. Did you try hard enough?'

So she thinks it's my fault...again.

My dad's arm wraps around her shoulders and he pulls her in closer. Her face relaxes for a moment, like it does every time he touches her.

'Come on, Nor. You know our Lani's a good girl. She knows the right thing to do.'

I am going to be sick. I can feel it in my throat. I put my hand up against my neck like that's going to stop it.

'I don't know that any of the young people know the right thing anymore. Look at Nick Larcombe.'

'How are Nick and Grace?' I realise I'm holding my breath...holding everything tight.

Mum shakes her head. 'They're getting married in a few weeks. And his father is happy about it. It's just wrong.'

My heart's pounding in my chest, thumping out a beat in time with my racing thoughts. I lick my lips, wondering if I'm brave enough to ask the question – to force her to try and think about it differently.

'They have a bond though, don't they? And that's what you want for me. So, you know, maybe it's a good thing. Maybe they should be together.'

The strength leaves my voice the more I talk. How can she still have that effect on me, even when she's physically so far away? She narrows her eyes. I can almost feel the anger rolling off her through the computer.

'That *girl* is not a changer so I don't believe for a second that it can be a true bond. It's wrong, Lani. Disgusting. That's it. No grey areas. He shouldn't be with her and yet, he's choosing to disrespect his heritage – his responsibility, to do just that.'

'What do you think, Dad?'

I can see him squirm in his seat. I don't want to put him on the spot but I need to know.

'I don't know, poss. It's good they're happy but...' He shrugs. 'It just doesn't seem right. She's not a changer and now he needs to keep it a secret from her. I think they're just too different. And their kids...well, it's not good for the community. It's not something I feel entirely comfortable with.'

'It's not something your brothers would ever do,' my mother cuts in. 'They know how to do the right thing.'

There is so much unspoken in that statement but I can hear it loud and clear. It's like it's sinking into my skin, poisoning me.

I smile again. It doesn't even feel close to normal. It's like an alien creature has taken up residence on my face.

'Well, I'd better go. I have to unpack some more and get dinner organised.'

Dad moves forward in his chair slightly.

'Are you okay, poss? With...well, with the break up and everything?'

I know how much it takes for my dad to ask me this. He usually tries to steer clear of anything even slightly emotional. I blink back the moisture that's suddenly sitting at my eyelashes.

'Sure, Dad. I'm okay. Thanks for asking.'

He nods and sits back, his relief clear. 'Okay. Well, we'll talk next week?'

'Sure.'

'We love you.'

'I love you too.'

My mother has her arms crossed and the scowl is back. Usually I get a half-hearted 'I love you' but there's nothing today. I've obviously disappointed her too much this time. And even though it's happened again and again, it still hurts. Even though I'm an adult, it still cuts me, like a knife drawing slowly over my skin. Not life threatening but painful, with small silver scars left on my heart to remind me.

I'm about to click off when she turns to my dad.

'She should come home. I knew she wouldn't be able to make it work.'

I close the program down before I have to hear anymore and lean back in the chair, shutting my eyes. Trying to breathe. Trying to be normal.

Sphenurus

It's only when I open my eyes again that I notice something sitting on top of the tall bookshelf in the corner. Something red. I stand and go over, reaching up to pull it down. The top is dusty and I wipe it off with my hand. It's a photo album. There's a square cut out in the bottom corner, filled with a photo. It doesn't take a genius to recognise Matt and Roxanne. Two kids at the beach, smiling at the camera. Happy. Matt looks to be about nine or ten, his body brown even then. I rub my finger over his image, my heart squeezing, aching.

I take it over to the bed, curling around it as I lie down, head propped up by my hand. I probably shouldn't look through it. It's private. Their memories that I'm no part of and have no right to. But it's too hard to resist. I want to see what Matt's life was like. I need to, just to make my soul feel better.

The spine creaks as I open it. The front page is a bigger photo, yellowing slightly at the edges. Their family – mum, dad and the two kids, in a garden somewhere. Their mother has her arm around Roxanne, matching flowers behind their ears. Smiling. Looking happy. Like they love each other. And their dad is nursing Matt, a baby still, wrapped in a blue blanket. Their father looks so much like an adult Matt that there's no denying they're father and son, the same shade of hair, the same eyes, the same stance. I wish there was something written next to it so I knew where it was taken.

The next pages are a montage of their life. Roxanne standing in front of a birthday cake, surrounded by friends, with Matt photobombing at the side. A picture of a dog – a brown bitzer – their pet, I'm assuming, with Matt's arm around his neck. Pictures of places they've obviously been. Matt coming in on a surfboard, his arms up in the air in celebration. And pictures of them with their mum, hugging each other and laughing at the camera.

The thought that she's no longer around, even though I

never met her, makes my chest ache. I think it's more the fact that Roxanne and Matt don't have this anymore – that they can't recreate the same photos, no matter how much they want to.

I'm so absorbed in the photos, I don't notice the person at the open door of the granny flat until they step inside. And it's only then that a realize it's Matt.

Matt

She looks so beautiful laying on the bed, her blue skirt tucked in around her legs, her hair hanging down the side of her face, that I just stand there and watch for a moment. She's looking at a photo album. One of ours, I think. It must've been one I didn't take with me when I left.

I don't know what I'm doing here. Well, I do. But I still don't know if it's the right decision. I've barely seen Zac over the last four days and each time I try and raise the subject of Lani, he just tells me I should go and see her before ending the conversation. The guilt is eating me up. Even though I haven't done anything wrong. I keep trying to convince myself of that, anyway. They were broken up. I didn't do anything until they'd called it off...

Last night he told me to just get over myself and go see her. He said he was okay with it. I don't know that I believe him but my need for her has got bigger than the guilt. So here I am.

Lani runs her finger over one of the photos. It's like she's touching my skin – touching me – and I take a step into the unit, needing to be closer. Her eyes flick up, widening as she sees me and she is up off the bed quicker than I would've thought possible. She straightens her skirt down around her hips in a way that's incredibly hot, even though I don't think she's aware of what it's doing to me. I have to make a conscious effort to look away from her hands and back up to her face.

She looks scared. Or maybe uncertain is a better word.

'Hi.' Not my smoothest line, but at least it's broken the silence.

'Hi.'

I look around the flat.

'I see you've you settled in?'

She nods. She's not making this easy but maybe I deserve it. I've been a coward – not wanting to put myself up there for more hurt until I knew where Zac really stood. But four days. She must think I'm a real arsehole.

'And how's it going at the shop. Are you enjoying it?'

'It's great.' She clears her throat. 'I mean, Roxanne's great to work for.'

There's a silence again.

'How is...the surf shop?'

I get the feeling she was going to ask about Zac. I don't know if that's a good thing or not.

'Good. Good.'

I stick my hands in the pockets of my shorts, feeling like a complete idiot. What is it about her that makes me feel like I'm revisiting my adolescence? I nod at the album still sitting on the bed.

'Found any dorky photos of me yet?'

She turns her head but I can still see the blush colouring her face.

'I wasn't snooping or anything...'

I hold up my hand. 'Hey, it's okay. I don't mind.'

Stepping past her, I pick up the book. I can see where she's lain on the bed. God, even that does things to me!

I look at the first page – the one with the photo of all of us – and smile.

'That was taken on a trip up to Cairns, apparently, not long after I was born.'

She comes over next to me. I can smell the shampoo she uses, the smell of the soap on her skin. It's all I can do not to touch her, lean closer in to her.

'You look a lot like your dad.'

I run my thumb over his face. 'Yeah, I guess I do.'

'What did he do? Your dad?'

'He was a builder. And Mum was a dress maker. I guess that's where Roxanne gets it from.'

She nods.

'What about your family? What do they do?'

She gets this look on her face. I don't know if it's a smile or a grimace. Probably something in between.

'Dad's an accountant. And Mum's...mum. She's always stayed home to look after us, support Dad, organise things.'

I try to remember what she said about her family before. 'And you've got two brothers?'

'Yeah. Greg, he's an accountant like Dad. And Tony is a dentist, owns his own practice.'

'Wow. High achievers.'

This time she does grimace. 'Yeah.'

She looks up at me. I want to lean down and kiss her – taste her lips, breathe her in. Bring her in close against me. I hear her breath change and hope that means she wants me too. I think it does.

But I want to take this slow. I want to make sure it's not just physical. That we're a good match. If it's going to stuff up my relationship with Zac – even though he said it won't – then I want to make sure it's the real thing and not just hormones on overdrive.

'Why are you here, Matt?'

I sigh. It's a fair enough question, especially since it's taken me this long to actually work up the courage to come.

'You left before we had a chance to talk.'

'That was four days ago. You said we'd talk the next morning.'

'I know. And I wanted to. But I wasn't sure...with Zac...and I didn't...well, it's complicated.'

She steps away from me, down to the foot of the bed, closer to the door. It feels terrible, like she needs distance from me, when all I want is to be closer. Her fingers play along the rail of the bed for a second before she looks up at me.

'How's Zac?'

I hesitate and then shrug. 'He seems okay, considering, well...considering the last few days.' I take a deep breath, trying in some way to stop my heart beating like a drummer on steroids. 'He told me I should come and see you.'

She raises her eyebrows. 'Did he?'

I nod.

'Why would he say that?'

It's my turn to feel the heat on my face. 'Apparently, at the restaurant, you told him you liked me.'

She ducks her head, looking away, eyes flicking to her computer before coming back to me and then skittering away again. I want to touch her – turn her head back to look at me – but I keep my hands in my pocket. I need to know where I stand first – if she wants me, now, in this moment. When she's doesn't have the alcohol in her system to make her brave and has had a few days to think about it.

She flicks her hair over her shoulder and suddenly there's a smile on her face. It's the smile that doesn't feel right. Like she's trying too hard.

'Well, it was pretty obvious when I got back to the house that I like you. I don't kiss just anyone like that.'

It feels like there should be a 'but' at the end of that sentence. I don't say anything, leaving space for her to fill it in. But my body is tight, waiting for her.

She shrugs. 'Like you said though, it's complicated.'

I nod, slowly, and rock back on my heels.

'Are your reasons for saying it's complicated the same as mine?'

Her eyes flick to the computer again and her smile gets bigger, brighter, like it's a mask keeping me from really seeing her.

'Well, there's Zac, obviously, and my parents met him, sort of, and where happy for me to come up here to see how it went...'

I don't understand what her parents have to do with it. She's an adult, after all. But if it's important to her, then I can do whatever needs to happen.

'Is that important to you?'

'What?'

'That Zac's met your parents? Sort of.'

'They're my family. They want to know I'm okay. Be a part of my life. They want to make sure...'

She stops, letting the sentence run over the cliff to a silent death. I chew on the corner of my bottom lip before deciding the words are worth saying. 'I'm happy to meet your parents. If you want me to.'

For a split second, she looks almost panicked. I'm missing something here. Something big. I plough on anyway, trying to make this work. Trying to convince her, even though I'm the one who's taken four days to get here. Even though I'm the one who said it was complicated first. I want her to want this as much as I do.

'And Zac's okay with this. Like I said, he wanted me to come here.' It's the truth, even if I don't truly believe he means it. Not yet anyway.

She nods. 'I know he says he's okay with it but I don't want to hurt him.'

That throws me; steals my voice away, leaving me with an open mouth but no words. It sounds like she's brushing me off. Like she doesn't want me anymore. And yet, she acknowledged the kiss. She told me she likes me. I lace my fingers on top of my head and look at her for a second, trying to work out what I need to say.

'I don't want to hurt him either. He's my best friend.'

She nods, licking her lips like she's nervous. But she doesn't say anything, even though I wait for her.

'So where does that leave us?' I'm almost afraid to ask.

The smile is back on her face. I'm beginning to really hate it. 'Well, you know, I like you. You're a nice guy.'

I take a step towards her. Her eyes are wide, watching me.

'Don't, Lani. Don't do that.'

'Do what?'

I take another step closer, standing at the corner of the bed, close enough that if I just leant forward, I could touch my lips to hers.

'Pretend you're all good. Use that smile like a mask to keep me out.'

The smile slips from her face then and she meets my eyes. I feel like I'm seeing Lani again. I bring my hand up to her face, cradling her cheek in my palm. Her eyes don't leave mine and for a moment, she holds herself stiff, controlled, before she leans into it – just slightly – and shuts her eyes. Giving up on whatever it is that's been holding her back from me.

My voice, when I talk, is ridiculously husky. 'I want to know *you*. I want to see you. I want to kiss you.'

She opens her eyes again but doesn't say anything. She's just looking at me. I lean down and put my lips on hers. The smallest touch. It's hard to pull back but I manage and I'm absurdly gratified to hear her suck in a breath.

'Do you want that too, Lani?' I kiss her again. Softly. Gently. 'Do you want me?'

I wait for her nod and when it comes, I kiss her again. Harder this time, but still with enough hand on the reins to hold myself back. I want to be sure. I want to hear it from her lips.

'Tell me.'

'I want you.' It's a whisper but it's enough.

My hand goes around her back, pulling her against me, and then my lips are on hers again, tasting her. Her mouth opens and her tongue flicks against my lips in a way that makes every cell in my body jump to attention. I groan, pulling her even closer, crushing her against me. Her hand comes up around my neck, her nails scratching against my skin, hard without being too hard, like she's marking me. Making me hers. It feels like each mark is coursing through me, changing me, feeding my hunger for her. Jesus.

'I want you.' She says it again, the words hot against my mouth. 'I want you.'

I don't know if I can stop. I don't want to and yet, I know I need to. Slow. That's what I wanted. That's what sounded like a good idea before she started kissing me. I want to get to know her, to be with her, to know it's just not physical. But I can't bring myself to stop kissing her, tasting her, feeling her. I'm overwhelmed by everything Lani.

In the end, she's stronger than me. She pulls back, her lips slightly swollen from the passion of our kiss. I let her go, grateful she could do what I couldn't.

Her hand goes up to the back of her neck and she looks uncertain again.

'Are you sure?' Her voice is just above a whisper.

'About what?'

'Are you sure I'm worth it? If it changes your friendship with Zac...?'

I hold her eyes for a moment, trying to make her understand that I'm serious – that I've thought about it. Over and over and over in the last four days...

'I'm sure.'

She bites her lip and then nods.

'Okay.' She looks down at the floor and then back up at me. 'Do you want to stay?'

I smile. 'More than anything. But I'm not going to. Not tonight. I want to take you out and wine and dine you.'

She smiles back at me. A real one, even if it's smaller than the fake. 'A date.'

I nod. 'A date. Tomorrow night?'

'Tomorrow night.'

I lean over to kiss her. It's more chaste than our last one but only just.

'I better go before I forget what I've just said.'

She laughs and the sound fills me with air, buoying me up, making me lighter. I laugh with her.

And then I go, while I still can. A last look back at her from the door shows that she's still got a smile on her face. The real one. The one that says she's happy with giving this a go.

And I'm sure I can keep it there.

Lani

I watch him go, fingers to my lips, feeling the touch of his on them still. I sit on the bed and then almost immediately get up again, pacing the carpet, unable to stay still. My brain feels like it's at war with itself. Happy – no, more than that – ecstatic over the fact he wants me. Maybe not as much as I want him given it took him four days to come and see me but that doesn't matter. He wants me. He said so.

And yet, all I can see is my mother's face when she said how disgusting it was for Nick to be with Grace – with a human. And I know, without a shadow of a doubt, that if I choose to be with Matt, she won't change her mind just because it's me. She'll think our relationship is disgusting. She'll think *I'm* disgusting for making that choice. She'll hate me, more than it feels like she does already. And I don't know if I'm strong enough to face that.

I kneel on a floor and bend my head down to my knees, trying to take deep breaths, trying to stop myself from hyperventilating at the choice I've made by telling Matt I like him. Acknowledging the bond, even if just to myself. God. It's not supposed to be like this. The bond is supposed to make every-thing easier. That's how I've always imagined it working anyway.

I jerk my head up at the knock on the open door, thinking it must be Matt again. And that he's going to see me like this – an emotional mess – and think I don't want him.

But it's not. It's Roxanne. Not that that's much better.

She takes a step forward into the flat.

'God, Lani, are you okay?'

I nod, trying to pretend everything's fine. That it's totally normal for me to be on the floor, trying to breathe. I don't think she believes me. She comes over and rubs her hand on my back. Round and round in circles. It's kind of nice. Reassuring. She's quiet, waiting until I've got my breathing under some sort of control. I feel like an idiot though. At this rate, she's going to regret hiring me.

I smile at her, grateful for the support nevertheless, and stand before moving over to the bed. I feel weak, like all this emotion has drained me.

'Thanks.'

She's watching me with her hands on her hips.

'What's Matt done?'

I grip the bed cover in my hands, screwing it up into balls of material in my fists. I don't know if I can do this. Not at this moment. Not with his sister. So, I just shake my head, hoping she'll take the hint.

She rolls her eyes.

'Don't give me that. I saw him come over here and then I find you like this. What did he say to you?'

'Please, Roxanne... he didn't say anything.'

'Bullshit.'

'He didn't, truly. It's me.'

She narrows her eyes at me. I wish she'd just stop but I don't think she's going to.

'Is this about Zac? Did Matt say something about him to upset you? Because if he did, I'm going to have to give him a piece of my mind.'

I shake my head again and then sigh. She's obviously not going to let it go.

'It wasn't about Zac. Not really.'

'What do you mean, not really?'

I make a conscious effort to let go of the bedspread, spreading my hands over my lap, smoothing my skirt down.

'When I broke up with Zac...' I stop, trying to think of how I can say it in a way that doesn't make me seem like a bitch. 'The reason I broke up with him was that I wasn't...in love with him. I like him, he's a nice guy, but not...like that. I didn't want to be with him.'

'Yeah?'

'I wanted to be with someone else.'

Her eyebrows look like they're trying to work their way up her forehead.

'Don't tell me that Matt came over here to have a go at you about that! I mean, I know that Karli hurt him, but it's none of his business –'

I put my hand up and she stops.

'He didn't come over to have a go at me about anything.' My heart's tripping over itself as I look at her and I rub my palms against by skirt again. Because I'm suddenly wondering what she's going to think about this – about me and Matt. Wondering if she'll think I'm good enough for her brother and maybe she won't and I'll be out of a job and a place to stay... I take a deep breath.

'Matt is the other person. He's who I wanted to be with.'

Her mouth drops into an 'o' for a moment and then she snaps it shut.

'Well, that's okay then.'

It's the last thing I expected her to say. 'Is it?' My voice comes out as a squeak.

'Of course. I've known he's been interested in you from the first moment I saw you two together.'

It's my turn for a mouth drop. 'Did you?'

'Absolutely. It didn't take a genius to work that out. He's my little brother. I know him.'

'Oh.' I don't know what to say. It feels wonderful to know she could see it but weird. What else have I missed? Was Zac able to see that too? Have I been hurting him even before we split up?

'I wasn't sure how you felt though. You seemed to really like Zac.'

So maybe Zac hadn't been aware of how I was feeling. My emotions feel like they're attached to a yo-yo and I was never good at them as a kid.

'I do like him. But as a friend. What I feel for Matt is...more.'

It seems so inadequate for how I feel but I don't know how else to say it. Not in a way that wouldn't lead to further questions anyway. And not in a way that's not going to make me sound like a rabid stalker.

She nods. 'Well, that's good.' She pauses and I feel myself tense, waiting. 'If you like him though, and he likes you, why were you on the floor looking like you wanted it to swallow you up when I came in?'

I look down, away from her. 'It's complicated. Us being together. I just panicked for a moment.'

When I look up, I can see the concern in her eyes.

'But you like him, yeah? You two are going to see how it goes?'

It's a bigger question than she imagines but I can't tell her that without revealing everything about our community. And that's not something I can do. Not when the importance of keeping it a secret has been drummed into me since I was old enough to understand what it meant.

So I just nod. Only one little movement and yet it feels like I've agreed to something both terrible and wonderful.

She smiles. 'Good.'

'You're okay with it? With us?'

She laughs. 'Not that I have much say in my brother's life anymore, but yes, I'm fine with it. I think you might be good for each other.'

I don't ask her how she knows that. I don't know that I want to hear the answer. But it's nice that we have *his* family's approval anyway.

'Thank you.'

She cocks her head at me. 'What for?'

'For coming in to see me. For wanting to know I was okay. For thinking I'm good for your brother.'

She laughs. 'Well, you haven't had a chance to make any friends up here yet and, in these circumstances, a girlfriend's support is needed, I think.'

I smile at her. 'It is nice. I've never had a girlfriend to share stuff with before. Not a good one, anyway.'

'Really?'

I nod. 'I'm not usually good around other women. I don't know why. I just find it easier around guys, I suppose.'

She comes over to hug me and I allow it. It actually feels nice.

'Well, I'm honoured to be the first.'

She steps back and smiles before heading out the door, only turning back when she's outside.

'You know, I had a good feeling when you first got here. That's why I offered you the job. I'm happy you're with Matt.'

I watch her go. And wonder if she'll continue to be happy.

Matt

I 'm locking up the shop when I hear someone behind me and spin around, adrenaline pulsing through my body. It's Karli, hair down around her shoulders, in a dress that shows her body to the best advantage. She looks beautiful. But then, she always has. Even when she was cheating on me.

'Shit, Karli, you scared the hell out of me.'

She laughs, and even now, even after all this time apart, even after she broke my heart like glass smashing against concrete, it still makes everything in me clench.

'Sorry.'

I slip the keys in my pocket and frown. She's not moving. She's just standing there. Waiting.

'What do you want, Karli?'

She pulls her hair over to one side, smoothing it down, taking her time.

'I just wanted to see how you were?'

I don't believe her. 'I'm a bit busy actually.'

She nods but still doesn't move.

'The weekend away was nice.'

'The weekend away?' I don't know that I'm doing a good job at keeping the impatience out of my voice. Maybe that's not a bad thing.

'You know. Brent took me away. I told you about it, down at the park.'

I'm not sure why we're having a discussion about this. But I *am* sure I don't want to know the reason. 'Oh, right. Well, good. Great.'

There's silence again and this time I push past her, unlocking the car and putting my things on the passenger seat. She follows me over. I pretend not to notice but when I turn around she's right there. Close. And I can't step back.

'Look, Karli, I've got things to do. What do you want?'

She runs her tongue along her top lip. 'You. I want you.'

My grip on the door tightens. 'What?'

She slides her hand along my forearm, lightly, like she's trying to be sexy. With me. Like she thinks it's something I want. I let my arm drop and her hand falls away. She purses her lips, as if I've disappointed her, and takes a deep breath.

'I realised, on the weekend away, that I'm still in love with you. Actually I think I knew that before. This just confirmed it. I miss you, Matt. And I want to be with you. I want to give us a second chance.'

'So, what, while you were off with another guy – the guy you cheated on me with – you were thinking about me; about us? You're a piece of work, you know that?'

'Don't say it like that. That's not how it was.'

'It sounds like it was exactly like that!'

She shakes her head. I can see moisture glistening in her eyes. But it doesn't do anything to me – not like it used to anyway.

'Please, Matt. Give me another chance. I promise, I'm different. I've grown up. Please, I love you.'

I push past her again, not caring that she has to back up into the bushes at the side of the car to get out of my way.

'Yeah, but I don't love you, Karli. Go back to Brent. Or wherever. I really don't care.'

My heart's thumping. It feels like anger. Or maybe hurt. God knows, she's given me enough of that to last a life time. Maybe there's a little bit of smugness too. I can't say that I'm not too petty for that. For the fact that she screwed me over and is now regretting it. I try not to think about the fact there might still be some left over feelings for her that's making me react like this. There can't be. I can't be that stupid. I climb in the driver's seat and she taps at the window.

For a second, I weigh up whether I can just be a real arse-hole and drive away. Then I sigh and wind down the window. Damn Mum for teaching me good manners.

'So, you won't give me a second chance? You won't even think about it? Everyone makes mistakes, Matt.'

I shake my head. 'I'm not into second chances. Not over something like that. I can't trust you. And without that, there's no chance of a relationship.'

'Please. I've changed. Please.' She hugs her arms to herself, as if she's in pain...how I kind of felt six months ago. But God, this is going nowhere. I feel like a shithead, which I shouldn't. It's not me that chose to have an affair and then regretted it.

'I've got to go, Karli. I have a date.'

She steps away from the car like I've pushed her.

'Who with?'

I shake my head. 'You don't know her. Not that it matters anyway.'

'Do you love her?'

'That's none of your business.'

There's silence as she just looks at me, like she's waiting for me to tell her anyway.

'We aren't getting back together, Karli. Get it out of your head because it's not going to happen. Move on with your life. Be with Brent. I don't care.'

She doesn't say anything else, not that I give her a chance. I want to get away from her and her pleading and the look in her eyes like I'm the one being unreasonable. She just stands there, watching me as I back out.

Which is a relief. I know I've made the right choice. I'm glad she isn't in my life. And that she doesn't have the opportunity to hurt me anymore.

Lani

I look over at Matt and his eyes meet mine for a moment, a
grin on his face, before he looks back at the road.

'So, where are we going again?'

'Stop trying to get it out of me. It's a surprise.'

I fold my arms. 'What if I told you I don't like surprises?'

He laughs and the sound of it makes me...fizz. Like it's
giving my blood more oxygen by osmosis. I feel young and light
and carefree.

'Then I'd say you'll have to get used to them because I love
giving surprises.'

I laugh back. 'Well, that sucks.'

He grins at me and reaches over to touch my hand resting
on my lap, running his fingers lightly over my fingers. The feel
of his skin on mine makes everything in me tighten. I want him
more than I've ever wanted anyone. This has to be right. How
can it not be? Does it really matter that he's not one of us? I
shove those thoughts away. Not tonight. Tonight is just about
Matt and me. I'm not going to think about anything else.

When he pulls up in the park behind his shop, I turn to

him, eyebrows raised. I can just seeing the answering quirk of his mouth in the fading afternoon light.

'What? Are you trying to impress me with how successful you are or something?'

He laughs. 'No. Trust me. You're going to like it.'

He unlocks the door and takes me into the back office. Everything is neat and tidy – all in its place. Not that that really surprises me. It fits with the Matt I feel like I know.

He takes my hand and leads me to a staircase at the end of the room, going up in front of me and unlocking the door at the top. When he opens it, I draw in a breath. It's perfect.

The flat roof of the shop, protected in part by a low wall, has been set up for an intimate dinner. Candles are set up in groups on the floor with citronella sticks next to them flickering in their tall holders, casting a golden glow over the table set for two. It looks out over the beach and the sound of the waves, washing up on the sand, reach out to me.

Perfect.

'Do you like it?'

There's a tremor of doubt in his voice, which warms me. Not because he's unsure but by the fact he cares about how I feel. I squeeze his hand.

'I love it.'

He pulls out a chair for me before pouring a glass of wine from the bottle already cooling in ice.

'I'll be back in a moment. I'm just going downstairs to get our food.'

'Do you want a hand?'

He shakes his head, running his fingers over the back of my neck, making me shiver.

'No, you stay here and relax. I won't be long.'

He flicks the speaker set up in the corner as he leaves, and low notes fill the air. It's a song I love. I lean back in the chair, taking a sip of the wine. It's sweet and cool. I think this is most relaxed I've felt since I came to Noosa. Everything feels right. I have my job, which I love. A place of my own to stay. A friend in Roxanne. And I have Matt. Which feels better than everything else put together. I want him and he wants me. And I'm determined just to enjoy that fact for the moment.

I look out over the beach, the street lights casting a low glow. There are a few people out there still, enjoying a night walk on the beach. One of them stops – it's too dark to know if it's a man or a woman, although the shadows make me think they have long hair – and seems to be looking up at the roof. At me. Staring. Which is stupid. Why would someone be looking up here? Especially for as long as they are. They must be looking at something else. Or thinking about something else maybe.

And yet I can't shake the feeling of being watched.

So it's a relief when I hear Matt come to the top of the stairs. I smile and look away from the beach.

The plate he puts in front of me looks amazing. Chicken breast with a creamy sauce and vegetables that look crisp and delicious.

'Wow, I'm impressed.'

He puts his own plate down before sliding into his chair.

'Yeah, well don't be too overwhelmed. Remember the full disclosure from the other day – I'm not a great cook. This is actually from a little restaurant down the road.'

I laugh. 'Good. It's nice to know you're not great at everything.'

I glance back at the beach, expecting to see the person still there, watching us, but they've gone. And I can almost convince myself that I was being stupid in thinking they were watching me.

We talk and laugh so much over dinner that I'm hardly

aware of eating my food. It's easy to be with him. So easy. Maybe this is what the bond means. Maybe it's just like a clue to who you'd be a good match with. The someone you fit with, like two puzzle pieces. It's a nice thought and I smile.

He reaches over to touch my hand.

'You're beautiful. Have I told you that?'

I can feel the heat on my skin at his words. I've been told that before but it feels different from him. Like he's not just talking about my looks, but about all of me. And I want to be beautiful to him. I want him to like who I am. Me. Lani. Not the girl I think I need to be. Not the Lani that always has to change. Not the Lani that can never make my mother happy.

Maybe I can get that with him. Maybe I'll be good enough.

He stands up, coming around the table, and holds out his hand.

'Do you want to dance?'

I smile up at him, taking his hand. 'Sure.'

He pulls me close as I stand, my body against his in a way that makes me pull in a sharp breath. Our hands are still together and he wraps his other arm around me, his hand on the dip of my back. I'm aware of every place his body is touching mine – our hands, our chest, our hips...God, how am I going to remember to move my feet when all I can think about is his body and how he smells and his hold on me.

He's looking at me, his eyes shadowed in the candlelight, but his breathing isn't any steadier than mine and for a moment, it's too much. Too intense. I duck my head to his shoulder, feeling the strength of his arm as it tightens around me in response.

His hand traces my spine, my backless dress meaning it's skin on skin. Intimate. All he'd need to do is slide his hand under the material...

I mentally shake my head, trying to take a steadying breath, trying for control. He wants to take this slow. And that's a good thing. It must be. To get to know each other first. To do this differently than I have with other guys. I want it to be different.

His head slips down to my neck and I can feel his lips on me, their touch light, almost not there, but it doesn't matter. It's like they're leaving a burn mark wherever they touch me, attuning my body to every movement he makes. The moan escapes me and he makes his own noise in response, pulling me against him like he's trying to make us one. I can feel his desire for me, hard and wanting. And then his lips are on mine and I forget everything else – where we are, what time it is...it is just us.

He moves us back over to the table, still kissing me, and sits on one of the chairs, bringing me down onto his lap, wrapping his arm around my waist. His hair is soft under my hands as I bring them up to the side of his head, needing to be closer to him and his hand is pressed wide on my back, warm and strong.

I don't know how much time passes before I pull back. Just enough to be able to look at his face and wonder how I can feel this way. Every part of me wants every part of him. Totally. I want to talk to him and laugh with him and touch him and kiss him.

I slide my palm down the edge of his face and he turns his head to kiss my fingers. Even that small gesture has every part of me pulling tight like a wire ready to snap.

He grins at me – a cheeky grin like he's up to mischief.

'What do you say about going for a paddle with me?'

I laugh before I realise he's serious. I glance out at the water. It looks dark and dangerous in the night – like it's hiding something.

'I'll look after you. Being out on the water at night is amazing. You've got to try it.'

I don't know what to say. Mainly because I don't know how I actually feel about it. So I go practical instead.

'But I didn't bring any bathers.'

He shrugs. 'You won't need them. I won't let you get wet, I promise.'

I take a deep breath, because even though the thought of being out there on the water at night is actually kind of scary – give me the air any day over the water – I trust him. And I want to show him I do.

'Okay.'

He squeezes my hand. 'Come on then.'

Hurrying down the stairs, he takes me through to the front of the shop, and I laugh at his enthusiasm. A blue board of some sort leans in a stand near the front door, and he tucks it under his arm, grabbing a paddle as well, which he hands to me.

'I hope you're not expecting me to drive.'

He grins back at me as he unlocks the front door.

'Nah, I think I'll do all the driving tonight.'

His words seem to allude to more than just our upcoming watery sojourn and my chest tightens around my heart, squeezing it. I want him to drive...to be the one in charge. At least for tonight. It's like sweet torture.

He holds the door open for me and I walk out in front of him, turning while he relocks the door. We wait for a car to drive slowly past and then cross, walking over the grass, wet with dew already. I kick off my high heels, using his shoulder to lean on, and he puts down the board for a moment to take off his shoes and socks. He takes my hand as we walk onto the sand, still slightly warm from the sun's heat. The water washes up lazily on the beach, the sound encompassing us in the night, surrounding us, and I take a deep breath, sucking in the salt air.

Sphenurus

It makes me want to fly. Not that that's going to be happening tonight. At least, not while I'm with Matt.

I look at him then, still in his long pants and shirt.

'I think you're a bit overdressed.'

Truly, I wouldn't mind him getting it all off but I'm not going to say that out loud. Not yet.

'It'll wash.'

He wades in enough that the board is floating and looks back at me, his face a mixture of light and dark shadows in the moonlight.

'Are you ready?'

I grin. He is gorgeous. Everything I want. Except he's not one of us.

But tonight, it doesn't matter. I don't care. I step into the water.

Matt

I love her spirit. The way she laughs. The uncertainty you see in her eyes sometimes. The way she moves, the curve of her neck, the golden streaks in her hair, the way she wrinkles her nose.

I love her.

God, I can't believe I'm actually thinking this already. But it feels different with her. Better. Easier. Like I don't have to try at it, even though I want to do everything I can to make her laugh and be happy.

That's definitely something I'm keeping to myself though. For the moment, anyway. I'm being a coward after Karli. After what she did. Just in case. And I'm man enough to admit it.

Lani is sitting in front of me on the board, her long legs stretched out and my legs either side of hers. I grip the paddle in front of us, like I'm wrapping my body around her. Protecting her. The feel of her body pressed up against me isn't doing much for my self-control and it's harder to concentrate – to keep us upright and dry – than I thought it'd be.

She leans over slightly, letting her fingertips trail in the water

'This is beautiful.'

'Told you.'

There's nothing like being on the water at night. The stillness of it, like we're in our own world, the moon on the water, casting ever moving patches of light and dark.

'Do you do this a lot? Come out at night?'

'I try to. I love the water. I'm happy just to be on it whenever I can, whatever mood it's in.'

She runs her hand down my thigh. It's enough to make me stop paddling for a second, like my brain can only focus on her touch, and it takes a wave to tip us slightly before it jars back into action again. Focus. Jesus! I promised she wouldn't get wet.

'So I have to share you with her – your ocean mistress. Is that what you're saying?'

I laugh at the teasing in her voice and lean forward, my voice soft near her ear.

'I hear she's happy with threesomes.'

She laughs and flicks water back at me, covering me in the warm drops.

'Well, I do think I need another surfing lesson. Does that count?'

'Sounds perfect.'

We sit in silence for a moment, only the noise of the paddle in the water filling the space. Her back against my chest is warm, soft...perfect.

'Tell me about Karli.'

I stiffen. It's a reflex action when it comes to that topic I think.

'What do you want to know?'

'I don't know. Whatever you want to tell me.' She's quite again for a second. 'She hurt you, didn't she?'

I roll my eyes, even though she can't see it. 'You've been talking to Roxanne, haven't you?'

She doesn't answer me and I sigh.

'Yep. She did. We started going out just after I left school. It was really good for the first couple of years but we were young. Looking back now, I think the relationship was probably just dying a slow death though. I don't think either of us was really happy. Although maybe that's just hindsight. And we had a history together – it's hard to give up on that. And then she decided she'd see if the grass was greener and I found out. She tried to blame it on me, which is sort of how Karli works. I'm glad to be rid of her. End of story.'

But even I can hear the resentment in my voice still. I can't work out how to get rid of it. Maybe being with Lani will help with that.

'What about you? What relationships have you had?'

I almost want to suck the words back in as soon as they're out. The breakup with Zac is still too fresh – like a new born ghost of relationships past. And I don't know that I want to hear about other guys she's liked. But she's answering me before I have the chance to change my mind.

'I've had lots of short relationships. Nothing serious. Not really.'

Not until Zac. It seems to hang out there, even though she doesn't say it. Although maybe Zac wasn't serious. They'd really only talked on line. Except she did come all the way up here to be with him. And they had the week together. A week where they looked like they were happy. I feel jealous and lucky and like a total dick, all at the same time. And so I go for some lightness...anything to make it less awkward.

'What? Are all the guys in Tasmania total morons? To not want to be with you? I would've thought they'd be lining up.'

She rubs my leg again and I don't think my attempt at lightening things up has worked. Her next words still have a flavour of seriousness to them.

'There were always reasons why we broke up. And my mum and dad are fairly protective. Well, my dad is anyway.'

'And what would they think of me, taking their little girl out for a moonlight paddle, totally at my lecherous mercy.'

I wait for her laugh but it doesn't come.

'My mother...' She stops like she's trying to find the right words. 'My mum is hard to please. Especially when it comes to anything I do.'

And there is enough in that one sentence to make everything clear. Her self-doubt, how hard she works to make herself what she thinks other people want. I want to wrap her up in my arms and tell her that she is absolutely good enough – more than good enough – but I don't think she'd believe me anyway. I think it'll take time to prove that to her. And time, I can give.

I lean in to kiss the top of her head.

'Well, then she must be crazy.'

She does laugh this time, but it has a harsh note to it.

'Yeah, let's go with that. But you can tell her that theory.'

I look out over to the horizon. There are clouds forming, dark in the night glow, and the wind has started to pick up. Enough that there feels like there's a change coming. Bad weather on the way, more than likely.

'Come on, my lady. I better get us back on solid ground. Smells like a storm's brewing.'

'Yes, it does,' she says, and it feels like she means more than the weather. But I don't ask. If she wants to tell me, she will.

It's not long before we're back to the beach. The waves have started to pick up and it's easy to surf them in, even with the extra person on the board making it slightly uneven. I help her off and kiss her softly on the lips, tasting the salt spray.

'Thanks for coming out with me.'

She is still serious.

'Thanks for wanting to take me.'

She takes the paddle and I tuck the still wet board under my arm again, wrapping my other arm around her as we walk over the road. We head around the back, where the door is still unlocked, and I put the board at the end of the office, ready to be washed off tomorrow, and turn back to her, smiling.

It doesn't last long though. Because she's not looking at me. She's staring at something on the desk. Something that shouldn't be there. It's a pair of panties, red and lacy, laid over the computer keyboard like a frigging beacon. I stride over and that's when I see the note.

I miss you and I'll wait. I don't care who she is. Whenever you want me, I'm yours.

There's no name but I don't need a signature to know who they're from. I know the writing.

Karli.

I scoop both the note and the pants into the bin with a ruler. I don't even want to touch them. Lani is watching me, her eyes wide, her face blank. That scares me more than anything. I take her hand, bringing it to my lips. She lets me do it, which is something, I guess.

'This is nothing. Karli must have broken in and put them here. Maybe while we were on the water.' It's only then that I wonder if she might still be here but a quick glance around tells me she's not. That's not her style anyway. I shake my head. 'She came over here this afternoon. Tried to tell me she wanted me back. I told her to get lost, that I was seeing someone. But I guess she wasn't happy with that.'

Lani's still just watching me. I touch her face.

'I swear. I don't want her back. She just likes to cause trouble. And she's selfish. Doesn't think of anyone but herself.'

Sphenurus

I don't know what I say that makes a difference to her but thank God something does. She leans into my hand.

'I think I saw someone watching me while you were down here getting our dinner. But I thought I was just being silly.'

I swear and bring her into my chest.

'I'm sorry. She doesn't mean anything to me. I don't want her. Ever again.' I take a deep breath. 'I just want you.'

She runs her hand over my chest and then looks up at me. She looks afraid. I don't know what of. Not me. I don't think so anyway. She licks her lips.

'Will you stay the night with me?'

I search her eyes, trying to work out what's going on.

'You're not going to lose me.'

'I know. But I want you to stay the night anyway.'

I don't think she believes me, even though she says she does. And yet, it's hard enough to stay away from her as it is. Harder than I thought. I want her, despite my good intentions.

'I'd like that.'

She sighs like she was holding her breath and I kiss her before leading her out the door, making sure it's locked behind us. I definitely don't need any more surprises waiting for me tomorrow. I open her door to the car and close it after her, moving around the front.

I feel like my body is full of small electrical currents zapping each organ, filling me with a nervous anticipation like I'm an eighteen year old. I glance at her as I get in and she seems as jittery as me. The drive back to Roxanne's feels like it takes forever and I reach over to hold her hand. Her fingers trace patterns over my palm and it's hard to concentrate on the driving. But I don't move it.

When we pull up, I turn to look at her.

'Are you sure?'

She smiles and she doesn't look scared anymore. She looks...determined. Like she's happy with the decision. It only heightens the effect of the currents in my body.

It's her turn to lead me this time. She gets the key out of her bag and unlocks the door. I kiss her again before we go in. Teasing. Small kisses that start at her mouth and follow the curve of her neck, down to her shoulder, her collar bone. Tasting her.

I hear her breath catch and I moan before I can help it. God, I want her.

She brings my face back up, crushing her lips to mine, her tongue tracing the edge of my teeth, her body against mine, pushing against me and we lean against the partly open door, almost falling into the room. I shut it with my foot, before my lips are back on hers, my hands in her hair, bringing her closer in. Her hands push up my shirt, her nails gently scraping against the skin of my stomach at the waist of my still damp pants.

She moves her mouth down my collarbone, pushing my shirt aside, biting gently against my skin, and I almost explode with my need for her. Christ!

I fumble with the buttons on the halter neck of her dress, wanting to touch her skin, stroke her body. Finally they're undone and it drops down, exposing her breasts, her nipples already hard. I cup them in my hands and lean down to kiss them, taking them into my mouth, rolling them with my tongue, sucking, biting gently. She moans, her hands in my hair, and I bend to scoop her up, taking her the four steps over to the bed, laying her down gently. She looks like an angel laying there, golden hair spread around her, watching me with a longing that matches mine.

And I don't care anymore about keeping my heart safe or about waiting or about anything except her.

I lay down next to her, my leg over hers, my thighs pressing against her, her skin warm under my hand. I look at her eyes, mesmerized by the golden flecks, wanting her to always be looking at me like this.

'I love you,' I say.

And I've never meant anything more in all of my life.

Lani

I stretch out in the bed, pushing my hands against the wall, and smile. I can still smell Matt on my sheets, even though he's gone into work. Late but he's there. He told me I was worth being late. Sweet. Wonderful.

And he loves me.

I've lost count of how many times he's told me that in the last week. When we've been out on the water, getting the next surfing lesson, and when we've shared lunch in our work break, and as a text during the day, and when we've been in bed each night, and each morning when he leaves me, punctuated by kisses.

And I've been able to say it back to him. I can't deny what I feel anymore. Despite the fact he's not a changer. Despite the fact that I haven't yet told my parents. I love him. It doesn't matter if they approve or not. That's just the way it is.

But I didn't think I'd ever be in this place.

Ever.

And now I have to tell Mum and Dad. I want to do it today

when I have a day off and Matt isn't here. Well, I don't really want to but I'm been avoiding talking to them because part of me thinks they'll know just by looking at me. I feel like it's written all over my face – how happy I am. And I've been enjoying the week of just being able to revel in it without judgement.

Each day I'm with him though, I feel like I'm becoming braver with what's happening. What we've got is real. I'm sure of it. Surer than I've been of anything in my life before. It's time to tell them.

Doesn't mean I'm not nervous though. Actually terrified is probably a better word. The fact that there's a huge number of kilometres between us helps. A little anyway. Then I don't have to deal with the in-person disapproval and try to find a way to escape.

A light knock at the door pulls me out of my thoughts and I don't even have time to get out of bed before the door opens. Georgie is standing there, hair in a tangled mess around her head like she's just got out of bed, highlighted by the morning sun.

'Hello.'

She grins and walks in, climbing up beside me on the bed, totally at ease, totally sure of herself. Is it sad that I'm a little bit jealous of a five year old? Probably. She reaches over to touch my hair.

'You have really pretty hair.'

'Thank you. So do you.'

She cocks her head at me, the curls bouncing on her head so that she has to push them back off her face.

'Is Uncle Matt living here now?'

I blink at the unexpected question and give what feels like wobbly smile, trying not to think about where this conversation might lead. While I'm finally feeling a little less awkward around Georgie, I'm so not up to knowing what I can and can't say about my relationship with her uncle.

'Umm, no. Not really. We're just enjoying spending time together. We're good friends.'

'Do you love him?'

Well, so much for the friend route. I take a deep breath. Maybe this is the easy place to start. Tell a five year old and then tell my parents.

'Yes, I do.'

Her little brow furrows. 'But didn't you love Zac?'

God, oh God, what do I say to this? I sit up in bed, smoothing the covers around my lap, trying to give myself some time.

'Well, I was really good friends with Zac.' I cringe at how lame this sounds. 'I mean, Zac and I only knew each other for a little while.'

'But you kissed him.'

I chew my lip, trying to think of the right words. My brain feels like it's frozen – in need of a reboot, and I'm trying really hard to channel either Roxanne or Matt who always seem to know the right thing to say. It's not helping.

I plaster a bigger smile on my face, going for confidence. 'I did. But now I love your uncle.'

She nods, like that makes perfect sense, and I can breathe again.

'Are you going to get married? Can I be your flower girl if you are?'

I can hardly keep up with her change in thoughts.

'I don't know. We haven't talked about anything like that. You'd make a gorgeous flower girl though.'

'Maddi was a flower girl. She had her hair done at the hairdresser – it was all curly, like mine, only neater – and she got to carry her own flowers. And she had a princess dress. It was yellow, although I don't really like yellow. But it was still pretty. Can I have a dress like that too?'

'Umm, sure.'

'And can Mummy be a bridesmaid. She'd love it. And we could dress up together. And have our hair done.'

'If Uncle Matt and I get married then she can be a bridesmaid.'

I'm sort of proud of the fact that I can say that without feeling like I'm going to hyperventilate. The thought of me marrying a human a few weeks ago would have had me in a panic. Funny what love can do. Georgie looks around the room, taking everything in.

'Has Uncle Matt been having a sleep over?'

'Yeah, I guess.'

'Maddi's slept over before but only for one night. That's all we're allowed. I wish she could sleep over for a whole week like Uncle Matt.'

'Maybe you'll be able to when you're an adult.'

'Mummy doesn't have sleep overs though and she's an adult.'

'Doesn't she?'

God, I don't know what to say. I've been learning really quickly in the last week that little kids seem to say whatever comes into their head. So the relief I feel when I see Roxanne at the door is almost overwhelming.

'Here you are. I was looking for you. Are you annoying Lani?'

Georgie scowls at her mother. It's sort of cute.

'I'm not annoying her. I was just asking her about Uncle Matt.' She takes my hand like I'm her new best friend. 'Lani said I could be a flower girl.'

Roxanne shoots me a startled look and I shake my head.

'Georgie just said she'd like to be one like her friend,

Maddi. And I said if anything like that happens, she could. But we haven't even spoken about it – Matt and I , I mean. And it's not something that I've even really been thinking about but Georgie just asked this morning...'

I'm rambling and I shut my mouth tight, trying to stop the flow. I feel like I've been caught out doing something wrong, even though I'm not sure what it is. Georgie turns back to me.

'But you love him. You said you did. And when a princess loves the prince, they get married and live happily ever after.' She smiles at me. 'You could even have birds to help you, like Cinderella. And I could sing the song. I'm a good singer.'

Roxanne laughs and comes in to pick Georgie up off the bed. The little girl pushes her mother's hair back and holds her face in her tiny hands, giving her a kiss. It's beautiful. What a mother and daughter should be like. Accepting, unconditional...

'I think we need to give Lani and Uncle Matt a little bit of time together before they get married, poppet. Come on. Let's go get breakfast.'

I smile my thanks at Roxanne and she winks at me as she goes out.

'How come you don't have sleep overs like Lani and Uncle Matt, Mummy?'

I can't help but laugh. Roxanne has probably had more experience at answering those sorts of questions though.

I swing my legs out to the side of the bed and sit there, contemplating for a moment the enormity of what I'm about to do. I feel like I should have a shower and get dressed – be perfectly ready – meeting all of my mother's expectations before I ring them. Being the perfect daughter. In looks, anyway, but there's another part of me that just wants to get it over and done with. A small part of me that doesn't want to do what she wants me to. A part that's sick of trying to please her.

I grab my phone before I can change my mind, texting that I'd like to chat to them if they're available. I have time to make a cup of tea before I hear the signal sound from the computer.

I shut my eyes for a second, feeling like I'm going to be sick – right here, right now, all over the computer keyboard. Which would be an awesome start. Mum would probably think I was pregnant. Another disappointment. Something else to screw up her face at.

I take a sip of tea – hot and sweet in my mouth; fortifying – and swallow hard before clicking on the icon.

Mum is already dressed, as I knew she'd be, hair done, makeup on – ready for whatever the day brings. Untouchable. Thank God Dad's still in his pyjamas. I don't feel like such a loser.

'Morning, possum. How's things in sunny Noosa?'

I smile at Dad, feeling a small bit of tightness release from my chest. This normal greeting, this term of endearment. Something so small but important. Especially today.

'Good, Dad. Sorry I haven't had a chance to speak to you in a while – I've had a busy week.'

Kissing Matt...but I don't need to start the conversation with that.

'That's alright. And how's the job. Still good?'

'Yeah, it's great. Roxanne's been looking at my designs. She's really interested in a few of them. Thinks we might be able to make them up and sell them in the shop. In fact, we're going to start making some up next week.'

'That's awesome! Don't you think so, Nora? What a clever daughter we have.'

'It's nice that she likes them. But be careful. You're too trusting. She might just be telling you that to make sure you stay. Is she paying you the right rate? Maybe that's what she's trying to do – butter you up so you don't realise you're being underpaid. And does she really know what she's looking at when it comes to design. Does she have any experience herself?'

I make a conscious effort to relax my jaw.

'She makes and designs most of the clothes in the shop herself and they sell really well. And she has orders coming in all the time. She's a good business woman, especially since she's done it all herself.'

'I'm sure she is, but it's not as if she's saving lives or like she's got a degree. It's just clothes, Lani. It can't be that hard.'

There's an awkward pause and I take another sip of tea, trying to hide from them how much my hand is shaking. It's my dad that fills the gap, like he always does. I wonder if he ever gets sick of being in the middle of us.

'And have you met any other changers up there yet, possum? Anyone we might know?'

'Just the ones I met during the Aurora.' When I was still in a relationship with Zac. I know they're thinking the same thing. 'It's been pretty busy, trying to get my head around work and moving in to the flat and getting the designs drawn out so we can cut them out...'

My mother frowns. 'You're just working in a clothes shop, Lani. Surely it can't be that hard. There must be time to go out and meet other people. Maybe you just need to come back home, where you know everyone and you know where you fit.'

That thought is almost unbearable. To be trapped again. To be there without Matt. I lick my lips. 'I've met other people.'

My heart's hammering as I wait for her to make the connection. Her lips narrow as she presses them together and I know she isn't going to disappoint.

'Not changers though.'

'No, Mum, not changers.'

'Well, that doesn't matter.' My dad's rubbing my mum's

hand, like he can feel her disapproval. I've got no doubt he can, considering I can feel it up here on-line. She must be practically radiating her displeasure down there, like sitting beside a sullen wood heater. 'It's good to have friends from all different walks of life.'

'Except, David, she's not going to find someone to bond with if she's choosing to only be around humans all the time. And isn't that what you want, Lani? Isn't that why you moved up all the way up there? To try and get a bond because it wasn't happening down here? You're not getting any younger, my girl, and those looks won't last forever. If you don't find someone shortly, I think you should just move back here – then at least you can be around your nephews and nieces. Help your brothers even if you are on your own.'

I can feel my heart beat in my eardrums, thumping, thumping, thumping and it's taking everything in me to stay seated when all I want to do is get up and pace the room. I try to smile. It doesn't work. But this is it. I have to say it.

'Actually it's happened already. The bond, I mean.' I take a deep breath. 'I've met someone and there's a bond between us and I'm really happy. It's amazing, Dad, just like you said it'd be. And I'm happy. Really happy. Honestly.'

I bite my lip, trying to stop the flow of words pouring out of my mouth. They've both gone absolutely still, like I've shocked them into paralysis. And then my dad is smiling, happy for me in a way that I've never seen from Mum. He wraps out a beat on the desk and turns to her.

'There. Did you hear that, Nora? Our Lani's found someone.'

'Yes. I heard.' She narrows her eyes at me, as if she can smell the whiff of a possible disappointment from there – always digging for the weak spot. 'Who is it? Do we know him?'

I shake my head, my movement's jerky, smile straining my face. 'No. No, you don't.'

'And what sort of changer is he?'

I take a deep breath. I don't want to be here. I want to run and run and run. Get away. But I want to be with Matt as well. And that need is stronger, making me stronger.

'Actually, he's not a changer.'

There, it's out. The words seem to hang in the air like a flashing neon sign, highlighting what a terrible daughter I am. That I'm no good. A failure. That I've disappointed her. Again.

It's Dad's turn to frown now. My dad, whose support I need more than anything. I willing him to just accept it, move on, still love me despite what I've just hit them with...

'What do you mean?'

But I don't have to find the words to answer him. Mum's face has gone hard, uncompromising – she's always been faster than Dad at finding the tarnished, damaged parts of the silver lining – and I know she'll be able to fill him in.

'It means, David, that *your* daughter stupidly believes she's bonded with a human.'

His mouth drops open and I can see the hurt in his eyes. It's too much. Not Dad. My main support. My rock. Tears start to form in my eyes and I blink them away but there are more there, ready to take their place.

'Is that true, Lani?'

Lani, not possum. Not anymore.

I nod. It's all I can do. This is so much harder than I thought it'd be. Or maybe it's harder than I *hoped* it'd be. But there's no turning back now. The damage is done. All I can do is to try and make him understand.

'His name's Matt. And he's great, Dad. You'd really like him. And he treats me really well and I'm happy. Happier than I think I've ever been in my whole life.' I can hear the pleading in my voice – the begging for him to understand and say he's okay with what I've done.

Mum doesn't even let me get all the words out before she's talking over the top of me.

'There is no such thing as a bond with humans, Lani. You're imagining it although that doesn't surprise me – you've always been dramatically in need of attention. I can't understand why you'd choose to say such a horrible thing to us, though. To your father. When we've given you everything you've ever wanted.' She dabs at her eyes like she's crying. I don't trust her for a second. She's done this too often, just to get her own way. To make Dad take her side. To make me give in. God, how cynical has she made me? Not that she's finished yet. 'You're doing it to just punish me, aren't you? You're always trying to find ways to hurt me. After all I've done for you. After all the time I've given you. I don't know why you want to treat me like this.'

My mother's voice wavers and Dad puts his arm around her, tucking her into his side. She's won. Again.

Which can't happen. Not this time. I'm shaking my head before she's finished talking.

'I'm not, Mum. I swear. Dad, it's a real bond. I'm not making this up. It's just like you told me it'd be. It's amazing. I want to be with him, be part of his life. I love him.'

My voice catches on the words, like a jagged fingernail on fabric. I wipe the tears away with my fingers, angry with myself for crying. I want to be strong. I want to make them understand how much he means to me. Or make Dad understand because Mum is still not listening. Not that I honestly thought she would.

'You're being stupid. You're just a stupid, little girl who doesn't think about the consequences of what you do or think about how it effects other people. Selfish. You always have been. And now, look, you've ruined your life and if we let you, you'll ruin ours. We should never have let you go up there.'

I shut my eyes for a second, shutting out the sight of her face, screwed up in disapproval, all her beauty disappearing into a mask of hatred. Aimed at me.

'I'm twenty-two, Mum. I didn't need your permission to come up here and I don't need your permission to be in a relationship.' I can hardly believe the words have come out of my mouth and for a moment, the panic that's making my chest feel like it's wrapped in concrete makes me want to suck the words back in. But I don't.

'Well, if you think we'd ever give you permission to be with this...human, then you're sadly mistaken. I will never, *ever* think this is okay, no matter how much you'd like to wear us down. But I suppose that doesn't worry you. You don't care what we think anyway.'

My dad squeezes my mum's shoulders and she stops talking, her mouth pressing together. I've never been more grateful for her silence.

'Are you sure, Lani? A bond? With a human?'

I nod at him, trying to control my breathing. Trying to get it together. 'Nick was telling the truth, Dad. It can happen – it *has* happened. To me.'

My dad shakes his head, slowly, like he's suddenly twenty years older. And I'm the one who's done that to him. Maybe Mum's right. Maybe I am a terrible daughter. Selfish. And yet, that doesn't stop me loving Matt. If only they could meet him... see us together... then they might understand.

'I don't know, Lani. I'm just finding it hard to believe.' He rubs his thumb and finger over his eyes. 'I can't comprehend it to be honest. And I don't know what to say to you at the moment. You've caught us by surprise with this. I'm going to have to think about it, okay?'

'Okay.' It's something, at least. Some indication he doesn't totally hate me.

My mother lets out a snort.

'Don't be ridiculous, David. It's not a bond. She doesn't know what she's talking about. It's just a way for her to avoid her responsibilities, like she always has. You baby her too much and it has to stop. See what it leads to!'

My father's voice is patient as he turns to her. I don't understand how he can still be so nice to her, after all this time. 'It could be real, Nor. It could be. I think we have to give Lani some credit with this.'

'You are always far too easy on her, that's why I have to be tough.' She draws herself up, running her hand over her hair, patting it down, even though it's still perfect. 'You're mistaken, Lani, it is *not* a bond. And anyway, even if it was, like you're trying to convince us it is,' I can hear the sneer in her voice, 'then there are ways it can be broken.'

Every organ in my body sinks, like my blood is suddenly not there to keep everything in place. She is not going to give in. There was a part of me – a tiny, little, malnourished part – thinking she'd eventually have to come around to the fact that the bond existed and live with it, even if she wasn't happy about it. But not this. I never expected this.

'What do you mean?' I don't want to ask but the words are out before I can stop them.

'I mean there are ways a bond can be broken. It's not easy and there's a price to pay, but it can be done.'

I actually move my chair back slightly, away from the screen.

'I don't want to break it. I love him.'

'Well then, I guess you have a decision to make, young lady. You can have him or you can have your family. But you can't have both.'

And before I have a chance to respond, or before my father can say anything else, she clicks on the button, sending the screen blank. The last image I have is of my father, looking pale and sad.

And all I want to do is to fly away.

Matt

The text message from Roxanne is short and to the point.

Come to the shop in your lunch hour. I need to talk to you.

Sometimes she just doesn't know how to stop being a bossy, older sister. I sigh as I read it. There's no point in ignoring it. It won't make her go away. She'll just get more annoying.

I wait until Dan starts his shift and then go over, the bell announcing my arrival as I open the door. Roxanne's helping a customer when I come in, laughing with her. I stand by the front counter and wait and by the time they're done, the woman's walking into the change room with a pile of clothes over her arm.

I shake my head when Roxanne comes over to hug me.

'God, you're a good salesperson.'

She winks at me. 'You don't need to try hard when you have high quality merchandise. Besides, you don't seem to have problems in that area yourself.'

'Must be in the blood. Anyway, what's so urgent that I needed to come over here during my break?'

'I just wanted to ask how you were. Since obviously you've been at my place all week and I haven't seen you once.'

I lean back on the bench and smile at her. 'I've had other things on my mind.'

She rolls her eyes. 'Yeah sure, other things.'

'Come on, Rox, that's not why you asked me over here. You could've come and said hello this afternoon if that was your problem. Spill it.'

'There's no problem as such. I just wanted to see how you and Lani are going.'

'Good. I think so anyway. Why?'

I suddenly have visions of Lani and Roxanne talking – of Lani telling her that it was all a mistake and she doesn't know how to break it off with me, that she's feeling guilty about Zac or can't deal with the jealous ex-girlfriend crap. I stand up, lacing my hands on top of my head, and narrow my eyes at my sister.

'Has Lani said something?'

'Only if you count telling us that she's in love with you and caving to the pressure from your niece to be a flower girl in a princess dress should you guys ever get married.'

I grin. I can imagine how that conversation went. And is it weird that the thought of marriage with her doesn't make me break out into a cold sweat? Even though I haven't known her that long. Not that I'm about to propose or anything. I'm not that impulsive. But still, it's nice to know it isn't terrifying.

'What's wrong then?'

She straightens the collar of her shirt, dragging her fingers down to the points on each side, and her eyes scuttle away from mine for a moment.

'Have you spoken to Lani today?'

I hesitate, worried where this is going, before shaking my head. 'It's been a pretty busy morning. Why?'

'Well, I don't know what happened but when I was getting ready to leave to drop Georgie off before coming here, Lani ran out of the flat and took off in her car. She looked...upset. Like she'd been crying. I didn't have a chance to catch up to her to find out what had happened or if she was okay. So I thought you might know.'

'She was upset?'

'It looked that way. Is everything okay with you guys?'

I frown. 'I think so. As far as I know.'

But maybe I don't know much. Maybe she's keeping something from me. Not secrets necessarily but how she's really feeling. Maybe talking to Georgie about the possibility of marriage has freaked *her* out. Maybe I'm more in love with her than she is with me. That thought has my stomach rolling, twisting in on itself. The thought that I might be hurt again makes me want to disappear.

I take a deep breath, trying to calm everything down – my thoughts, my breathing, my heart. It might be about something totally unrelated. Something to do with home. With her mum maybe. I need to get a grip.

I pull out my phone and take a few steps away from Rox, turning my back. She takes the hint and moves over to the clothes racks. I don't know what she's doing but I'm glad she's not standing there, listening to us, watching me.

Not that it matters anyway. Lani's phone rings and rings before the message clicks in. I tap my fingers on the wall as I wait for it to finish.

'Hey, it's Matt. I just wanted to check that everything's alright. Give me a ring when you get this message, okay?'

Totally inadequate for what I want to say. God, any

message would be. I just want to talk to her. Roxanne's looking over at me, her eyebrows raised.

'It went to message bank. I'm sure she's fine.'

Roxanne nods. 'I'm sure she will be. Maybe she just needed to be on her own for a moment.'

I nod. 'Yeah, maybe. Anyway, I better...' I wave in the general direction of the door. 'You know, get back to work.'

'Let me know when you hear from her?'

'Sure.'

It's only when I'm sitting in the car that I do the thing the previously-hurt, stupidly-suspicious part of my brain wanted to do as soon as the phone went to message bank. I take a deep breath. This is stupid. Idiotic. I've got no reason to doubt Lani. No reason at all. But I can't help it. I dial Zac's number.

It goes to message bank too. Which means nothing. Hell, Zac could still be asleep. It doesn't point to anything. And yet, all I know is that I feel sick.

Lani

I tuck my wings in to my side and spear down to the ground, feeling the wind rush past me. Excitement spreads through my body as I get closer and closer, and then, at the last moment, I spread my wings out again, catching the currents underneath them, gliding over the waves that only serve to remind me of Matt and our surfing lessons.

Matt. Who I want to be with without question.

Matt. Who loves me. Accepts me for who I am. Makes me smile and laugh. Makes me feel sure of myself. Encourages me.

And yet, according to my mother, I can't have both him and my family.

All I can picture is my father's face.

I flap, pulling myself higher in the air again, trying to leave the image behind. It doesn't work.

I don't know what to do. I don't want to lose my family, even my mother. She's my mum, even if she's a crappy one. But I don't want to lose Matt either. I can't. And there's no way I want to break the bond. I want to be with him, despite the fact he isn't a changer.

It's no good. There are no answers up here. I'm not getting the peace I normally do from being able to spread my wings and follow the currents. I turn back towards the secluded part of the beach where I stashed my clothes. There's no running away from this. I have to deal with it.

It's only as I come in to land that I can see another kite, spiralling in the air, and know that it's Zac. Today of all days, I don't know that I can handle this. But then, maybe he'd be a good person to talk to. He knows Matt, he knows how I feel and he knows about being a changer. I catch up and move with him, trying to convey that I want him to land with me. Within a matter of minutes, we're on the ground, changing back.

I don't know what to expect from him – sadness or anger maybe, aimed at me. But I don't get any of that. He looks good. Settled. I didn't realise how much of a relief that'd be until right at this moment.

'Hi Lani.' His voice is quiet. Controlled.

'Hi.'

'How are you? How's Matt? I feel like I haven't seen him in the last week. It's like I've got my own place.'

I smile – it feels tight – and turn to take my underwear from the branches of the low tree I put them in.

'He's good. We're good.' I turn back to him. 'Thank you. For being so...understanding, about all of this, I mean.'

He shakes his head. 'Nothing to thank me for. I'm happy for you guys. Especially with the bond. I know how important that is for you. I'm not going to say that it wasn't a bit of a blow to the ego to start with but it's all good. I'm just glad it's worked out for you.'

I nod but I can't smile this time. Because right at this moment, it doesn't feel like it'll work out. It feels like I'm going to lose someone I love from my life no matter what I decide. I pull my underwear on, not answering him. It's only when I've done up my bra and he's started to get dressed himself that I feel like I can get the words out.

'I told my parents about him this morning. And about the bond.'

He stops, pausing with one leg in his shorts and one out.

'I'm guessing from your expression it didn't go well.'

I shake my head, blinking away tears. Zac finishes putting his shorts on and comes over, wrapping me in a hug. It feels nice. Something a friend would do. Comforting. This is what we always were, I think. Friends. Even if in the start I wanted to try and force it to be more than that. Having felt the bond with Matt – knowing how good our relationship is – I know what I had with Zac was always friendship. I hug him tighter and then step back. Deep breath.

'Mum told me I'd have to choose between my family and being with Matt.'

'Shit, that's harsh! Aren't they glad you're happy?'

I shake my head, feeling the tears again, trying to hold them back, swallow them down.

'My dad looked really upset and my mum...my mum told me I was being ridiculous. That's it not a real bond and that if it was, there's a way to break it. So that's what she wants me to do. If it's real.'

'Are you kidding?' He sounds angry now. Angry on my behalf. 'I can't believe she'd even suggest that. Jesus! She's your mother! Did she tell you what breaking a bond involved?'

I almost go to defend her...like I've done every time before... every time someone has told me she should treat me better or one of my friends has had a go at her...but I don't this time. She doesn't deserve it.

'No, she just said it'd be hard to do and there'd be a price to pay. Whatever that means. That was it. Why? Have you heard about it?'

'Yeah. And believe me, it's not something you want to be thinking about.'

'Why?'

'It can kill you. What you have to go through to break the bond is so frigging full on that changers have died! That's part of the reason I've never been hung up on having a bond. Jesus, I can't believe your mum even suggested that!'

I'm numb. Empty. I can feel the sand sticking to the soles of my feet and the material of the clothes in my hand, hear the sound of the waves crashing in on the beach, but I can't tell how I'm actually feeling. It's as if my brain has trapped all of my emotions behind a glass wall.

Because all it can deal with at the moment is that my mother would rather I be dead than to have a bond with a human. She would rather risk my life than be happy that I'm happy. This is a new low, even for her.

'What am I going to do?' I'm not actually asking Zac, it's more just talking out loud, trying to get my brain to work. He answers me anyway.

'Do you love him?'

I nod. There's only a slight tightening of his jaw. That's all I notice anyway.

'Then go and be with him. Stuff your mum and all the stupid 'changers only belong with other changers' shit. It doesn't sound like she's doing an awesome job at being a mum anyway.'

He's right. There's no way to argue with that. It makes logical sense. But still, she's my mum. I keep coming back to that. I want her to be proud of me and what I do. I want her to love me. And she's not the only one I have to think about. She's not the parent who has been the most important one in my life.

'What about my dad?'

Zac looks uncomfortable for a moment, his brow furrowing into deep grooves.

'God, Lani, I don't know. This is so out of my experience. Maybe he'll come around when he's had time to think. He loves you, right?'

Yesterday, I would've said yes without hesitation. Today, I'm not so sure. So I shrug. It makes me feel terrible that I don't know – wrong, like my skin is only just managing to keep everything together. Something I thought I could always be sure of and now I don't know. How did everything get so screwed up? How could the bonding be so right and so wrong?

I don't know if it's the look on my face or the fact that I don't answer but he wraps his arms around me again. I hug him back but it's more because my body knows what to do rather than really feeling it. My brain isn't functioning.

'I'm sorry it's got shitty. I know how important the bond was to you.'

Shitty. That's about the only word for it. Still, it's not Zac's fault.

'Thanks for being a good friend.'

It's his turn to shrug as he releases me.

'You and Matt are my friends. And you belong together.'

I smile. It's weak but at least it's a smile. 'Let's just hope my parents come around to that thinking.'

'Are you going to tell Matt about any of this?'

I can't keep the shock from my face. That had never occurred to me. Not even for a second. All my life, the importance of keeping our secret has been drummed into me. To never, ever, *ever* reveal it to someone who's not a changer. And despite the fact I love Matt, he's not a changer.

'No. Why would I?'

His brow creases. 'I don't know. It just seems like an obvious thing to do – with the bond, and everything that's going on with your parents. How's he going to understand what's going on for you otherwise? Why your mum and dad are objecting so strongly to you guys being together when they were happy for you to come up here to see me and yet, disapprove of your relationship without even having met him? Or are you just never going to introduce him to them?'

I know my mouth is hanging open as I listen to him. Part shock and part amazement, I think.

'But what about keeping it a secret? Weren't you always told that growing up? That it's important not to tell anyone who's not a changer?'

'Yeah, sure. But this is different. I'm not suggesting you rush out and tell the whole world or anything. Just Matt. How can you be with him – have a bond with him –

if he doesn't know who you are? What happens during the next Aurora if you guys are together when it happens? He's going to freak out if he sees you in pain and doesn't know why.'

How stupid am I that I hadn't even thought of that? But Zac's right. What happens when I'm forced to change? How do I explain that to him?

And yet, if I tell him, that's only going to disappoint my parents further.

I shake my head. It doesn't have any effect on my scattered thoughts.

'God. I don't know what to do. I'll have to think about it.'

Zac nods. 'I wouldn't take too long to decide. Secrets aren't a good thing – especially for Matt.'

'I know.' My stomach is churning so much it wouldn't take much for me to throw up, right here on the sand. I swallow hard. As if on cue, my phone rings. It's Matt. And there's already been two missed calls from him.

I look at Zac. 'It's Matt.'

He winks at me. 'I'll see you later then.'

I hit the answer button as he walks away, back up the track to the car park.

'Hey.'

'Lani. Thank God.'

I can hear the relief in his voice and my heart jolts in my chest with the thought of what might have happened while I've been flying.

'What's wrong? Has something happened to Roxanne or Georgie?'

'No, no, they're all good. But I was talking to Rox and she said she'd seen you leave this morning and thought you were upset. And then when I couldn't contact you...'

I feel a rush of love for him, spreading from my chest to the rest of my body, washing over me, making my skin tingle. He was worried for me.

'It's okay. I'm fine.'

'Are you sure?'

'Yeah. I spoke to my parents this morning, that's all. And my mum was being her usual charming self. She just got to me, so I thought I'd go for a walk, try and clear my head.' The half lie sits heavily on my tongue but I need to think about what Zac said before I just blurt everything out.

'I tried to ring...'

'Sorry. I left my phone in the car. I didn't want mum trying to call me.'

It's a worry how quickly these lies come to me. And I don't want to be lying to him all the time. Maybe Zac was right about telling him...just not yet.

'Okay. Well, I'm just glad you're good.' There's a pause, like he's trying to work up the courage to say something. All of my stomach muscles clench, wondering what it could be. I've had enough emotion for today.

'Do you still want me to come over tonight?'

'Of course.' I don't even have to think about it. But then I wonder if he doesn't want to – is that why he's asking? 'If you don't want to though, that's okay. If you have other stuff you need to do or you want to sleep in your bed or something.'

There's another pause. I don't understand this one. I wish he was here in front of me so I could see his face because all I can think is that something has changed and I'm not good enough to hold him. And my mum will be right about me.

'I want to come over.'

I let out a sigh. 'Great. I'll see you tonight then.'

'Okay, see you tonight. Around five? I'll go back to the house first for a shower and then come over. Is that okay?'

Relief courses through me, warm in my veins.

'Sounds great.' I can picture him, standing at my front door, his hair still wet from the shower. I can feel his lips on mine already. 'I love you.'

'I love you too.'

And I wonder if he still will if I tell him who I really am.

Matt

I help a guy load the paddle board he's just bought onto the top of his ute and go back inside the shop. Dan looks up as I come in.

'I might take off now.'

He nods. 'Sure. I've got everything sorted.'

I head over to the computer, leaning over the desk to log off. The email icon is blinking at me and I hesitate for a second, just wanting to go and see Lani. But a few more moments aren't going to make much of a difference.

The image comes up as soon as I open it, saved within the email rather than as an attachment, and I take a step back before I can stop myself. For a moment, I can't breathe, can't move. No, no, no. It can't be right. It must be photo shopped. It must be. I tap my fists on my forehead, struggling to make any sense of the image in front of me.

Lani, dressed in her underwear, hugging a half-naked Zac.

Fuck. I can't do this. Not again.

It doesn't make any sense. Lani loves me. She said she did. I *know* she does. And Zac. Christ!

I pace behind the chair, needing the movement, needing to do at least something. My whole body feels like it's revolting against the image that's seared itself into my brain in those few seconds. I don't know what to do – how to make this better.

It's only when my brain finally kicks into gear that I actually think about the sender, and I almost leap over to the mouse, moving it to see the top of the email.

Karli.

I should've known. Some of the panic leaches from my body, enough that I can breathe again. It must be photo shopped. I don't know how she's done it but it can't be real. It's just the next step for Karli. That's what she does. And it needs to stop. There's no way I'd ever go back to her. Ever. She needs to understand that.

I delete the email before I shut the computer down and almost run across to where I keep my keys and wallet.

'Are you okay?'

Dan's standing there, watching me, our new supply of leg ropes in his hands.

'Just need to take care of something.'

It's only when I get to the door that I turn back.

'Hey, if Karli comes here, don't let her in, okay?'

'Don't let her in the shop?' His eyebrows are shooting up his forehead but I'm not about to explain it to him.

'Yep. Tell her I said to fuck off.'

And then I'm heading out before he can ask any more questions. I almost rip the door off in my rush to get in the car, and back out so fast the tyres squeal. It's only when I realise I'm doing eighty in a sixty zone that I take my foot off the accelerator and take a deep breath. No point killing myself over Karli.

I can't believe she's done this though. This is a new low, even for her.

It seems to take forever to get to her place and I don't even take the time to park properly before I'm out of the car and striding up to her door. I pound on it, the screen door rattling under the abuse. It only takes a few seconds before she's there, unlocking it and holding it open to me.

Jesus, she just doesn't stop! She's in a bikini that barely covers her breasts and a short sarong that shows off most of her legs.

'Matt, I'm so sorry. I didn't want to send it to you but I thought you should know.' She actually looks like she feels bad for me. I didn't realise she was that good of an actress.

'Cut the crap, Karli. I don't know what you think you're doing but know that it's not going to work. So stop fucking with me. I don't love you. I'm not getting back with you. In fact, I don't want to lay eyes on you ever again. Just leave me the fuck alone.'

Her mouth is hanging open and I figure it's a good time to leave before she recovers. But I don't even make it half way to the car before she comes after me, grabbing my arm.

'Matt, stop!'

I don't want to but it's pretty hard to walk when she's dragging on my arm. I swing around and it overbalances her enough that she lets go of me.

'I didn't make them up. The photos. They're real.'

'Bullshit!'

'They are! I'm not that desperate. God! Is that what you really think of me – that I'm some sort of psycho ex-girlfriend?'

'You broke into the shop and left your underwear there for us to see. We were on a date, for Christ's sake. Yes, I think you're that psycho.'

But I'm not sure. Not really. There's a small part of my brain telling me it could be true. Not that I want to think that or acknowledge any part of it. For both Lani and Zac to do that to me is beyond what I can deal with. Way beyond.

Karli is watching me, her arms folded.

'Look, I didn't want to send it to you. It was a difficult decision to make. I don't want to make you sad...not anymore.' She looks down for a moment and when her eyes come back up to meet mine, she's the one who looks sad. 'I didn't want this to happen to you again.'

'Then why *did* you send them?'

She frowns at me. 'I thought you deserved to know.'

It feels like there's a war happening in my head. Mortar fire, tanks, the whole fucking shebang. And I don't know which side's winning.

'I don't believe you.'

'I can show you the other photos if you want.'

I don't want. Not at all. What I want is to be back at the beginning of the day when I was lying in bed, kissing Lani, and everything was good. Great. Wonderful. That's what I want.

But maybe I should humour her. Maybe I should let her hang herself with this. She's probably not expecting me to say I want to see them. Bluffing. In that moment, it makes perfect sense in my head.

'Okay. Show me.'

She just nods. No hesitation. I try to ignore the heavy feeling that's settled on my chest. Lani and Zac wouldn't do this. They wouldn't.

It feels wrong to be walking into Karli's apartment. Like my life is in reverse, taking me back to where I never thought I'd be. I follow her through to the kitchen and she picks up her mobile from the kitchen bench.

The feeling in my chest gets heavier as I watch her, pressing on me, squeezing my ribs until I wonder if they're actually going to snap under the pressure. I want to get out of here...now...before I can see anything else but I'm paralysed. And then she's passing me the phone and my hand reaches for it automatically.

And there it is in front of me. The photo she sent me. Lani, half dressed, in Zac's arms. I want to be sick.

'There's more. Just scroll through.'

Karli's voice is soft. Caring. I want to tell her to shut up but then my finger is moving on the screen and there's another image. And another. And another.

All of them with Lani and Zac in various stages of undress. Talking. Hugging. Together. Too many of them to be fake.

'Where did you see them?'

I don't know why I ask the question. I don't know *how* I ask the question. Maybe to check that it's real and I'm not just stuck in a nightmare.

'In the national park while I was doing some research work. I swear, I didn't follow them or anything. It was just pure chance.'

Pure chance. I want to laugh. Except I don't think I'd be able to stop if I started. But for it to be by pure chance that my life has been turned upside down... How can that be right? It's not fair. I don't want to know. And yet, if it's happening, I need to know.

Fuck!

'When?'

'Today. This morning. Just before twelve.'

The time when I couldn't get either of them on the phone. The time that Lani told me she'd gone for a walk. Except she's obviously lied to me.

I want to throw the phone. Smash it against the wall. The part of my brain that still seems to be working is actually proud of the fact that I manage to put it on the bench. But I need to get out of here. The walls feel like they're pressing in on me. Suffocating me. I start walking but I've only gone a few steps and then I'm running. Running away. From the pictures. From the look in Karli's eyes. From what I thought I had. From the lies. From everything.

Lani

Five o'clock comes and goes and I'm still here on my own. I tell myself that he's just running late – probably stuck at the shop – and busy myself with painting my toenails. Anything to stop thinking about my parents and their reaction. Anything to stop thinking about the choice I'll have to make if they don't change their mind.

It's twenty to six before I finally pick up the phone to ring him to check where he is.

It's Matt. I can't come to the phone. Leave a message.

I smile at the sound of his voice.

'Hey, it's me. I'm picturing you in the shower so hurry up and come over.'

I know he'll love that message. He'll smile that sexy smile and maybe even laugh. God, I want him here. I want to be in his arms. Feeling his love wrapped around me. Tonight more than any other night. To know he still loves me even if my parents don't.

It's not until six o'clock comes and goes that I start to worry.

Especially since I still haven't heard from him. Not even a text to say he's got my message. Nothing. I hold the phone tight against my ear as I try to reach him once more. The message plays again.

I try to keep my voice even. Casual, so that the panic building inside me doesn't have an opportunity to warp my tone.

'Hey you. You're probably just caught up at work but I thought I'd check if you're still planning to come over. Call me okay. And hurry. I miss you.'

I hang up and throw the phone on the bed, pacing across the floor, before putting my head out the door, just to check. The birds, finding their roosts in the trees, are the only movement. This doesn't seem like Matt. Not the Matt I've known over the last week anyway. The Matt who rang me today to check if I was okay. The Matt that's been doing sweet little things for me, loving me.

That just leaves the thought that something's happened to him – that he's hurt somewhere. A car accident or that he's been robbed in the shop and is laying there, bleeding to death.

I chew on my fingernail, staring at the phone still laying on the bed like it's going to give me the answers. As if it's going to tell me what to do. Already another ten minutes has passed. Ten minutes where he would've rung me if he could've. I'm sure of it.

I grab the phone and hurry out the door, trying not to run because that'd make it an emergency and I'm trying really hard to believe it's not. I hear Roxanne and Georgie laughing inside the house and pause for a moment to see if I can hear a deeper voice – Matt so caught up with his family, he's lost track of time. I could absolutely forgive him for that. Except that doesn't seem like something he'd do either. I can't decide if I'm disappointed I can't hear him or glad he wouldn't make me worry like that.

I knock on the door, short and sharp. Even though all I want to do is bang and bang and bang until it's answered. I tap my foot as I wait for them to come. Trying to breathe in a normal way. In and out, slow, calm. It's not working. I check the phone, just in case. Nothing.

Georgie's face smiles up at me from behind the screen door.

'Hi, Lani.'

'Hi, Georgie. Can I speak to your mum?'

She opens the door for me and Roxanne looks up and smiles from the kitchen bench where she's chopping vegetables. Normal. Like nothing's wrong. I take that as a good omen.

'Hey there, neighbour. How are you feeling?'

I know she's talking about this morning, when she saw me rush off but that seems so long ago. And so unimportant at the moment. I don't care if Matt's not a changer. I don't care if Mum and Dad never speak to me again as long as he's okay.

I peek at the phone again. The screen's still black. Black and silent.

'I'm okay. Thanks.'

I wait for a second. But a second is all I can manage before the words push their way out of my mouth.

'Do you know where Matt is?'

She stops chopping and frowns at me.

'No. Why?'

I shrug. It's stiff, tight from the panic that isn't going away.

'When I spoke to him this morning he said he was going to come over around five but he isn't here and it's...' I look at my watch, 'six seventeen. I've rung but he didn't answer. So I left messages but he hasn't rung back.'

I can hear my voice getting higher. Shrill almost. I stop and take a breath. Well, try to anyway. It's shaky.

'I mean, I'm sure he's okay. Just held up at work or something...'

I wait for her to tell me I'm right, that of course that's all it is but she doesn't. All she does is reach for her phone, like she's worried too. Which is crazy. He's only an hour late. Everything will be okay. His phone's probably flat. Or his car's broken down. He's fine. Fine. Roxanne has to believe that even if I can't.

I suck in air, holding it, holding it, as I watch her call him, waiting for him to answer. Waiting to hear that I've been stupid and of course he's okay.

'Matt, it's Rox. Where are you? Call us.'

A message. For a moment, when she's said his name, my heart thought he'd answered and had somersaulted in my chest. But it's fallen again, heavy. God. God!

Roxanne tries to smile at me but it doesn't reach her eyes and I take no comfort in it.

'He'll be fine. He's probably just caught up at work. Actually, I'll ring the shop now.'

It's a relief that I don't have to be the only one to worry anymore. Selfish, but as long as I don't have to do it on my own, it makes it a tiny bit easier to deal with. I watch her, willing him to answer. And then I realize I haven't rung Zac. Stupid! I dial his number. It rings three times before he answers. I know, because I count each one.

'Lani. What's up?'

I can hear the smile in his voice and, for a second, my soul believes everything will be okay.

'Have you heard from Matt this afternoon? Is he at the house?'

'Um, no. I'm at home now and he's not here. I don't think he is anyway. Do you want me to check?'

'Yes. Please.'

I can hear him walking, can picture him going down the hallway to Matt's room, wait for him to say that he's there...

'No, he's not here. Sorry. I thought he'd be with you.'

I drag my hand through my hair. It feels like this is the last resort. If he's not at home, I don't know who else to call.

'No. He said he'd be here around five but he hasn't got here yet.'

I want to keep on talking...to explain it all out so he can tell me I'm being stupid...but I'm afraid he won't, so I pinch my lips shut, trying to keep it all in.

'Do you want me to go and check if he's still at the shop?'

'Would you? That'd be great? Is there anywhere else that he might be?'

There's a moment of silence. 'Not unless he's gone for a paddle or a surf?'

Shit. Stupid. I didn't even think about that. That's why he wouldn't answer his phone, but I can't believe he'd be this late. Not if he said he was going to be here. And now all I can think is that a bloody shark has got him and we'll never find him.

'Okay. Can you let me know when you get to the shop?'

'Sure. Don't worry. He'll be fine.'

It's what I want to hear. Except it's not making me feel better. When I hang up, Roxanne's watching me, eyebrow's raised.

'Zac. Matt's not at home but Zac's going to go down and check the shop for us.'

She nods. 'Great.'

'He also said he might be out on the water.'

'No. If he said he was going to be here at five, he wouldn't be this late. He just wouldn't do that.'

It reinforces what I was thinking. I don't know if it makes it better or not.

'Is there anywhere else he'd be?'

'I can't think of anywhere. Nowhere that he'd go and not have his phone. Or ring to let you know what's happening anyway.'

Georgie comes over from in front of the TV and grabs a bit of forgotten carrot from the chopping board.

'Is Uncle Matt okay?'

Roxanne puts her hand on the top of her daughter's head. 'Sure he is, poppet. He's probably forgotten to charge his phone.'

She rolls her eyes. 'He always does that.'

I hope she's right. I hope it's as simple as that. Except where is he?

Roxanne puts some of the salad on a plate and gives it to Georgie.

'You can watch some TV for a while longer if you like. Just for tonight. I want to talk to Lani for a moment, okay?'

She takes the plate, happy to go and watch her cartoons again. Happy. I wish. I want to be back to this morning. Or to our date on the roof of the shop. When I was happy. Well, most of the time. The ex's underwear put a little dampener on it.

I look at Roxanne.

'Matt's ex has been hanging around lately. She wants to get back with him.'

'Karli?'

I nod, trying to stop the swirling of my stomach at the thought of them together. But he wouldn't do that. He's not that type of person.

'Matt would never go there again. She broke his heart. And I've never seen him as happy as he's been with you. Don't even think about that.'

I take a deep breath in. 'Do you think she might know where he is? Is it worth a call?'

Sphenurus

Because it's now six thirty-two and he's still not here. I leave that unsaid. It doesn't need to be. I know Roxanne is as aware of it as I am.

She hesitates, looking at her phone and then back up at me.

'I don't think she's going to be able to tell us anything but there's no harm in calling.'

I sit on one of the stools at the front of the kitchen bench while she calls, watching her as she waits for it to be answered.

'Karli. Hi, it's Roxanne.'

There's a short silence while Karli speaks. I wish I could hear the other side of the conversation but I don't want to hear her voice, imagine her with Matt.

'Listen, we're just wondering if you've seen Matt recently. If you know where he is?'

Silence. This one is longer.

'So, he was at your place this afternoon?'

God, oh God. He's back with her. Sick of me already. I watch Roxanne's face change, her eyes flicking to mine and then away again.

'But –' She's silent again as Karli talks. 'No, that can't be right.'

I bite the inside of my cheek to stop asking what that means, watching her. She's pacing now. Agitated. This is so not right. Something bad has happened. I want to leave now before I know what it is. But I stay on the stool anyway.

'I don't believe you.'

Her voice is flat. Emotionless. I don't know what else Karli's said but Roxanne presses the button to hang up and stares at the phone for a moment, like she doesn't want to look at me.

It's hard to talk past the lump in my throat but I manage to get the words out anyway.

'What is it? What did she say? Where's Matt?'

Roxanne takes a few steps back over to the kitchen bench, placing her phone carefully down on the marble like she's worried it's going to break. She looks at Georgie, still engrossed in the TV, and it's only then that her eyes meet mine. I don't like what I see in them.

'She said that she saw him this afternoon, after work. That he went over to her place.'

I shut my eyes for moment. It's too much. He's taken her back, even though she cheated on him. Even though he said he was in love with me. When I open them again, Roxanne's still looking at me, as if she's unsure about my reaction.

She takes another step back, leaning on the kitchen bench behind her, further away from me.

'Karli said she showed him some photos. Photos of you and Zac together.'

I frown. I don't understand what she's trying to say. 'From when I was going out with him?'

Roxanne shakes her head.

'What do you mean then?'

She folds her arms. 'She says she has photos of the two of you together. From today. This morning.'

For a second, I don't understand what she means – how that could even be possible. I haven't been with Zac. I love Matt. That's all there is. But then I remember the hug after we changed back. The hug of a friend. But to an outsider, it would've looked like more than that, especially when we were only half dressed. How did she get the photos though? We were surrounded by bush. Alone. Although obviously not. And I was too caught up in telling Zac everything – wanting to feel better – that I didn't do a proper check. Stupid!

My heart is pounding in my chest and I can feel the panic rushing through me, making my thoughts swirl, my stomach cramp. Roxanne is still watching me and I can see the look on her face for what it is now. She thinks I've cheated on her brother. She believes what Karli said and I'm suddenly the bad person in this situation.

I shake my head, standing up from the stool and going around the bench to her. Her arms are still folded and I stop.

'It's not true, Roxanne. It's not.'

She's silent, looking at me.

'Please. You have to believe me. It's not true. I haven't cheated on him with Zac.'

'Matt obviously believed the photos showed that.'

And there it is. It doesn't matter if she believes me or not. Not really. Because Matt does. Matt believes I'd do this to him. He hasn't been in an accident. He's not in mortal danger. He just doesn't want to be with me. He thinks I've cheated on him with his best friend. How trite does that sound? But I guess the photos prove it. Except they're not what they seem.

I struggle to breathe, struggle to think – the panic making it all too hard. It feels like everything that's been good in my life has suddenly turned to ash and all I want is to find him – find him and beg him to understand.

And I know what I need to do if I want to make this better. There's no option, despite what my parents – my community – have always drummed into me.

I need to show him what I am.

I can't keep this secret any longer. There's no choice anymore. Not if I want to convince him. Not if I want him to believe me. To love me. And I want that more than anything. More than keeping our secret.

If he gives me the chance.

'Please, Roxanne, I need to talk to him. Did Karli say where he'd gone?'

She shakes her head and then sighs.

'I think I know where he's gone though. It's where he went when it happened with Karli.'

I blink, trying to stop the threatening tears. I don't want to cry. I want to be strong. I want to fight for him. I grip the bench and take a deep breath.

'Please. You need to tell me where he is.'

Matt

I'm numb. A big ball of nothing. My brain still can't process the images it saw. Can't or doesn't want to, I'm not sure which.

I move out onto the veranda with my coffee, sitting on the bush chair my granddad made just before he died. This little shack feels like a haven, stuck up in the middle of the bush of the Sunshine Coast Hinterland. Maybe that's what it was for him too, after my grandma died.

Last night was a complete cluster-fuck in my head. That's the only word I can find that fits. All I could picture was Lani in Zac's arms, her body pressed up against him. In a strange way, this feels worse than Karli's betrayal. Maybe because that relationship was on the way out anyway. And this involves two people I love...two people who know what I've already been through. Two people who obviously didn't care enough about me to give a stuff.

And if I'm honest, what I feel...felt...for Lani was a lot deeper than what I felt for Karli. Even in that short period of time. Sitting here now, all I want is her next to me. And yet, I don't want it. I don't want to have to look at her and still want her and yet know what she's done.

My fingers get tighter around my phone. I don't know why I brought it out with me. It's still off. I just can't talk to anyone. Not even Rox. Which I know is an arsehole thing to do but I can't tell her what's happened to me. Again. What is it about me that means this keeps happening? Fuck. I obviously just need to steer clear of relationships. Maybe that's my lesson here.

I know it's not fair though. Rox will be worried. And I shouldn't do that to her. I turn it on before I can change my mind and it's only a few seconds before there's a barrage of whistles as messages flood in. I stare at the screen, contemplating whether I actually have the strength to listen to them. Leaning forward in the chair, I hesitate for a second before pushing the icon for message bank.

The first one is Lani. I only listen to the first two words before stabbing at the button to delete it. Even those two words make me feel like crap – like I've been punched in the stomach, winded and sore. I don't know that I can listen to the rest. I thought I was strong enough but I don't know that I am.

I call Rox instead. She answers before the second ring.

'How are you?'

She must know then. I'm not surprised. She's always been pretty resourceful.

'Crap.'

'Are you up at the shack?'

'Yeah.'

'I'm sorry.'

'You've got nothing to apologise for, Rox.'

'I know. I'm just sorry this happened.'

Happened *again*. I can hear the word echo around in my head, filling up the empty, numb place.

'Shit happens.' It sounds more blasé than I feel.

'Are you sure? That it happened I mean. Lani's been here, worried about you. She said it's not true.'

I lean back, pushing my fingers hard against my eyes.

'I saw the photos, Rox. I wish I hadn't but I did. It's true.'

'You know how Karli's been. Are you sure she hasn't just...I don't know...photo shopped them or something?'

'They were real.'

I would give anything to say they weren't but there's no doubt in my mind that they were. There were too many of them. Of Lani and Zac, both half-dressed, caught in an embrace that's definitely beyond friend limits.

'Is there anything I can do?'

'Not really. Dan's looking after the shop for a couple of days.'

'Okay. Call me if you want anything.'

'Thanks.'

'I love you.'

'I love you too.'

I hang up and stare out over the view, trying to get my brain working. I don't know what to do; how to handle this. Especially at home. I don't want Zac there. I don't want to have to face him but I don't want to talk to him either. I don't know how to do this. It's all too hard. I just know I'm not putting up with it. I can't.

I sigh and take a sip of my coffee.

Jesus, how am I in this situation again?

I stand up, pacing, needing to get away but there's nowhere to run to. My thoughts are coming with me wherever I go. I'm trapped in a fucking cycle of the images. I lean against the pole at the edge of the veranda, squinting against the morning sun. It's only the squeak of the wood that clues me in that someone's there and I swing so quickly, I splash coffee over my hand.

I fling the hot liquid from it and rub my skin against my shirt. 'Shit.'

And then I look up.

And my heart stops. Just for a moment.

It's Lani.

Lani

My whole body is trembling as I come up the steps of the little cabin and see him, looking out over the view, coffee in hand. He looks sad. I hate that I'm the one who's done that to him. Unintentionally, but that doesn't matter. There's a part of me that thinks maybe it'd be better if I just leave before he sees me and I start this whole process that there's no coming back from. Easier all round.

But I don't want to do that. Because I want to be with him, despite the fact that my dad may not support me. Despite the fact that my mother will probably never talk to me again. I've decided I need to chase the life I want, not my mother's approval. I might never get it anyway.

But first, I have to get Matt to listen to me. And I don't think that's going to be easy.

I'm only just brave enough to take the final step onto the veranda. It squeaks under my weight and I wince as he swings around, splashing coffee over his hand and swearing. Not the way I'd hoped this'd start but then I wasn't really expecting it to go well anyway.

He's glaring at me. 'What are you doing here?'

I run my hands down my skirt, wiping the sweat from my palms.

'Roxanne told me about the photos. I had to talk to you.'

'Did she tell you where I was too?'

I nod.

'Fuck. She should just keep her nose out of it.'

'She didn't want to tell me. Not to start with. But I convinced her I needed to be able to talk to you. Needed to be able to give you my side of the story. She finally gave in and told me a couple of hours ago.'

He puts the cup he's holding on the table. Carefully, like he's trying to be controlled. When he looks up at me, his face is tight. Hard.

'Were they real?'

'The photos?'

He nods.

I can barely get the word out and when I do it's only a whisper. 'Yes.'

His jaw clenches and he closes his eyes.

'Then there's nothing to talk about.'

I step forward, closer to him. It's a mistake. His eyes snap open and he flinches before taking a step back. My chest is so tight it feels like there's one hundred rubber bands encircling my ribs. But I have to make him understand. It's time to stand up and grab at the life I want. The life I had for a week.

'They're true. But there's something you don't know.'

He laughs. It has an unmistakable bitter edge. 'And what's that, Lani? It happened before we were together? Except that it was yesterday, when you told me you'd gone for a walk. When you lied to me. Or how about that you and Zac didn't mean to do it? You just couldn't help yourself. You'll never do it again.

You love me. It was nothing. You're just friends with him. Which one is it? This thing that I don't know. Fuck!'

He swipes his hand, knocking the cup off the table, sending it smashing to the floor, brown coffee staining the wood. He's breathing hard, chest heaving. I want to step forward and take him in my arms. But I stay where I am.

'There's something you don't know about Zac and me. We're...different. Our whole community is.'

This is not how I wanted to tell him. On the drive up here, I'd gone through what I wanted to say, over and over, but now I'm here, facing him, seeing his hurt, all the carefully rehearsed words have fled, leaving me to fumble with these inadequate ones. And I can see the anger on his face.

'What the hell are you talking about? Jesus. Just go! Fuck off, Lani.'

The words pierce my heart but I can understand his anger – know he has the right to it. I shake my head, trying to keep that kernel of strength inside me, even in the face of his hurt.

'I'm not going. Not until I show you.'

'Show me what?'

'How we're different.'

My fingers are trembling as I start to undo the buttons on my shirt. So much so that I fumble with the first one, trying a few times to push it through the hole. It's only when I'm on the second button that he seems to understand what I'm doing.

His face is a mottled red as he looks at me.

'Stop it, Lani. Jesus! I don't want...you can't...just stop!'

I take a deep breath and look him squarely in the eyes. Brave. Sure of who I am and what I want. For once. I hope it's enough.

'The only reason I'm undressing is to show you what I can do. It's not to...tease you or anything. That's why in the photos

Zac and I are only partially dressed. I'm assuming that's what they're of, anyway.'

He stares at me like he's going to say something. And then he just nods and my fingers start to move again. He watches every movement, his eyes not leaving my fingers. It feels...intimate and my lower body clenches in response, wanting him. I need this to work. It's not until I draw my shirt off my shoulders that he looks away, out over the scenery. I can see the muscles tight in his neck where he's clenching his jaw. I don't know if it's because he's still angry or if it's from watching me undress. Maybe a bit of both.

I strip the rest of my clothes off quickly, just wanting this over and done with now. Wanting to know if it'll change what he's thinking.

'Okay, you need to look now.'

My voice is soft but it doesn't matter. He hears me anyway and when he turns his head, his eyes are sad again.

'God, Lani, what are you doing?'

'Just watch.'

I close my eyes, feeling the change wash over me, like my organs are melting away, moulding to a different form. And I am no longer Lani, the woman Matt loved. I am the other side of me. And I need him to love that me too.

Matt

If I hadn't seen it with my own eyes, I'd never have believed it was possible. Even now, I don't really know if I'm dreaming. Or hallucinating. Maybe this final betrayal has sent me over the edge without me knowing and I'm having a full break down.

I take a step back, I can't help it, and stumble over the chair, falling hard on the floor. It feels real. So does the pain in my shoulder. I can't seem to move. I just lay there like an idiot, staring at Lani. Or at what Lani's become.

She's a bird, for fuck's sake.

A bird!

I can't wrap my head around it.

She...it...she walks over closer to me and I still don't know what to do. What to think. What to say.

I'm not sure if it's the fact that I'm still just lying there, mute and staring, or if she *has* to...change back or something but there's suddenly a shimmer around her outline, moving, changing and she's back. Lani. The woman I love. Loved. Shit,

I don't know. I don't know what any of this means. Nothing make sense.

She's naked, sitting on the floor with her legs tucked under her, her skin golden in the morning light. Beautiful. Even having seen what she can do. Even with the photos, my body wants her. I want her. But still, I haven't said anything.

She reaches up to the table where she put her clothes and slides her arms into her shirt, bringing it around in front of her, covering her. It's a relief and a regret, all mixed into one.

'Say something.'

I sit up, taking my time, trying to get my brain to work, and rub my hands through my hair, back and forth, back and forth. Playing for time.

'What do you want me to say?'

She watches me, like she's trying to work out what she wants to do. I'm glad it's not just me.

'I've never shown that to anyone else. Anyone who isn't a changer, anyway.'

I don't know what she wants me to say to that. Thanks? It doesn't seem to fit with the whole weirdness of this situation. I don't know what she's making of my silence but her face tightens and she shakes her head slightly, like she's having an argument with herself in her head.

'Right. Everything in the open. I'm a changer. I can change from human form into a bird. Into a kite. As you saw.'

A kite. Huh. That's what she was. My brain feels like it's on drugs, like I can't connect with my thoughts; with the importance of all of this.

'Zac is one too. That's how we hooked up in the first place. Through the changer community.'

Zac. My best mate. The guy I've known for years.

'How come I've never seen him do this?'

'It's not something we show to non-changers. We're not supposed to.'

And yet I've shown it to you. The words hang in the air, obscuring the view. I pretend to look right through them.

'So you're all good at keeping secrets then.'

She doesn't even flinch.

'Only this one.'

My thoughts are like a jumble of the messed up Christmas tinsel that mum used to drag out every December. And no matter which way I tug, they're not coming apart.

She lays her hands on her bare thighs, like she's a school girl about to recite a poem, except she looks nothing like a school girl.

'You know I left the flat yesterday morning? That I was upset.'

I nod. It's brief but it's there.

'I went flying. I just needed to get away. Get some air. I saw Zac out there. He'd changed too. It was a pure co-incidence. He landed when I did and he asked me why I was upset. He was giving me a hug...as a friend. Trying to make me feel better. He actually said I should tell you about this. About being a changer.'

I try and ignore that. 'You were both half-dressed!'

She shrugs. 'Nudity between changers, especially when you've just changed, is... well, it doesn't mean anything. It's nothing. Part of our life. Otherwise we wouldn't have any clothes left. They'd all be torn apart. It's not a big deal. It's not even a small deal.'

'Well, it is for me! And what about in the bathroom that time, when you walked in on me? You couldn't get out of the room quick enough.'

She tightens her lips like she's trying to stop the rush of blood to her cheeks. It's not working.

'That was different. You're not a changer.' She takes a deep breath and rushes the next words out like they're tied to the exhale. 'And besides, I already liked you. I was already really attracted to you. That just made me want you more and I was there to be with Zac.'

I can't stop the momentary stab of satisfaction deep in my gut. Stupid. Stupid, stupid, stupid.

I don't want her. I don't want to want her. I can't want her.

Even with knowing this secret. Even then, it's too dangerous.

Lani

It's not working. I can see it in his face, in his body. It feels like I can see it in his bones. He doesn't want to believe me. Panic makes the words tumble out of my mouth.

'When I was upset...you know I was upset...you rang me, remember? It's because I'd contacted my parents to tell them about you. To tell them I was in love with you.'

He looks down, away from me. And in that moment, I understand that he doesn't love me anymore. That the photos have killed the love he promised. My whole body aches with that thought, like the air pressure around me has increased so much it's pressing in on me, weighing me down, crushing me like my bones are made of craft wood.

'What did they say?' He's still not looking at me.

'My mum took it like I thought she would. It's just another disappointment to her. Another thing I've done wrong. I think she'd prefer I was dead than in a relationship with someone who isn't a changer.' I try to laugh but it doesn't come out well – it is cracked and chipped from years of living with her.

His eyes are back on me now but I can't read what he's thinking.

'It was my dad's reaction that was the hardest though. He's usually...supportive. Loving. But he was disappointed too.' I'm going for a rational voice – one that says I'm taking this well, composed, adult-like but it warps at the end, wrecking it.

'Maybe it's better if we're not together then. If it's going to wreck your family.'

No. No. No, no, no. That's not what I wanted him to think.

'I don't care. I don't care what they think or if they love me or if they never want to see me or if they think I'm dead. I don't. I love you. I want to be with you. That's what I told them.'

He rubs his hands through his hair and shuts his eyes, letting out a guttural noise that sounds like it's been eroded from the acid in his stomach.

'Shit, Lani. I don't know. This is just...too much to take in. You and Zac and this whole changer thing and your parents. And the photos. I don't know what to think.'

'The photos were real. I'm not denying that. But there was nothing to them. It was just a hug. There was no kissing, was there? None. Just a hug.'

Indecision wavers on his face, like an image shifting on a computer.

'Zac told me to show you. That's what he said to me. That I shouldn't keep this a secret from you. Not if I loved you. And he's right. That's why I wanted to show you. Now. Before it's too late. I love you.'

'Don't.'

But it's different. Quieter somehow. Like he feels he needs to say it but maybe he doesn't really want to.

I get up, moving closer, kneeling in front of him. I touch his face and his eyes don't leave mine.

'I love you. I would never hurt you.'

Sphenurus

He doesn't move. But he's not pushing me away either. I lean forward, closer.

'I love you.'

And my lips touch his, a pressure so soft that it's barely there, before pulling away just enough so I can see his eyes. And he can see mine.

'I love you.'

I kiss him again. Harder this time. He groans and I can feel the vibration of it – feel it travel down my body, through my cells, into my soul. And then his hands are on me. In my hair. Under my shirt. Against my ribs. Down my back. Against my thigh.

Touching.

Stroking.

Needing.

Branding me with contact.

And I am his.

Matt

The bed is only just wide enough for the two of us. Not that it matters. I like the feel of her body pressed up against mine, my legs wound through hers. I move the hair away from her neck and lean in to kiss it. She smells of the soap in the shower. And me. She smells like me, which is just so fucking hot.

She moves so that she's on her back, cradled in my arm. Her eyes are sleepy still, despite the fact that night's just fallen. And that we've spent all day in bed, even if we haven't been doing a lot of sleeping.

'Hi.'

I kiss her again, on the lips this time, and her hand comes up to the nape of my neck, pulling me in.

'Hello, right back at you.' I can hear the smile in my voice.

'Thank you.' She smiles up at me.

I laugh. 'Well, ma'am, the pleasure was all mine.'

She smacks my chest. 'Not for that. For believing me.'

The terrible thing is that I don't know that I do...not one hundred per cent. Not yet anyway. I think there's still a small part of me that wonders. But there's a bigger part that's okay with taking this leap of faith. With taking the chance that the photos show a different reality and it all has to do with this... changer thing, rather than Lani and Zac wanting to be together.

'So tell me more about being able to change.'

'What do you want to know?'

'I don't know. How long have you been able to do it?'

'Since I was about five.'

'And your whole family does it?'

She nods. 'It's a genetic thing. Carried down.' She smooths the covers with her hand, little movements that highlight the sudden tenseness of her face. 'That's why my parents are so against us being together. Because it means I can't...carry on the genes, if we ever have kids.'

I put my hand on hers, lacing our fingers together.

'Are you okay with this then?'

She smiles and it's one I almost believe.

'I want to be with you, no matter what. I know that, totally and absolutely. I'd love them to be happy about it. But if they're not, they're not. I've decided I can't spend my life trying to get Mum to like...well, me, I guess. I'm more than that.'

'What about your dad?'

She doesn't say anything for a long time. I let the silence sink around us, rubbing my thumb against the side of her hand.

'I didn't think Dad would be like this. I thought the fact that I'm happy would be enough for him.'

'You love your dad?'

'Yeah. I've just never had to think that his love might have conditions. It's hard. He's always been there. Always supported me. Always tried to make it easier with Mum. It's hard to think I might've hurt him. Hurt him enough that he can't just be happy with this.'

I bring her hand up and kiss the back of it.

'I'm sorry.'

'Don't be. Being with you is right. I want it. The other stuff doesn't matter.'

'Are you sure?'

'I'm sure.'

I kiss her again. This one feels like it's sealing the deal. We're together. We want to be. We're choosing it.

I stroke the hair back from her face. 'Well, I better be the hunter and go into town to get us something for dinner since there's not much here. Unless you want to go out?'

She shakes her head. 'Can we just be here? Just the two of us?'

'That's what I was hoping you'd say.'

'Do you want me to come?'

'No, stay here. Be comfortable. It might take me an hour or so by the time I get there and back. I like the thought of you still being in my bed when I return.'

She smiles and this time, it uses her whole face. 'I can certainly do that.'

I pull on my clothes and lean over, kissing her again, my hands travelling down her side, the sheet the only barrier.

'See you soon.'

'I'll be here.'

I grab the keys and shut the door behind me, taking the stairs up to the carport two at a time. I'm driving up the path when the phone rings. Rox. Worried about me. As usual. I press the answer button on the steering wheel.

'Hey, big sister.'

'Hey.' There's a second of silence. 'Are you still talking to me?'

'Yes. Although it was a shitty thing to do. You could've at least warned me you'd told her where I was.'

'Oh yeah, like that would've worked. You would've been out of there in a second.'

She's right but I'm not going to tell her that.

'Do big sisters ever know when to back out of their brother's life?'

She laughs. 'There'll probably come a time when that happens but I wouldn't hold your breath.'

I laugh with her. It feels good.

'So, you guys are okay? You sorted stuff out?' There's still a hesitancy to her voice, like questions are waiting to come out of her mouth.

'Yeah.'

She pauses. 'What is it?'

'What do you mean?'

'I can hear something in your voice. Something wrong.'

'It's fine.'

'What is it?'

I sigh. She is the dog with the proverbial bone. Or maybe she's the t-rex with the bone.

'It's nothing. We're together. But we'll take it slow. I think we probably went into it too fast.'

Protection. That's what I need. So I don't get hurt again. I want to be with her. There's no getting round that. But I want to be sure. I want to be strong. And I want to give myself some space. Just in case...

'So what Karli said...?'

How can I explain that to her? Well, Rox, the photos were real but, weirdest thing, my best friend and the woman I love can change into birds and they were just doing it to provide comfort over the fact that her changer parents are freaking out because I'm not one of them? Seems a bit much.

'It's all good. Trust me.'

'Okay. I do. And I like Lani. I didn't think she'd do something like that. Not when even I can see how much she loves you.'

I laugh. It echoes through the car, bouncing off the windows, filling the space.

'Well, good to know.'

'Tell her I'll handle the shop tomorrow. You two spend it together.'

'I'll definitely tell her that. Talk to you later.'

'Okay. Bye.'

I feel the smile fade from my face.

Because what I said to Rox was right. It is good. I'm glad we're back together. But the photos are still real. The images are still there – front and centre display in the Matt James mind gallery. And I'm not one hundred per cent sure that I'm doing the right thing.

Lani

I roll over to Matt's side of the bed. It still has some of his body warmth and I want to stretch out in it, like a cat in the sun.

We're good. Not great – I can feel the resistance in him still, even when we were making love. That slight pulling back like he's still thinking...about the photo, about the changing, about me. That's understandable. I have to show him I'm not Karli. Prove it. And I'm happy to wait however long it takes to do that.

Happy to be with him.

Happy to prove to my parents that it's important.

Happy.

My phone, thrown on the lounge yesterday when we came inside, starts to sing. I'm tempted to ignore it but it might be Matt and I can't resist hearing his voice again.

When I look at the screen though, it's not him. It's my oldest brother. He must know about the bond – Mum and Dad must've told him – and I know he'll hate the fact I'm with Matt.

I know he'll ask me what the hell I'm doing. And yet, even though I know this, I still answer. Because maybe he won't.

'Hi, Tony.'

'Lani, thank God. You need to come home.'

'I'm not doing that, Tony. I know Matt's not a changer but that doesn't mean any-'

'I don't know what the hell you're talking about. And I don't care. It's Dad.'

Everything around me seems to stop. The air, the noise of the birds in the trees, my heart...it is all still.

'What about him?'

'We're on our way to the hospital now. The ambulance has just taken him in. They think he's had a stroke.'

'What?'

I've heard him. But my brain refuses to acknowledge the word. He must be wrong. Must be.

'Dad. He's had a stroke.'

My words have gone. All of them. Flown from my brain like a terrified flock of birds.

'Did you hear me? Lani?'

'Yes.'

'Okay, so get your ass back home. He's not good. I don't know...' There's a break in his voice. That scares me more than anything. 'Just hurry okay.'

'Yes.'

And then he's gone and I'm left with the silence. I sink to the floor and stare at the black screen of my phone.

My dad.

My dad.

My dad.

No. It must be a mistake. Except I know it's not. Tony wouldn't have called me otherwise.

What have I done? Slightly less than forty-eight hours after

Sphenurus

I told him about Matt and he has a stroke. My dad. The man who has loved me no matter what. Maybe this was too much for him. Maybe by being selfish, I've killed him.

A sob breaks free, running away before I can call it back. I put my hand over my mouth, keeping the others in. There's no time. I need to go, go, go. To the airport. To home. To my dad, before it's too late.

I scroll through my phone, fingers jabbing at the screen, made uncoordinated by the desperate need to be with him now. Before anything happens...

But finally I'm on the airline site and the tickets are booked and I know I'm going home. I shove clothes on, not caring how I look. And grab my keys.

I can make the phone call from the car.

Matt

The pizza is still hot in my hands as I carry it from the car. The light on the veranda is on and I smile to think that Lani's turned it on for me – thinking about me in even this small way...coming home when it's dark.

But it's not Lani waiting for me at the table. It's Zac. On his own. My confusion is so encompassing that I stop short, pizza sliding in the box with the abruptness of it. Zac stands up. He looks tight. Like he doesn't know what reaction he's going to get.

I don't know what reaction he's going to get either. My brain has yet to catch up with the realities of the situation.

'Where's Lani?'

'She's not here.'

That doesn't make any sense. I left her here only an hour and fifteen minutes ago. Left her naked, waiting for me in bed... And now Zac's here.

'What do you mean she's not here?'

He points to the other chair, not looking at me.

'How 'bout you sit down.'

'I don't want to sit down. I want to know where Lani is.' My hand's tightening on the box and it's starting to buckle.

He sighs and scratches his forehead, eyes closed for a moment. When he opens them again, I can see sorrow and the fact that it's probably for me almost makes my knees buckle. 'I'm sorry, Matt, but she left,' he says. 'She had to go back to Tassie.'

That doesn't make any more sense than the rest of our conversation so far.

'What? What the fuck's going on, Zac?'

He puts up his hands, like he's trying to calm me down. 'This has nothing to do with me – I'm just the messenger.'

'The hell it doesn't. Those photos...' I can't even finish talking. The anger that's building up in me is locking the words in, trapping them.

'Yeah. She told me about them. She also told me she showed you the change.'

'Well, sounds like you two have had a cosy conversation since I've been gone. Anything else I need to know.'

He stands up straighter, shoving his hands in his pockets. 'I didn't see her, if that's what you're worried about. She rang me, on her way to the airport.'

'And why did she ring *you*. Why not me?'

'She said her dad's had a stroke. Apparently, her brother called her and said he's not in a good way – that she needed to get home straight away.'

That grabs me around the neck, like a tie being done up too tight. I want to be the one to be there, to hold her, to make her feel okay. Because I know this is going to be making her feel like crap. But instead, she's fled. Run from me. And called on Zac.

'That still doesn't tell me why she rang you instead of me.'

'Just sit down, okay. And then I'll tell you what she told me.'

I want to say no. I want to throw the pizza out into the darkness and stomp away like a kid. Except I stopped being a kid ages ago. So I sit, shoving the pizza away from me on the table, definitely not hungry anymore.

Zac's eyes meet mine and then move away to just over my shoulder, like he can't bear to look at me. 'She blames herself for her dad's stroke. She said it's all her fault even though I told her that's bullshit.'

'Why would she do that? She wasn't even down there.' And then I stop, mouth still open, as it hits me. 'It's because of me, isn't it? Because she's in a relationship with me rather than a…a changer, and her parents don't like it. So she's blaming herself for it.'

'Yeah. That's what she said to me anyway.'

I slump back. 'Fuck.'

'Yeah.'

I don't know how to combat this…how to make her see it isn't her fault. That choosing to be with me has no bearing on what's happened to her dad because how can that be – it's ridiculous.

'Has he died? Her dad.'

Zac shrugs. 'I don't know. When she was talking to me an hour ago, she said he'd been taken to hospital and that it wasn't looking good and her brother, Tony, said she should come straight away.'

I slump back in the seat. 'Fuck.'

We sit in silence for a moment, listening to the cicadas filling the night with their calls.

Zac taps the table with his fingers, like a drum beat of unspoken thoughts, and then stops, looking at me. 'Listen, I'm sorry about the stuff in the photos. It was nothing though. I was just being a friend.'

I squint my eyes, like I'm trying to see something in the

blackness. Because I don't want to answer him. I don't want to say I'm not sure if I can trust that. Or trust him.

He sighs but doesn't push it. He knows me well.

'Why didn't she call me and tell me?'

I think I know the answer already. I know how she thinks, why she'd blame herself. But I want to hear him say it.

'She said she couldn't.'

'Why?'

'Because if she did, she wouldn't be able to do what she needs to do. She said if she heard your voice, she wouldn't be strong enough. And she said she had to be strong for her dad. That she thought her being there for him would make a difference over whether he lived or died.'

'What did she need to do?'

He sighs again. This one is longer and filled with that shitty sorrow again, which I just want to shove back down his throat.

'She said she needed to break up with you. For her dad's sake.'

And there it is, out in the open like an uncovered ulcer. Just when I thought I had her back, she's lost to me again. She doesn't want me, not enough to fight for us to be together. I stand and pick up the pizza and this time, I do throw it out into the night. It doesn't make me feel better.

'What are you going to do?'

I turn back to Zac. 'What?'

'What are you going to do?'

'What do you mean, what am I going to do? She's made it pretty fucking obvious she doesn't want me. Flying to Tasmania before I even have the chance to see her again, calling you instead of me, telling you to tell me to get stuffed. She's made her choice. It's not up to me.'

'Bullshit.'

'What, so none of that's true?'

'Well, no, it's all true. But she loves you. And you love her.'

I snort. 'Yeah, sure looks like it.'

He shakes his head.

'Don't be a dick. I gave her up for you.'

'Yeah, well that worked out great, didn't it?'

I can hear the bitterness in my voice. I don't want to hurt this much. It's like my whole body is building its own exoskeleton, bit by bit, weighing me down until there's nothing to see but shell.

It's not that I don't feel for Lani and what she's going through. I do. I would give anything for her not to have to go through this. Anything to hold her in my arms and make sure she's okay. But, right now, all I can think is that she didn't choose me – she's taken what we had and rejected it. It doesn't matter why – she has.

'Whatever it is that she thought she felt for me wasn't enough, was it?'

'Are you shitting me?'

I can't understand the incredulousness in his voice. But then, I can't understand most of what I've seen and heard over the last twenty-four hours. I guess this one doesn't make much of a difference.

When I don't answer, Zac leans forward.

'Did she tell you about the bond?'

'What bond?' I'm sick of riddles and new things and the world as I know it not actually being the world as I know it.

He shakes his head and sits back in his seat. 'Sometimes, with changers, a bond forms. Not just affection – it's more than that. That's what she was hoping for with me – why she came up here to live, but it didn't happen to us.'

I wait for the rest of it. My heart's thumping in my chest, like a board slapping on the waves. I don't know why. Maybe it knows something my brain doesn't.

Sphenurus

He taps on the table again – three short beats. 'And it didn't happen for us because, for Lani, the bond happened with you. Which is not something that normally occurs. It's usually between two changers, even if they're not the same type. That's why her parents were freaking out.'

'What is it? This bond? How does it work?'

He screws up his face.

'It's like a...I don't know...soul mate thing, I guess. It doesn't happen to everyone – hasn't happened to me obviously, or my mum and dad. But Lani said it'd happened to all of her family. It's supposed to be pretty special.'

'Does it make her fall in love? Like if she had a choice, it wouldn't have been with me.'

He laughs. 'Like love is ever a choice, whether you have the bond or not. You may not act on it but you don't have a choice. Not really. And the bond doesn't make you fall in love, it's supposed to just happen with the person you're most suited to – the one you're meant to be with.'

I want that. I thought I had it...I thought *we* had it.

'And we come back to the choice thing. Whether she was meant to be with me or not, she chose to leave. She *chose* it. She doesn't want me.'

'So chase her. Give her some time to see what's happening with her dad then go to Tassie. See her. Convince her. You don't normally give up this easy.'

I shake my head. I can't. I just can't do it. Because what if I go there and it's still not enough? What if I'm not enough, even with this bond thing that Zac is telling me exists?

He pushes back from the table. 'Well then, you're an idiot. If it was me, I'd be down there quicker than she could.'

I don't point out that he's a changer and that, obviously, that would be perfectly acceptable. Whereas I'm not. I'm just me... Matt...a non-changer.

'Well, you go then, if that's what you think. Go and be with her.'

Even though it tears at my soul to say that. A big long rip that makes me feel like I'm no longer intact.

I want to take the words back, scared suddenly he might actually do it. But I don't. I stare out into the blackness, pretending to not care. Not wanting to be alone and yet desperately wanting it, all at the same time. I'm a screwed up mess.

I don't look at Zac as he gets up and goes. I don't move until I hear his car drive off. And then my head sinks to the table.

Lani

The taxi ride to the hospital feels like it takes forever. Every red light is like an extra torment – I feel every tick of the clock as I sit and wait, wondering if that's the tick that heralds my dad's time. I've rung both of my brothers and, as a last resort, my mother, but none of them have their phones on. Probably still at the hospital. That's what I'm hoping anyway. Because it's been ten hours since Tony's phone call, so I'm taking it as a good sign rather than something negative.

They haven't rung so he must still be alive.

It's not too late.

And yet, I'm a mess for more reasons than being worried about Dad. I cried the whole way on the flight from Brisbane to Hobart. So much so that the flight attendant offered to move me to first class. I don't know if she felt sorry for me or just embarrassed. Either way, I couldn't move. It didn't seem physically possible. And it wouldn't have fixed anything anyway.

Because all I want is Matt.

Every further kilometre I travel away from him – every bit

of physical distance between us – pounds in my head, reminding me that it's over.

Over.

Over.

I can't fix it. Not if it means my father's life. Not even with the bond. Not even when every cell in my body is aching to be back with him.

I'm not crying anymore, thank God. I'm just numb. Laying-on-your-hand-for-twelve-hours numb.

I throw money at the taxi driver and jump out. It must be enough because he doesn't come after me. The front desk is awash with people though and it's another ten minutes before I get to speak to the nurse.

She directs me to the intensive care unit. Not good but good at the same time. Because at least he's still alive. I run, unable to walk anymore. I'm just outside the unit when my mum and two brothers come out the door. They look tired – all of them – but my mum looks the worst. She looks skinnier, although I don't know how that's possible after only half a day. Maybe it's her face – skeletal and drawn.

She frowns when she sees me – I can feel the pressure of her disapproval like a force pressing me back. It stops me walking towards her. Walking towards them. It's only Tony coming over and hugging me that changes it.

'How is he?'

'Still fighting. They gave him some medication to help with the clots when he first came in and they're hopeful it's working. He's asleep now though. Has been for most of the night. They don't think he'll probably come around until later this arv. Maybe not even until tomorrow. But they can't be sure how he is – what the stroke's done to him – until he's awake.'

It is just as well Tony's arms are still around me, giving me some support, otherwise I'd be on the ground, weak from a mixture of relief and no sleep. Alive. I'm not too late.

'Can I see him?'

'He's asleep, Lani. Fighting for his life. Don't be so selfish.' Mum is glaring at me.

Tony's arms fall away and he and Greg look at each other before looking out the window, away from us, like they'd rather be flying. Me too. But I'm not about to take this from her. Not anymore. I've given up Matt to make this better. I'm a good person. And I deserve some respect.

'I'm not going to wake him. I just want to sit with him. See him.'

There is a long pause – long enough for me to understand that the lack of answer is the answer. Greg squeezes her shoulder.

'Come on, Mum. We were just in there.'

She looks at him in a way that I don't think she's ever looked at me.

'I'm just worried about him.'

'Course you are. But Lani won't do anything.'

'Alright, but I'm going to go back in there too.'

Tony takes a step towards her. 'Come on, Mum, you need a break. And something to eat. Lani will be fine.'

'No. I'm going back in. You boys go and get something to eat. Or go home. I'll ring you if anything happens.'

Part of me wonders if she'd do the same for me – ring me if I needed to come. Not that I care anymore. All I care about is Dad getting better. The boys know better than to fight with my mother though.

'Righto. But we'll be back in later this afternoon unless you ring us.'

She smiles. 'My good boys. Your father would be proud of you.'

There is so much left unsaid in that sentence. And I know it's all directed at me. I refuse to let it affect me anymore. I'm over trying to please her when so little does.

Tony and Greg both give me a kiss on the cheek as they leave. When I walk over to my mother, she doesn't touch me. She doesn't look at me. She turns and walks into the ward in front of me.

I stop at the door to his room, even though my mother has already deposited herself on the chair nearest to him. He looks small, swamped by the bed. I can't remember him ever looking so...slight. And there are tubes and IVs attached to him, monitors screening the changes in his body, beeping, flashing. I want to back out, just for a moment, to be able to take a breath. But I step into the room.

His skin is cool when I touch him, my fingers running over his the back of his hand. Not cold but not warm either.

'Hey, Dad.'

It's soft, barely above a whisper, but my mother frowns at me.

'Don't wake him.'

I don't point out that her hiss is louder than my whisper. I just turn and pull the second chair up closer to the bed. And then I sit in silence, watching his face, taking in everything, like I'm never going to see it again. It scares me that I almost might not have.

'I don't know why you even came.'

I'd almost forgotten Mum was still in the room and when I turn to her, it's obvious the anger has been building in her, ramping up as she's looked at me, until it's exploded from her mouth. But a frontal attack is so different to what she normally does. Better, though, I think. I can deal with this.

'He's my dad. Of course I was going to come. I wanted to see him.'

'You weren't thinking about him when you decided to be with that human. To bond with him.'

'You know you can't choose who you bond with, Mum.'

'But you could've broken the bond. I told you that.'

'You didn't tell me that it could kill me though. Is that what you would've wanted? Me, dead, rather than happy with someone you don't approve of?'

She tilts her head, her jaw jutting towards me.

'Yes.'

I don't know what to say to those words that feel like they cut into my flesh, even though I'm not bleeding. It's a new low, even for her. But it's not a shock. Not really. How sad is that?

'Dad's stroke isn't my fault. And you know if he was awake, he'd say that too. I'm not taking that on.'

'You shouldn't be here.'

'Yes. I should. I've given up the man I love to come down here, to be with Dad. Do you understand how hard that is? How much harder the bond makes it? To give him up? So don't tell me I shouldn't be here.'

'So you've ended it.'

'Yes.'

'Well, that's something at least.'

And then she shuts her eyes, like she can't bear to look at me. Like she's imagining me somewhere else. And part of me feels sorry for her, which is new. It's only when she starts to softly snore that I realise how tired I am. Emotionally dry, like an already juiced lime And I shut my eyes too.

The nurses wake me when they come in during the day but there's no change. I think that must be good. And my mother doesn't speak to me again. Which is definitely good.

Both my brothers come in again at seven, just as night is starting to deepen outside the window. Not that there's anything we can do. Not that there's anything anyone can do.

Just wait. And wait. And that's what we do, all through the night. Tony tries to convince me to go for a while but I just can't. Frightened that something might happen while I'm gone and that Mum will never let me see him again. Never let me say goodbye...

It's not until the next morning, when the sun starts to paint patterns on the lino floor, that Tony forces me to leave for twenty minutes just to get something to eat. Not that I'm hungry but I know I need food. And yet all I want is the two most important men in my life. And neither of them are available to me.

I eat the food so fast it's a wonder I don't get indigestion but I can't wait to go back up to the ward, in case there's a change.

Tony smiles at me when I come back in, like he understands what's happening for me. Maybe he does, although I'm not sure if he knows about Matt. I'm not telling him though. Not now.

'We were just saying that it's a shame there's not an aurora coming soon so that dad could heal.'

I nod. 'Might be a bit hard to explain to the hospital staff though.'

'Yeah.'

The gasp from my mother startles us both. But the sight of my father blinking his eyes is the most wonderful thing I've ever seen. The relief courses through me, like it's illuminating my veins in a golden glow.

'David, oh my darling. My darling.'

My mother is kissing his hand, sobbing. She loves him. If for nothing else, I can respect her for that.

I can see my dad trying to smile. It looks lopsided. But it's a start.

'Nora.' It's slurred but he recognises her. That has to be a good thing.

Sphenurus

As if on cue, I step with my brothers to the end of the bed.

'Boys. Possum.' The words come out in a slurred whisper but it fills my heart with joy and hope.

And then he's closing his eyes again. Sleeping. But we are all smiling. Smiling and crying.

Matt

I am still so frigging angry that she's left. And that there's been nothing from her, although I know that sounds selfish, even in my own head. No call, not even a text.

Nothing.

Like I'm nothing.

And yet, I can't understand that. Because she is everything. And I would give everything to have her back.

Lani

I t's not until early the next morning that he opens his eyes
again. Twenty-four hours of waiting and waiting.
Twenty-four hours of thinking – thinking about what
Dad will have to go through when he wakes, thinking about
how I can help him recover and hoping Mum will let me. But
mostly thinking about Matt and what he's doing and what *he's*
thinking. Wondering whether he hates me. And aching for him.
Wanting just to call him, hear his voice, tell him I love him. But
I can't do that. I can't do it to either of us. Even though it's
killing me...slowly decaying my soul.

It's only Mum and I in the room again when he moans and
opens his eyes to look at us. I don't begrudge her the need to be
with him. But I'm not leaving either. Not yet.

He's able to move his right hand when my mum kisses it
this time. Enough to stroke her face. Weak but useable. And
then he turns to look at me.

'How are you, possum?'

It's hard to understand him but I get enough.

'Good, Dad. Worried about you.'

He shakes his head. 'Unstoppable.'

And I have to smile at that.

My mother squeezes his hand. 'And you don't have to worry anymore. She's broken it off with the...well, with that man.'

All my good thoughts for her fly away like birds in the presence of a predator. And all I want to do is slap her.

My dad turns wide eyes back to me.

'But the bond...'

I shrug, like it's nothing. Easy. Except it's not.

He shakes his head. I can see the agitation on his face, which scares me.

'It doesn't matter, Dad.'

'No. Not right.'

He shuts his eyes for a moment, like it's all too much. My mother is glaring at me again. I don't really know what she thinks I've done this time.

When he opens his eyes again, he seems calmer. Centred.

'You should...be with him.'

'But David, he's not a changer. You're not thinking straight. It's the stroke. Don't worry about it. Lani's not going back to him. She said she wasn't. You just need to focus on getting better.'

He ignores Mum. His eyes meet mine instead and he shakes his head.

'Doesn't matter. You love him?'

All I can do is nod.

'Then it's okay.'

I don't know whether to believe what he's saying or not. Is it the stroke talking? Will he change his mind? I don't know and I don't want to hope. Just in case.

'Nick and...Grace. Go.'

I don't know what he's talking about and he looks at my

mother, nodding his head, like he wants her to explain. It's just as well she loves him otherwise I don't think she would.

'They're getting married. This afternoon. On Bruny Island.'

'Go.' My dad is looking at me, like he's trying to get everything he means into that one word. And I get it. Enough that a small hope grows in my soul, like a plant germinating, pushing a green leaf just out of the soil.

'David, are you sure?'

He squeezes Mum's hand and tries to smile.

'Want her happy.'

I go over to kiss him, my lips on his forehead.

'I love you, Dad.'

'Love too.'

And I don't even look at my mother as I leave the room.

The taxi ride from the hospital to our home doesn't take long and I change out of the clothes I've been wearing for the last three days, grateful, for once, that I actually had to leave some clothes here when I went to Queensland. Not my favourites, but clean. I try and pick something suitable for a wedding. A wedding between a human and a changer.

I ring Tony to get the details and tell him about Dad waking. He sounds happy. I like that I can do that for him.

Because I'm happy too.

It's only when I'm on the ferry to the Island that it suddenly occurs to me that Matt might not want me back. Despite the fact I love him, despite the bond, despite how I think he feels about me...it might not be enough. He's forgiven me once – taken all my differences in his stride, tried to understand about the photos between Zac and I... maybe he won't be able to do it again.

I bring up his number on my phone what feels like a hundred times on the way over to the wedding. But each time I hang up again. He deserves more than that. I need to be brave. If I want him, I need to see him face to face.

There's a small bus waiting in the Island parking lot for the guests to take them to the wedding. I pretend I'm invited and no one calls me out on it. Because I need to see them with my own eyes. I need to see that they're happy. That, after four years of being together, they're still in love. That it's possible.

The wedding is in a park, overlooking the water, and they're standing in front of a tree. It looks like it has something carved into it but I don't get close enough to read it. It's not important. What is important is Nick and Grace. Standing with each other, holding hands, kissing, smiling, touching, loving. It's obvious to see, even from the back. And Nick's dad looks happy, even though Grace isn't a changer.

I hadn't intended to go up to them after the ceremony but, after watching them together, I can't help it. I need to be near them. Nick's face is slightly guarded when he sees me. I can't say I blame him after how I acted when they got together but I smile anyway.

'Congratulations to you both.'

'Hey, Lani. I thought you were in Queensland somewhere. Noosa?'

I nod. 'I'm going back there today, hopefully. If I can get a flight. I came home to see Dad.'

'Of course. Sorry. How is he?'

'Awake and talking, so that's a start.'

'Well, that's good.'

He pulls Grace into a one arm embrace and she smiles up at him, her red hair pulled into a loose bun that emphasises her grey eyes. I can see, even in that one look, how they feel about each other. How it doesn't matter what they are. They're just Nick and Grace. In love.

'Well, I just wanted to say congratulations. And that I'm really happy for you guys.'

Nick smiles, even though he's still looking confused.

'Thanks, Lani. Hope it works out for you in Noosa.'

'Me too.'

The ferry ride on the way back over seems to take forever. But I book the plane tickets on my phone so at least it feels like I have a plan. I am going to win him back. Even if I need to try over and over. Even if it takes me forever.

Tony is waiting for me when I get off the ferry. It's an unexpected surprise.

'How was the wedding?'

'Nice. They seem happy.'

He nods. 'Seems weird to me, being with someone who's not a changer, but if they're happy, I guess it's all good.'

He's looking at me strangely and all I can think is that Mum's told him about Matt. Which sort of makes it easier really.

'Yeah, happy is good. Do you think you can take me to the airport? Now that Dad's awake, I need to go back to Noosa. For a while anyway.'

'I don't think you're going to be wanting to fly anywhere today.'

Fear clutches at me, like I'm surrounded by spiders with nowhere to run.

'What's happened? Is Dad okay?'

'Yeah, he's good. Shit, sorry, I didn't mean to scare you. The doctor said she was happy with his progress when she saw him earlier. But I picked something up from the hospital. That's why I'm here. Thought I'd bring it down to you.'

I'm totally confused. Actually beyond confusion.

Until he steps to the side.

And I see him.

Matt.

Standing on the stairs.

Waiting.

I look at Tony and he's smiling at me.

'Thought you'd like the surprise. He turned up at the hospital looking for you. Seemed like a pretty decent guy. Least I could do was bring him down here, especially since Dad was so insistent.'

I hug him, even though I just want to go, go, go. And then I'm walking across the jetty, my heels clicking on the wood, the burble of people around me fading into nothing. All I can focus on his him.

His face is blank. It's enough to hold me back from running over to where he's standing. But finally I'm in front of him.

'Hi.'

Short but I'm happy he's spoken first. 'Hi.'

'Your dad's going to be okay?'

'I think so. It looks like it.'

He nods and I wait. Even though I just want to kiss him. Even though my hands are itching to touch him. Even though I love him.

He looks down for a moment and then back at me. I'm swallowed up by his blue, blue eyes, all over again.

'I love you. I know, with your mum and dad and everything...it's hard for you... but I just wanted to tell you. in case it made a difference. I love you.'

I'm crying and smiling again. It seems to be the theme of the last few days.

'I'm sorry I didn't call you to tell you what was happening. I was just stupid...crazy with worry over Dad...but I should've called you...told you...'

He touches my face. It's such an intense, sweet moment, I stop talking and sink into the feeling.

Sphenurus

'It doesn't matter. It's okay, I understand. I love you.'

'I love you too.'

He's still not smiling. 'What about your dad?'

'It's okay. We love each other. We can be happy. That's all that's important. That's all he wants.'

And as he kisses me, I know that's what we have.

Epilogue - Roxanne

The wedding is exactly what I would've hoped for my baby brother.

The afternoon light baths the beach in a golden glow, creating a halo around Matt and Lani. It's like they're being blessed by the universe. God, weddings always bring out the romantic in me, especially when it's with people I love.

He's smiling at her in a way that makes my heart light with joy and when her hand comes up to cup his face as she says her vows, I can feel the tears balancing on my eyelashes.

Georgie, in the lilac flower girl dress Lani designed for her, puts her hand on my chin and moves my head so she can look at me face on.

'Why are you crying, Mummy?' Her voice is a loud whisper and I smile at her.

'I'm just really happy, poppet. They're happy tears for Lani and Uncle Matt.'

She smiles back at me. 'And for the new baby.'

'Of course.'

It's been a close contest in the happiness stakes for her in the last few months between being a flower girl like her friend Maddi or the princess dress that she's been wearing every night for the last week since it was finished or the fact that Lani and Matt are going to give her a cousin in around six months. Our family is growing – another blessing.

Lani's belly is still only slightly rounded but the joy on her face when they told us two weeks' ago – the happiness on both of their faces – made me wish, probably not for the last time, that our mum was here to celebrate with us.

Lani's family are here though – her father, still recovering from his stroke six months ago, although you'd hardly know it to look at him, and her mother...what a piece of work she is. I don't understand how Lani can be such a loving, caring person, although it probably explains why she's been so unsure of herself.

But in the last six months, I've watched her blossom. Her designs are selling well at the shop and she's stopped questioning whether they're good enough, most of the time. She's more settled – grounded.

And it's not only her. Matt has changed too. He's less... intense, driven. Happier.

I watch as he takes Lani's hand in his and slides the ring onto her finger.

'You are my light, my love,' he says. 'With you, I feel like flying.'

Lani beams at his words, her laugh filling the air, and as he leans in to kiss her, I know that no matter what comes in their lives, they will have love.

THE END

Acknowledgments

Even though being an author is essentially, a solitary activity (after all, no one else can hear your characters whispering their stories), this is not something I'd ever be able to do without being surrounded by some absolutely fantastic human beings.

My family - Adrian, Jack, Gabrielle and Lawson, all of whom support me in so many beautiful ways - how did I get so lucky? Mum and Dad, who have never doubted (or at least, never let on if they have!). Toni, who goes above and beyond in reading stories and giving awesome feedback. And to the rest of my family - like a beautiful, huge web of love - for everything that you do, little and big, it is so appreciated.

My friends - what would I do without you guys? For your support, your feedback, your enthusiasm, your love, your laughter and for supplying a good cup of tea or glass of wine at times when it's most needed, know that I won't be able to ever offer enough appreciation (but I'll keep trying!)

My readers - without you, I'd just be someone who hears stories in their head! Thank you to my returning readers and to my new readers - I hope you enjoyed reading this story as much as I enjoyed writing it. Big (massive, huge!) love and thanks to you all.

About the Author

A writer of copious amounts of words – just because if they didn't come out, she's sure they'd make her head explode – Sue-Ellen is an internationally published author.

In her 'other' life, she is a social worker living in Central Queensland with her family, two dogs and a snake called Slide.

She loves quirky shoes, dark chocolate and good tea. An eternal optimist, she enjoys making things difficult for her protagonists but loves a satisfying ending.

You can find Sue-Ellen at:

www.sueellenpashley.com
https://www.facebook.com/sueellenpashleyauthor
Instagram – sueellenpashleyauthor

Also by Sue-Ellen Pashley

Afterword

I hoped you enjoyed *Sphenurus*. A million, heart-felt thanks to you, the reader, for taking the plunge with Lani and Matt.

Author's souls are nourished by reviews so if you felt so inclined, please leave one on your favourite platform. You'd have my undying gratitude and an unlimited virtual supply of chocolates.

Want to read more about Grace and Nick? You can find their story (before the wedding!) in *Aquila,* published through Penguin Random House. Read on for the first two chapters.

Aquila

True love can take you higher than you ever dreamed.

Eighteen-year-old Nick Larcombe is a self-confessed *non*-romantic. Until he lays eyes on Grace Carr, who has just moved to Bruny Island with her grandmother, Lillie.

Already bruised and battered by life, Grace isn't looking for any sort of relationship, but when Nick, the mysterious boy next door, somehow rescues her from sure death at the bottom of a windswept cliff, Grace needs answers.

But how can Nick give her the answers she needs when he's been sworn to secrecy, ordered to keep his true nature hidden from the girl he's fallen hard for? And what will his community do when they discover he's fallen in love with a human?

Intensely romantic, *Aquila* is a story of sacrifice and passion, and how true love can make you soar.

Published by Penguin Random House

Grace

There are still times when I want to curl up into a ball and die. When everything that's happened hits me again and I want to stop breathing and let it all wash away so it no longer has any control over me. When I feel like running away. Even after three months.

How can it still affect me so much?

It's stupid. *I* was stupid. But it's over. I need to keep reminding myself of that.

I square my shoulders and take a deep breath, trying to think about the important things, like Lillie and Casper and my music and the remoteness of our new home, and not the feel of his slap on my face or the way he looked when he said he was sorry . . .

Lillie is waiting for me as I step off the ferry, leaning against the bonnet of our little red hatchback, wrapped in a jacket, scarf, gloves and a hat. I can hardly see her beneath all the clothes which seem to swamp her tiny frame.

'You should've waited for me in the car,' I say as she hands me the keys and I slide into the driver's seat. 'At least it's sort of warm.'

'The cold makes me feel alive.'

I grin at her, deciding it probably isn't tactful to ask if she can actually feel the weather dressed as she is. My grandmother is the best thing in my life and always has been. Not that I would ever call her Grandmother out loud. She decided long ago that grandmotherly names made her feel old, so she is Lillie. Not Grandma Lillie or Nanna Lillie, just Lillie.

'Were you able to get what I asked for?' she asks, divesting herself of her hat and gloves and laying them neatly on her lap.

I hand over the bag; it contains the numerous tubes of oil paint that were the main reason for my trip over to mainland Tasmania that morning.

'Oh, you are a darling girl,' Lillie says, patting my cheek with her sparrow-like hand. 'I think this place is going to be good for us.'

It isn't the first time she's said this and I wonder if she's trying to convince herself or me. Not that I hate Bruny Island – hate's far too strong a word. It's just . . . different. Quiet and peaceful and idyllic and . . . quiet. Very quiet. Very different from Sydney. I sigh under my breath, missing, just for a moment, the frenetic pace of the place I was born. But Lillie had wanted to move to Bruny – had wanted to get me away, I'm sure – and I was in no fit state to argue. So here we are.

'Right,' she says as I start to drive, heater cranked up to full. 'I think we're finally set. Two weeks in and we have a beautiful little home, we have paint and canvas, we have wine and food. All we need now is to get you out and about again. Enjoying life.'

I roll my eyes, trying to ignore the rush of fear that her words bring. Which is stupid. Again. I never used to be the fearful type. Not before Ben, anyway. I grip the steering wheel, feeling the bumps press against my skin, trying to not let the panic take me over – take away who I am, just for a moment, like it does every time I think about putting myself out there again.

'Lillie, I don't need –'

'Nonsense.' Her voice doesn't allow for any argument. 'You're seventeen years old, Grace, on the verge of womanhood. You need to dive into life. Experience everything despite . . . well, despite the unpleasantness we've had in the past year. You've got no reason to hide away now that we're here. We have licked our wounds long enough.'

She puts her hand over mine on the steering wheel, still looking straight ahead, and I let her quiet strength settle me. Enough that the panic shrinks again, down to the size of a pea in the pit of my stomach. Manageable, even though I know it's still there, waiting for its next moment to swell. I trust Lillie. Really, I do. She is perhaps the only person who I can say that about.

After all, she was the only one who was there for me when my life went to shit. Both times.

Nick

'**F**or Christ's sake, Nick, will you stop bloody daydreaming and finish washing down that frigging deck before we run out of daylight hours?'

I mentally shake myself out of my brain fade and try to pretend that I haven't heard Dad and have in fact been working hard the whole time. I hear him grunt behind me as if he knows what I'm doing. Sometimes, it's a real shit working with family.

My hands are chapped and cold, even in gloves, and I can't wait to head back to the house and get warm again. Finally finished, I rip the gloves off, the stiff canvas scratching at my already tender skin, and stuff them in the box in front of the cabin, letting the lid close with a bang. The boat – *The Bruny Island Beauty*; I still roll my eyes every time at that sucky name. What the hell was Dad thinking? – is as clean as it's ever going to be and I just want to get out of the cold Antarctic wind that's roaring over us.

'Meet you back up at the house,' I call to him and he grunts again, not even looking up. Man of few words, my dad, except when he has tourists to take out – then he's charisma

273

personified. Not now, though: it's off season. If only that meant the boat didn't need attention. I jump onto the jetty, feeling a tug of resentment at having to waste my time down here.

I wander up the road that leads to our place, and tuck my hands in my jacket pocket, trying to get some warmth into them, kicking the loose stones on the bitumen like a sulky kid, listening to them click hurriedly over the other stones. A whole morning wasted. Probably not from Dad's point of view, but that's half the problem. I'm pretty sure he still sees my photography as a hobby. God, even having the exhibition at the gallery doesn't seem to have clued him in. I look out over the bay and try to picture how I'd compose the photo that's been bouncing around in my head. One taken in the early evening light with a really slow shutter speed . . .

'Are you finished being deck hand for the day?'

The call comes from behind me and I turn and walk backwards for a moment, watching Jake as he catches up with me. He looks the same as he did when we were five – red hair all over the place like a frigging Muppet – except taller. Which is probably a good thing.

'Yeah. Dad only made me scrub it today. Didn't have to take it out.'

Jake shakes his head and sticks his hands in his pockets, keeping pace with me.

'When are you going to tell him you don't want to do it any more?'

I roll my eyes at him. 'As soon as you tell your parents you don't want to do engineering any more.'

He grins at me. 'So, what? Never?'

I smile back. 'Yeah, that's about it.'

'But seriously, it's not like you haven't got anything else to do. You could be taking your photos full-time. Move away.'

I shrug, feeling his eyes on me. It's not the first time he's asked me about this.

'It's not that easy. He's my dad. It's just us.' I shrug again. 'I don't know.'

Jake's been my best friend for as long as I can remember. All through school we've had each other's back, spent holidays together, slept over at each other's houses, got in trouble together. I'd trust him with my life . . . but I'd never tell him the real reason I stay here with Dad, even though I'd rather be off taking photos. We walk in silence for a moment.

'So, Jess was talking about you today. Going on about how talented you are and how cool she thinks it is that you're still helping your dad. Shit like that. Like you're a frigging saint or something.'

'Yeah?'

I look out over the bay. I have absolutely zero interest in hearing what Jess thinks about me. We went out for three weeks in year eight and that was more than enough for me. Jake doesn't take the hint though.

'She wants you bad, man. God knows why. She's got absolutely crap taste if you ask me but you'd better watch out, anyway.'

'Yeah, whatever. Jess isn't my type.'

He laughs and I grin at him. His laughs usually have that affect.

'I don't think it really matters to her whether she's your type or not. Don't say you haven't been warned.'

I shake my head at him as he veers off to his house. He seems really pleased with himself – like delivering the bad news has put him in a good mood. What a friend!

The sound of a car coming up the road makes me look up and I watch it pulling into the driveway of the house next to us. The place had been on the market for a while and even though the new people have been here for about two weeks, the gardens around it make it pretty secluded and Dad and I haven't managed to meet them yet. Mum was always a big one for knowing your neighbours – being a part of your community. Probably as good a time as any. I hurry to make it up there before they disappear inside again. I don't want to have to go and knock on the door and introduce myself like a salesman. Much better to grab them while they're outside. The car engine stops just as I reach the top of the driveway and I slow down, not wanting to be right on top of them when they get out.

Up until this moment, I've never been anything like the soppy, romantic type. Movies where the guy and girl like each other, then something happens to break them up, then they love each other again, blah, blah, blah – they just leave me cold and I'm proud to say that I have *never* celebrated Valentine's Day – I mean, what a load of crap. And while I've had a few girl-friends over the years, I've never had a relationship that I'd even consider anything close to serious.

But as the car door opens and a girl steps out – a girl with long, flaming red hair that looks like it's on fire in the afternoon sun – my heart stutters, as though it's forgotten how to beat, and adrenalin floods my body, making it zing like the first time I flew.

And, as stupid as it is, I think this must be what love at first sight feels like.

Like to read more? You can find Aquila at:
Amazon
Booktopia
Google books